THE BIOHACKER'S ALMANAC
First Dan

JAMES KANE

THE BIOHACKER'S ALMANAC
First Dan

JAMES KANE

ISBN 978-1-77400-017-5

www.dragonmoonpress.com

Printed on Acid Free Paper

Carnage in the bush

It was early autumn and the hillside floor was covered in soggy biomass that clung to his shoes and occasionally gave way underfoot. As a professor of Political Science—a student of the human condition and social cohesion—he generally liked people, but not enough to spend his weekends with them. He had planned a solitary weekend, hiking through the lank bush behind Melbourne, passing beneath the sparse Mountain Ash, searching for a billabong near the source of Woori Yallock Creek while churning through a good internal monologue.

On this particular morning, he was considering Rousseau and the *Reveries of a Solitary Walker* when he was suddenly confronted by an unsettling tableau. His legs caught mid-stride and he clutched his stomach. A knot of vomit clogged his throat as he crouched in the undergrowth.

Several minutes later, he emerged into a clearing where a boy, clawing at the sky like an upturned beetle, lay on a fat slab of granite. Strewn over the grass and up the trees was carnage, blood and bone, the shattered wreck of a mother's corpse.

The professor stepped across the clearing, reached over the rock and gently lifted the boy, carrying him out of the clearing with arms outstretched, lurching down the hillside like Frankenstein's monster, the kid bawling loudly. He stopped and lowered awkwardly onto one knee, spreading a hiking jacket on the ground and gently placing the child inside, his movements deliberate and careful, as if the little thing might metastasize.

The boy looked pleased, wriggling and shitting in the warm jacket while the professor called the police.

A young bull is taught a lesson

The westering sun ducked its head behind the mountains like a perp cowering behind a fence line. Lieutenant Declan hauled himself up the rough hillside path as the distant fir trees collected shadows on their inky fingers. When he finally pushed his way into the clearing the boy was gone, lost in the bullshit stew of bureaucracy, but the flat granite rock remained jutting from the earth like an unholy altar. An icy frost was forming over the pink and magenta corpse, slowing the decay and suppressing the stench.

"The boy was found by a hiker," said a plum-faced officer, ushering Lieutenant Declan towards the rock.

"Who was the hiker?"

"Some professor from the university."

"He been interviewed?"

The junior officer mumbled an excuse and dashed off to talk with the others. Declan huffed, pushing his hands deeper into the large pockets of his coat. He didn't like young bulls; they were too jumpy, liable to kick out at any time, throw down their pad and storm off the scene, or worse, vomit.

Officers from Forensic Recovery were scouring through the shredded remains like crows hunched around roadkill, trying to collect as much as possible before the frost set in, carefully removing each piece of corpse, labeling, bagging and storing it for the file. Declan leaned down and picked up a twist of skin; it might've been the tip of a finger or a toe, it might've been anything.

"All this come from one victim?" He poked the unidentified piece of flesh with his finger.

"As far as we know." Another junior officer appeared at Declan's side. "She was the boy's mother—"

"Doesn't look like a homicide to me," he said, interrupting the eager new recruit. "Looks like a blender hit this bitch." The dark lieutenant shucked a grin, but the young bull obviously wasn't ready for lightheartedness. Declan turned away from the rock. "Looks like a mutant kill. You don't need me, you need a bounty hunter."

"We found blood," the junior put in quickly. "It's not on file, but it's a human haplotype."

Declan considered this for a moment. "Gen-mod?"

"Maybe."

"Just the two of them out here?"

"No sir—witnesses saw her leave with a man and a young girl too. We figure the victim was partners wi– "

"She was married." The lieutenant reached down and picked up a necklace from the muddy remains. He wiped mud and blood from the silver cross hanging at the end of the chain. He was back on familiar territory now; if a human did this, then it was a very angry human: a jilted lover, an estranged father.

"We're trying to agg more data on the victim, building the file so—"

"Forget about the woman." Declan thrust out his chest, stretching his shoulders and cleaving his lungs. "Track the man she was seen with. Bring him in."

The young bull hesitated. "Sir, we're already building a file on the victim. Her data should inform—"

Declan hawked a slip of sputum from his lungs, ending the officer's suggestion mid-sentence. "You can aggregate all the data in the hydra, still won't get this woman's story." He paused and sipped the loogie under his tongue. "This woman married God—how does that inform you?"

Declan shot the loogie at a tree with surprising accuracy. "Direct all resources to finding the male." He grimaced, examining the sludging spittle as it moved down the trunk. "If he's gonna act like an animal, I'll hunt him like an animal.

He tucked the silver cross into his pouch and walked away from the blood soaked clearing.

Mother Umami's Pot
Despite significant advances in the scientific method, it still remained that the fastest way to a lover's heart was through their stomach. In the case of Mother Umami it was a complex co-transmission of numerous neurochemicals, that for simplicity's sake we'll call love, that caused her to pinch and pluck and fold flavors into a bouillon of such emotional intensity that refined palettes would come to consider it beyond the bounds of reality—*gastronomique surreal*, in the words of the Parisian expats who would one day patronize her establishment.

Sadly, when Mother Umami was starting out, those sitting at her table were far from refined. She brooded over her pot for months, finding places at a molecular level to tuck aromas and surprises until her creation expressed her feelings in flavors and textures that were both intoxicating and blatantly contradictory—yet she was never given proper credit. Instead, the local wits quipped that Mother Umami's pot contained the original primordial ooze from which all life had evolved.

And so for many years she pursued her passion in secret, performing magic shows for the front of house, while stealing down to the kitchen at night to prepare her new form of food.

It was one of those endless working Wednesdays that had somehow slipped seamlessly into Friday when Mother Umami dipped her chubby pinky finger into the froth at the top of the pot and immediately recognized that her legacy was bubbling in the milky meaty soupiness, her future foretold in the oily swirls. That was the moment she knew she would build an empire.

PART ONE

INVISIBLE THREADS

The future influences the present just as much as the past—Friedrich Nietzsche

Trainsurfing 101

Dan1 slipped into the hydra and checked the train; still coming, right on time, sliding along the travelduct like quicksilver. The frictionless outer membrane poured around the final curve and swept into the straight. Dan1 leaned out from the railing, his hand pinched on a loose ligament.

A rustling susurration built to a low rumble as the train entered the tunnel, then a furious roar burst from beneath the overpass. He swayed back, a step away from death, trying to get his timing right.

Five... four...

He moved his hand up the ligament, making sure he was directly over the center of the train.

Three... two...

He took a deep breath and jumped.

The hunter and collector

Dex was stuck in traffic on 2nd Arterial. A truck accident had blocked the exit duct and bored-looking transit cops were standing around chatting while the driver of the Golgi Prime-Mover squatted ashamedly in front of his wrecked vehicle. Lines of cars stretched for miles up the arterial, their skins glistening in the waning sun. Occasionally the forlorn honk of a frustrated driver reverberated through the afternoon heat.

Dex was a hunter and a collector, wearing a patchy calfskin coat, fresh off the bone, stolen from the flock of an inattentive *drover a manger* on his way back into town. He had recently returned to the city carrying the head of a mutant caught terrorizing a small camp of prospectors in the proteome pits over at Bacchus Marsh. This had earned him enough credit to pass the season, but he kept working, chasing a collection job for a private client who was after a teen's DNA, probably to check the little yobbo wasn't his son.

Dex knew the boy would be at the arena watching the opening battle of the season, barracking on the blows with the rest of the bloodthirsty city. It was the kind of thing Dex knew instinctively—the exact thing he was paid for. It was going to be difficult finding his target in a crowd of thousands; tracking was always hard, but sampling was easy—snatch anything bio-vital: hair, nails, skin, body fluid.

He held himself above the restrained haunches of his panther-cycle—the latest in synthetic biology, a sophisticated hybrid of animal and machine—and shifted his thumbs along the motor cortex to relax the tense sinews in her hind limbs. She eased down onto the road and Dex walked to the edge of the elevated arterial, gazing over the cityscape, squinting into the sun, his eyes the color of nicotine stains.

A few miles away the arena rose from the suburbs like an enormous upturned clam. In front of the arching shell was a valet and train station, both connected to the main entrance via elevated walkways that snaked circuitously towards the building with fallopian symmetry. These vast conduits surged with spectators, streaming towards the arena like blood through veins. Somewhere in that relentless flow was his target.

Dex had hunted more elusive prey than teenagers. He had chased serpentine mutants through silted riverbeds, crashed through dense forest following lithe primates swinging high in the trees, tracked stealthy felines through endless marshes. He had never lost a target and despite the hopeless odds of finding one boy in a crowd of thousands, he felt confident.

He kicked his panther-cycle and the cat purred to life. He turned her round and headed the wrong way up the arterial, cars moaning loudly as he slipped over bonnets and dodged through the narrow gaps. He leaned into the soft curve of the panther's back while his hands delicately manipulated the controls: a tether to the left, a nudge to the right.

At a section where the road dipped lower, he shifted into the outside lane and leaped a motionless car. The driver hammered his horn, but Dex was already away, flying from the edge of the arterial and onto the roofs below, landing with a crash on a quiet suburban bungalow.

He padded through the backyard and leaped the fence into a narrow laneway, swinging hard right into a wider street lined with the low bungalows typical of outer suburbia—an endless collocation of Bondi blue, lemon yellow and coral pink. Every house was an incidental variation on the next, as if the same design had been passed from architect to architect, with each accidentally embellishing it.

Dex expanded the sat-map in his peripheral vision. The back blocks of Melbourne were a complex network of narrow lanes, one-way streets and cul-de-sacs. The map arranged itself, zooming and adjusting, controlled by imperceptible movements of his pupil. He selected the arena and requested annotated directions.

Easing back on his cat, he padded quietly through the calm Sunday afternoon, passing a group of children playing in a narrow lane. They were surprised to see such an exotic creature in their neighborhood. Dex's coat was made from shreds of black and tan snapped together with studs—his face, roughly speaking, fitted the same description. Down the middle of his bald head was a mohawk of tendrils that writhed and wriggled like a conga line of worms. He had a row of sharp spines across his forehead and a delicate spider web grafted to his neck. The neighborhood kids watched in reverent silence as he disappeared.

Half an hour later, after negotiating the tangle of throughways, he arrived at a flat expanse surrounding the arena and galloped for the valet, dropping off his bike and following the elevated walkways.

Inside the arena, there were security guards everywhere, busy directing people, answering questions and subduing over-stimulated spectators. Dex grinned as he approached a guard standing alone outside an unmarked door. The man grinned back.

"Excuse me…" began Dex, but the guard was unconscious before the sentence finished. He caught the slumping body in his arms and opened the door, shuffling them both into the supply closet with a skillful waltzing movement.

"I'm sorry," Dex breathed, "but I'm sure your medical plan will cover this." With a curt movement, Dex popped the guard's eyeball into his cupped palm, snipped the ocular nerve and deftly reattached it to his own system. He sprayed a dark substance into the vacant eye-socket to staunch the bleeding, then left quickly.

Five steps into the crowd and the arena's surveillance system had organized itself in Dex's peripheral vision—access to the security network, hundreds of eyes, every security guard optically linked.

As he passed a guard, he nodded at the man and smiled, watching himself smiling and nodding in his own peripheral vision.

Making the fence
A Wrigglers Pie sat way out at the end of the tray—enough clearance for Dan1 to snatch and gobble before the vend could object. He was three steps away with the pie already wriggling its way through his alimentary canal before the vend found him and threw a tentacle around his ankle, complaining loudly, "Sir, you'll have to pay for that pie."

Dan1 stamped on the slim pseudopod until it squished and broke. The vend boomed in a deeper voice, "Dan1 Kallikak, you have been identified. Your account will be..." But he was away before the vend could finish, the slim fingers of the pie kneading the lining of his stomach.

He raced across the crowded walkway towards the arena, his light-brown hair wiry and chaotic, like shaky lines on an Etch-A-Sketch, his face creased with the dirt and worry usually reserved for the long-term homeless. Even wearing baggy pants and a hoody he looked older than fifteen; his hurried stride lacked confidence, more like a quick shuffle, hunched over and hooded down, moving through the crowd like a mouse in the undergrowth—hidden, silent, unnoticed.

A crush of people carried him into the arena through a long colonnade of arches that looked like ribs attached to an elaborately decorated sternum. He stopped just inside and found a quiet corner to wait for his foster brother. Ten minutes passed before a creeping awareness distracted him, an ESP coming through the hydra, the slow dawn of an idea:

Sorry bro—a kitty cat wanted ur pass
+ i can't refuse a cut woman—Locky

Dan1 was disappointed, but not surprised. It was not the first time he had been ditched by his foster brother at the last minute.

He reached out to his network in the hydra, a few low rent "friends", mostly members of a DIYbio-clutch that troubleshot sequencing and incubation solutions—a pathetically small collection compared to Locky's hordes. A few of them were at the arena but their feeds were blocked, backs turned, so he figured he could watch the battle from the pit, a public viewing area in the bowels of the arena, exclusively reserved for Melbourne's most unwanted outcasts—not a place to be alone, filled with scum revved up on endo and looking for someone to pick on.

The aggressive crowd threw him around as he headed down the narrow passageway. He emerged into the bright roar of the arena, twelve enormous balconies teetering above him, stacked like an elliptical wedding cake, packed with more than a million fired-up fans.

This is where he was happy. He knew some people came for the spectacle, some for the roughness of the crowd, some just because that's what everyone else in Melbourne did, but he was here for the battle. He was here to see two giant beasts pitted against each other; to see strength, cunning and the will to win.

He shifted along the crowded strip through a loud and agitated mob, the battlefield's sandy surface turned warm gold under the houselights, stained with patches of blood—maroon, deep blue, and dark viridian—the cracked bones of past competitors pressed up against a high mesh fence at the edge of the field. He made his way towards the fence to find a good place to watch.

The crowd was a throbbing tumult of biopunk splitters—he passed a group of Modified Angels, their bodies bristling with spines, adventitious appendages and writhing tattoos. The splitters had marked their territory; the reek of piss stung his eyes, a blurred gang sign flickered in his peripheral vision. He grimaced and clutched his temples to massage the hack from his perineurals.

Among the splitters were tiny dryads—diminutive young girls sifting through the crowd at about hip-height, clear white skin shining beneath darkened hoods. Splitters and dryads always appeared together, like groupies and rock stars, or plaque and tooth decay.

He reached the Slayers of Leviathan, a particularly nasty mob, and pushed on, attempting to go unnoticed, his head down. He was exceptionally talented at going unnoticed—not blending into the background, but actually *being* background, like human muzak.

He gripped his hood and pulled it forward, accidentally stumbling onto one of the dryads. The fine-boned whiteness of her cheeks accentuated her shocked face. She cowered beneath him and bowed her head, her dark hood hiding peppered pixie eyes. Dan1 went to apologize but was seized by the shoulder and violently spun around.

"What are you doing to my little friend?" The growl came from an enormous cracked leather coat. Across the pitted skin on the splitter's neck was a rose-colored scar, surrounded by uneven patches of coarse hair. A raw red hand emerged from the coat and lifted Dan1 by the throat. "Did you touch my girl?"

"Mgnng," was all Dan1 could reply before a wasp-waisted woman whirled from the crowd, swore violently and spat, reaching forward to push something hard into the splitter's neck. Dan1 gagged at the heavy smell of smoldering rubber. The coat crumpled to the ground, taking Dan1 with it.

"That's for cheating." The tall woman kicked the fallen splitter hard in the stomach with a pointed leather shoe. Dan1 tried to scramble away but a fence of legs kept him trapped inside the circle. The bitch kicked out again, this time catching Dan1 across the chest. "And that's for doing it with a dryad freak."

"Don't call me a freak," shrieked the offended dryad. The bitch laughed and flicked her pointed shoe at the small robed figure.

Almost immediately, a wave of dryads swarmed the bitch, their piping voices raising a rallying cry. Dan1 jumped to his feet and scrammed, pushing against a tide of tiny people.

He finally reached the fence and clung on, jostling for space against an enormous organik. He wasn't in the mood to take shit, and even though the organik was wearing a preposterous orange cardigan, orange stovepipe pants and had a ragged sprout of green hair that made him look like a giant carrot, Dan1 clung on and shoved against him. Under normal circumstances, a giant carrot wouldn't be much of a neighbor, but in the pit it was his best option.

He threaded a hand through the mesh and threw his hood over to block the organik's smell. He'd found a good place to watch the opening battle of the gladiorg season, which was just moments away.

The opening bell

A slobbering mass moved through the passageway, a giant lizard-like gladiorg dragged by a powerful electromagnetic leash. The crest on his head was formed from thick plates of compact bone, which stretched down his back to the tail, where they divided and divided again into a whorl of spiny scales. Fully upright he stood over ten meters tall, using the base of his tail as a prop, whipping the spiked tip through the air, occasionally tearing it across the sand.

This animal was not the result of evolution—this was the result of human imagination. He had numerous eyes spread about his body, carefully concealed by nictitating membranes—gratuitous in a traditional predator but indispensable on the battlefield, capable of detecting a threat from any direction. This animal was a gladiorg—a contraction of *gladiator organism*—purposefully designed and bred for battle.

As he was led out the team responsible for his design flashed across the giant monitors. This was the elite. The lead, Theodor Slit, stood in front of the team and gazed down at his creation as it lurched across the sand. Dan1 wondered what it must feel like to watch your creation march into battle—the ultimate test of bioengineering skills—with a whole city hanging on the outcome.

On the other side of the arena, a giant scorpion emerged

onto the sand, its segmented body protected at the front by two hunched pincers. Arching from its rear was a whip-like tail tipped with a deadly telson. The arachnid's immense exoskeleton shifted and slotted with a curious creaking and cracking that could be heard even above the noise in the arena. Its six legs, like articulated tubes narrowed to a point, stabbed the sand as the beast marched into battle.

One by one, the crowd in the pit noticed the gladiorgs emerge. A surging avalanche of bodies tumbled towards the fence, crushing Dan1 closer to the organik. He was shoved into the carrot's thick cardigan, taking a mouthful of stale wool and a lungful of musty air.

The magnetic leashes were switched off and Rex Australis, the giant reptilian gladiorg, lifted to his full height.

The crowd bayed for the fight as a loud howl filled the stadium.

Both beasts hunched into the sand, tense and waiting to pounce, facing each other with their legs spring-loaded.

A siren sounded.

Rex Australis leaped forward, attempting to throw his claws under the scorpion's body, but the scorpion was ready, its abdomen flat to the sand. It easily parried Rex's advance with a swinging pincer, spinning its six nimble legs in effortless concert, following the huge pincer round and concentrating the centrifugal force into a powerful driving stab at Rex's side. The giant reptile stumbled sideways and almost collapsed. The crowd groaned.

Rex Australis was always the favorite—the hometown boy—designed and bred by the Biota Corporation, the city's raison d'être, its largest employer. Rex had survived three seasons, an incredible feat for a gladiorg in the champion's league, and would set a new record if he won another Grand Final. The arachnid from Monbiot should not have been a challenge.

Rex stumbled, lowering himself onto one knee. The scorpion

scuttled behind the tottering reptile, aiming for his exposed hindquarters. A blow to Rex's hamstrings would have left him badly disabled. The scorpion retracted a pincer, sliding out the serrated edge, and made for the soft flesh behind Rex's knee.

There was a brutal, splintering crash as Rex's tail crashed down on the scorpion's back. The arachnid was stunned, its legs smashed into the sand.

The crowd screamed. Dan1, crushed between the mesh fence and the giant organik, emptied his lungs. He pushed back with all his strength, just enough to take another breath. The giant reptile had feigned injury, drawn his opponent in, and then dealt a devastating blow from above—masterful tactics.

Rex whipped around and flung his tail into the side of the scorpion, sending it tumbling across the arena, a clattering collection of flailing limbs and shattered armor. It stopped rolling and collapsed into a bloodied pile. Rex charged straight for it, the scorpion quickly sinking the shattered points of its legs into the sand and awkwardly scuttling away.

The crowd booed and jeered as the giant arachnid desperately dodged the final, fatal strike. Trilling birdcalls filled the arena and the gladiorgs relaxed. Their magnets took hold, dragging them from the battlefield.

Protesters in the pit; teetering
At the end of the first round the crowd settled and moved away from the fence. With more room to move, Dan1 untangled himself from the organik's woolen cardigan. The strange carrot-shaped boy resumed his casual stance in the corner, leaning with one arm stretched up the mesh fence.

Dan1 glanced around, looking for someone to talk with. The sleeve of the organik's cardigan had slipped back to reveal a pattern branded into his wrist, not tattooed, burned into the flesh, a series of circular scars, each containing the other, like an archery target.

The expanding circle, thought Dan1, the symbol of PETSO— People for the Ethical Treatment of Sentient Organisms—a group violently opposed to gladiorg battles. *What's PETSO want here, today?*

Dan1 barely had time to think before the houselights were lowered. A spotlight cut a small circle onto the surface of the arena and a tall black beast appeared, its body like a panther-cycle, only larger and more robust. It paused in the light, throwing its mane from side-to-side and harrying the ground with its hoofs.

The crowd's focus was drawn to the horse when from out of the darkness a woman jumped onto its back, spurring it towards the middle of the arena. The spotlight followed them as they galloped across the sand. She was dressed in a beige leotard, her body toned and muscular, her hair a mass of dense dreadlocks tied with cord. She started a lap of the perimeter, holding the attention of a crowd multicasting straight into the hydra, and began to raise a makeshift flagpole above her head.

Dan1 was impressed—this kind of stunt was guaranteed to grab millions of eyes. She was perched in the stirrups, one hand on the reins, the other slowly unfurling the banner.

Apprehension washed through the crowd—an uncomfortable shuffling—a rippling disturbance that passed swiftly from person to person.

Dan1 looked back at the woman in the spotlight.

Oh shit.

She had only revealed half the flag, but she was clearly carrying the symbol of the expanding circle, the symbol of PETSO.

The pit remained silent for a moment, refusing to accept it was the beginning of a protest. Gladiorg fans were used to PETSO demonstrations—in front of the Biota offices, in the city streets—but the arena was the temple of gladiorg worship. Suddenly heretics had stormed the pulpit.

Dan1 turned back in the direction of the strange organik, but carrot-boy was gone, had disappeared up the fence and was now balanced precariously at the top untying a piece of cord. With a final heave the cord snapped and a huge canvas unrolled, scrawled with giant red letters: *Ban the Bloodsport*.

The crowd turned angry, their reaction visceral, sharks with blood in the water. The pit churned with bodies. The sudden rage was terrifying and caught Dan1 completely by surprise.

Splitters rushed the fence, trying to topple the tall organik. It didn't take them long to turn on the kid he was standing with. Dan1 was shoved into the fence, his neck snapping back as his skull hit the hard bone pole. His body sagged and he was buried under a great hulking pile of punks.

Then suddenly he was thrust above their shoulders, the splitters tearing him in every direction. A hand grabbed him by the collar and wrenched upwards. He took hold of the fence and scrambled to the top, sitting and catching his breath, just out of the mob's reach, the organik next to him.

Lines of security guards appeared across the pit, helpless in the face of the building riot. Dan1 and the human carrot clung to the mesh as swarms of splitters charged the fence. The jacked-up meat-axes were building a pyramid of bodies, slowly making their way up, scrambling over each other to the top.

The boys were trapped. They couldn't climb down the other side of the fence without being stabbed through the mesh. A splitter at the top of the pyramid was within reaching distance.

Dan1 looked down into the man's eyes—curiously calm—a delicate web grafted to his neck, the thin threads glistening in the light. The man moved up the mesh, planting his hands and feet as nimbly as a spider.

Dan1 turned and leaned out over the other side of the fence. Something had him by the foot. Instinctively, he struggled free, his balance tipping backwards as his shoe slipped off. It was a long fall to the sandy floor below. He sucked in his breath and closed his eyes.

The guards: Dex zeros in

Dex pushed through the crowded arena, target data pouring down his peripheral vision. A pic of the teen, uploaded into his perineural, combed through the thousands of images relayed over the network, assessing itself against every face in the crowd. Occasionally a near match was displayed, but so far no eureka.

Dex was not concentrating. He rounded a corner and found himself outside the supply closet where he had left the one-eyed guard. He stopped and pinched his thigh, angry for making a schoolboy error. Just as he was turning away two things happened: a group of guards rushed towards the closet and a pic of Dex's target appeared across his visual cortex.

Dex hunted his targets as doggedly as he fled from his past. When he needed to take a trick, he let ferocity trump stealth— force always being a higher suit than tact. Stealing a guard's eyeball for a biometrix pass was not the worst thing Dex had done, but in this particular case, it had seriously jacked off the other guards.

He fled as distress calls flooded from central security. Dex's picture flashed over the network, identifying him as the primary mark. From across the concourse a guard spotted him slipping quietly behind a vending machine.

Dex self-consciously scanned a shelf, pretending to be torn between a sweetfinger and a packet of piggel-E-nuts. Central security updated their primary target, replacing Dex with some organik sheila on a horse, but this didn't deter the guard. Dex edged further behind the vend.

"I need you to come from outta there, fella." The guard sounded cautious and a little rattled. Dex selected a sweetfinger from the shelf, flicked it at the guard's neck and rushed back into the crowd.

The guard took off after him, but only made it three steps before the vend responded, throwing a tentacle around his neck, bringing him to the ground.

"Sir, you'll have to pay for that sweetfinger…"

Dex moved deeper into the crowd. His system had a lock on his target's position, somewhere in the pit. It was a tough place for a kid—but a perfect place to get a sample. He moved slowly, keeping himself in the flow of people. Guards shouted at him to stop—four of them pushing through the congested corridor. He dashed forward.

The pit was unusually quiet, the arena dark, spectators standing in shocked silence, strangely motionless as they gazed out over the battlefield. Dex moved between them, making his way towards the front fence as the four guards pushed after him. If he could get the sample before being arrested, he wouldn't have wasted his evening.

Suddenly, and without warning, the pit exploded into frenzy. The guards following him were eclipsed by the riot. Splitters threw wild punches and bashed against each other.

On the other side of the pit, Dex's target was being crushed into the mesh fence. There was a sudden disturbance and the kid was hoisted up the fence, out of the crowd's reach.

Dex pushed through the violent mob, scrambling over the mound of punks to heave up the mesh.

The target locked in his perineural and samplers were sent out—a dozen tiny spiders swarming from his neck-web and along his arm. They reached the fence and started climbing, just ahead of Dex.

Several were pinched in the swaying fence and never made it to the top. Four of them reached the target and threw out webs. Dex could see them as bright pink spots in his vision.

The boy looked as if he was going to spill over the other side, so Dex reached up and grabbed at his foot, but the boy's shoe slipped off and fell to the sand—taking the remaining spiders with it.

Dex held the fence with one hand and cocked his wrist, a thin spine extending from his sleeve: hollow-tipped, designed to capture a sample and deliver it to the cryopac stuffed in his pouch.

He steadied himself on the fence, taking careful aim. The spine shot forward, but the boy was gone, wrenched away by a massive organik.

The target slips away

The organik leaped clear of the fence, dragging the boy down with him. The woman on the horse had discarded her flag and pulled up beneath them. The organik landed skillfully behind the saddle, but the boy missed the horse entirely and swung under its flank, hanging semi-conscious in his hoody, his bare foot dragging along the sandy ground.

Dex rolled over the fence and climbed halfway down, dropping the rest of the way and landing heavily in his boots. He took off across the sand, his lungs choking on the fine dust kicked up by the horse's hooves. The horse cut into an enclosed area about the size of an aircraft hangar where Rex Australis was secured in a web of dragline silk, handlers swarming around him.

The three riders disappeared under Rex's legs. As Dex followed two guards rounded on him, both copping a barb to the neck, launched with an easy cock of Dex's wrist. The ataxic venom pieced their carotid arteries and took immediate effect—their legs crumpled.

Dex burst through the rear exit and followed the chaos left behind the galloping horse. He found the black mare and her riders trapped on the crowded walkway leading to the train station.

His cat emerged from the valet and he kicked her to life, riding below, quickly gaining on the trio. As he reached the station the horse leaped the travelduct and disappeared.

He raced up the steep embankment and scanned the horizon for any sign of the horse and riders, circling back for a look in the other direction, his eyes keen but beginning to lose hope. The night had been an exhausting seesaw of good luck and misfortune. He was still wary of the mess he had made back at the arena.

He knew he should leave—the arena guards were still hunting—but he wanted the sample, otherwise the night had been a complete waste of time. He steered his panther round and headed down the travelduct.

A silhouette clambered from the embankment on the other side. The dusk had fallen into a dusty night but there was enough light being thrown from a nearby arterial for Dex to recognize his target.

He spun his panther, pressed his thumbs into her cortex, and leaped the travelduct. The three figures were fleeing on foot, clambering up the overpass.

Dex pushed faster. At the last moment he expertly twitched his heels; the panther leaped and roared onto the roadway. He pulled to the outside lane, moving quietly along the edge of the overpass, preparing to lay siege; there was only one way out—the way they had come in.

He swung his leg off the cat and looked down from the overpass. The three of them were standing at the edge of the railings, leaning out over the travelduct. A train was coming.

It suddenly twigged that they were preparing to jump.

Without thinking he rolled over the edge and lowered his body until he was hanging by his fingers. He let go, falling briefly. His boots caught the rail and his knees absorbed the downward momentum, but his bodyweight teetered slowly backwards. He scratched wildly at a loose ligament, swaying back as it slid from the skin, then suddenly took hold. He pulled forward and steadied.

The three figures were only meters away, standing in a row, holding hands. Dex's target was closest, the kid's bird's nest hair quivering as the train approached. In a loud voice he began to count down.

"Five… four …"

Dex shuffled along the railing, keeping one hand secured around the ligament. The train was rushing beneath in a furious torrent of silver.

"Three… two …"

Dex was almost close enough. He reached out and swiped at the boy's hair—and missed.

"One…"

The three figures dropped onto the back of the speeding train. A single hair remained caught in a looping updraft. Dex tried to grab it, but the last carriage on the train sucked under the bridge, carrying the delicate hair with it.

Dex was panting heavily, teetering above the travelduct, secured only by a thin ligament. He had lost his target, his sample, and he had no idea how he was going to get back up to the overpass, where his panther-cycle was waiting to take him home.

Sister Lickety-Split

The three of them were crouched on the roof of the train, nestled in, sheltered from the wind. A card pinged across

Dan1's perineural:

Dex Foo

is coming for you

He brushed away the ominous message with a twitch of his brow.

"Lucky you can ride a train," the carrot-shaped boy was reluctantly thanking Dan1. "That splitter punk was right up us."

"Yeah thanks." The girl's voice was muffled as she slipped a poncho over her body suit. Out of the poncho popped a head, round-faced and apple-cheeked, a stray dreadlock sticking up from her scalp like a blunt stalk. "You saved our butts. How'd ya know when to jump?"

"Me brother taught me t'train surf. Shit scary first time, eh?"

"It was a leap of faith." She fastened her poncho, still panting slightly. "Anyway, I'm Sister Lickety-Split and he's Brother Samson." She gestured towards her carroty friend, who was stretched out on the roof of the train with his back to them.

"That was some mean vehicle at the arena." Dan1 leaned towards her. "Where'd ya get it?"

"That wasn't a vehicle," the girl said flatly. "She's an Arabian mare, a mammal of the family equidae."

"Sounds pricey. Where'd ya buy that?"

"We didn't buy her, we bred her at our farm. We're organiks."

Dan1 snorted and spat into his hand. "I didn know ya called ya-selves that." He rubbed his palms together and looked down at them to make sure they were clean—or at least cleaner than they had been.

The girl gave him a heavy look and Dan1 felt strangely empty, like the weightlessness at the top of a rollercoaster just before the thunderous fall. She turned her shoulders slightly and stared out over the passing nightscape, the rhythm of the train gently rocking her hair, each lock bound in colorful cotton. A small piece of her coral armband worked loose and rolled across the roof of the train towards Dan1. He surreptitiously picked it up and pushed it into his pouch.

Locky had taught Dan1 a lot about talking to women and the number one rule was: pretend to be interested in what interests them. The second rule was: don't look like you're pretending.

"I didn't mean t'be rude or nothin," said Dan1, smoothly shifting over the roof towards her. "Just innerested in what PETSO's all about, ya know?"

She looked up and smiled. "That was the point tonight," she said quietly. "We speak for those who can't speak for themselves."

"Well that doesn sound so crazy." Dan1 grinned at her.

She laughed impulsively. "I've never thought of it as crazy. We just want to enforce the Charter."

"Aw yeah, what's that about then?"

"It's about protecting our dignity...," she paused, obviously gauging Dan1's reaction, which was a blank stare, "our dignity as human beings." A long blank stare followed by a non-committal nod. "The Charter prohibits the manufacture of conscious organisms."

"Aaahh." Dan1 got it now. "But ain't we humans manufactured? We is just manufactured by our mum's bodies."

"We are created by our parents' natural processes." Dan1 shrugged, "Same diff tho ain't it?"

"Not at all, if we allow corporations to manufacture machines that think like humans, what's to stop them from treating humans like machines?"

Dan1 suddenly found himself out of his depth. He was good with practical stuff, but he couldn't cope with philosophy and whatnot. It was like she had some deep brewing energy that shocked him whenever he drew near. And what was worse, she seemed pleased by his discomfort, like she'd been looking for a conductor all her life and then along walked Dan1, forgetting to wear rubber boots.

She sat back and wrapped her arms around her knees. Dan1 had endured a few failed attempts at talking to girls, but somehow this was the most comprehensive. He had been teased before, pinched and even punched, but this was much, much worse. He felt stupid. He decided it was time to leave.

An organik is tempted by the hydra
Brother Samson sat upright. "What direction are we headed?"

"Nor'west," replied Dan1.

Samson unfolded a small scrap of paper with a crude drawing of a map. Organiks didn't use sat-maps, or have perineural systems, or use any kind of auxiliary network at all.

"Where ya goin'?" asked Dan1.

"We can't tell you," said Samson.

"PETSO's location is a secret," explained Sister Lickety-Split. "Otherwise we'd be constantly harassed." She smiled at him, possibly to make up for upsetting him. Dan1 was unsure how to respond, so he picked a piece of Wriggler's Pie from his teeth. "We could tell you if you joined PETSO. What do you think, want to join us?"

"Nah," he said, "I'm not inta politics."

"Everyone is involved in politics," she replied lightly. "Maybe you don't know it yet."

"Yeah, maybe. Tell me what station ya want."

Brother Samson looked wary.

"We're looking for Orbdalak," said Sister Lickety-Split, ignoring her friend's discomfort.

Dan1 rolled his eyes and pulled a map of Melbourne's travelducts from the hydra, pinning it in his peripheral vision, shifting and zooming until he found Orbdalak.

"We're close," he said. "On this line, just two stops ahead."

"Thank you," said Samson curtly, obviously still uncomfortable relying on Dan1's perineurals.

"What happens when your eyes roll back like that?" asked Sister Lickety-Split, her voice lilting with mischief and curiosity.

"I'm looking into the hydra."

"But what do you see?"

He examined her closely, trying to imagine never visiting the hydra, never feeling the seductive tug of a perineural link.

"I see everythin'," he replied lamely. "If two heads are better than one, then consider a billion skulls broadlinked through a networked neural bank. Imagine all human knowledge, from intimate personal details to soaring philosophical treatises, swirling through an infinite ether that only exists in the impossible space defined by the idle thoughts of a billion minds."

"Wow. That's beautiful."

"Yeah, I stole it from some professor in Uppsala. He's linked in right now."

She laughed gently. "I really can't imagine it. Sounds blint though—like direct access to the collective unconscious. Makes me wonder who would bother memorizing a map of travelducts."

"Trainspotters," replied Dan1 automatically.

She tilted her head, surprised by his answer—surprised that he had an answer at all.

"There's a world'a weirdoes out there." He shook his head to clear his vision. He could see a train coming from the opposite direction. "I'm gonna grab that train."

"Can you do that?" asked El9.

Dan1 shrugged. "Course I can."

Life after Leviathan; Mother Umami's generous bosom
Locky and Dan1 had first met when the city was under the

shadow of Leviathan. The engineers at Biota were trying to figure out some way to kill the beast and stop the devastation. It was a dangerous time to be living outside the city.

Locky was twelve, yet he'd been surviving on his own for nearly eighteen months. His parents were among the first devoured by Leviathan on Black Saturday; he was left to find safety for himself, spending months in the rough camps spread around the Biota citadel, trying helplessly to get into the city. He was on the outskirts when he stumbled across Dan1, a three-year-old sitting in a muddy ditch bawling and scratching at himself.

When they finally broke through, Locky carried Dan1 into the city and up to the central square, intending to leave him for someone with authority, but nobody came. They spent a few months drifting around, sleeping on stoops, eating anything they could get their hands on, sometimes meat stripped from the sidewalk and cooked over bins. Eventually they were picked up by Biota caretakers and hustled into temporary boarding. The conditions there weren't great either. Dan1 was a feral little kid, always getting into scraps and being picked on. Locky taught him to blend in and avoid conflict—or simply hide.

After Leviathan went down the city started feeling a bit more normal. Adults were working for a future, not just scraping things together from day to day. For Dan1, who had grown up in the chaos, the slow return of civic order was a curious process, something foreign and unknown and for that reason suspicious. For Locky it was a relief, a return to life as it had been.

The boys were gradually weaned off the teat of the city, taken from their temporary accommodation and offered up as cheap labor. Their ward took them straight down to *Mother Umami's Magic Show and Lucky Protein Carvery du Jour*, a food franchise on the outskirts of the city, where they were brought before the great matriarch herself.

Dan1's first impression of Mother Umami was of a giant, living, flesh beanbag. She was a massive woman who insisted on wearing short skirts with fishnet stockings so tight that her thighs looked like two fat infants lashed together with red licorice. Her low cut top squeezed two half-moons up to a neckline that began in a deep fold of soft pink skin. She squinted at the brothers and whistled through the gap in her teeth.

"I reckon I gotta use for these runts, somethin' on the floor, in front-a everyone."

Mother Umami was a stickler for detail who firmly believed personal touches made a dining experience more authentic, and nothing says "family restaurant" like free child labour, so she offered the boys free board in exchange for a fair day's work, a scheme known by the local business fraternity as *rent-a-runt*. The boys started that day, serving behind the counter and clearing out the tables. They spent their first night curled next to each other on a gelatinous bag of pats in the pantry at the back of the store.

"We is on our way up," said Locky into the dry air. And Dan1 fell instantly to sleep, knowing that his brother was always right.

The dancing toy
Dan1 threw himself at a soft curve on the roof of the oncoming carriage, momentarily sinking in as the fatty frame absorbed his impact. Behind him, in the dark night, he could just make out the liquid form of the receding train.

Before him stood Central Melbourne, the citadel, an *organic urbanism* designed and grown by the Biota Corporation from spiraling skeins of DNA. It had been the first of the living cities, the pinnacle of bio-industrialism. At the height of the Leviathan panic the crumbling national government was replaced by local city-states operating under the protection of the WTO, creating a Neo-Hanseatic league bound by their loose interpretation of the Charter. Melbourne offered security to a society that had learned to fear government—a model of radical corporativism where most were contracted to Biota.

The train slipped over a cluster of hills to reveal the ghostly form of the city at night, the size of a mountain, about 800 meters high, and shaped like a spiraling minaret, its diaphanous walls emitting an eerie glow. The midsection was a vast empty space stretching from the atrium at the bottom to the opening eye in the roof. During the day this open section followed the sun as it moved across the sky, just as a flower cranes its neck to soak up sunlight. Criss-crossing the interior were veinlines and Metroducts—throughways delivering goods and people between the city's sections and levels—and trains emerged and receded along the travelducts in elegant symbiosis.

Dan1 reached the base of the city and slipped unnoticed from the train's roof, hopping onto a Metroduct heading for his pad. The interior of the city whizzed past his window—a riot of colors, hyperbolas dancing with parabolas to a syncopated rhythm, all dynamic, undulating, and flowing lines, the Mandelbrot motif insinuated into an art nouveau wet dream—a dizzying, gaudy, *fin de siècle* spectacle, as if the interior designers had seen the Great Barrier Reef and challenged God to be more flashy.

The city was designed at Biota's head office in Paris and reflected Parisian design, structured around 20 arrondissements that served as discrete neighborhoods. Dan1 and Locky lived on the Western slope in the 17th arrondissement, a bland corporate enclave known as the blubber belt.

Dan1 was exhausted and just wanted to be lying on the couch, but the sounds coming from inside told him Locky was entertaining. He stuck his thumb in the lock and gazed into the door's misty eye, stumbling in, ready to feign surprise.

Dan1 knew the conversation that was about to take place—he had been a part of it many times.

"Aw, sorry," he said, "I didn't realize…"

"No worries bro," said Locky generously. "This is Lijia."

"Hi Lijia," said Dan1 weakly.

"Hi," she returned.

She was attractive but bland—typical for Locky. While not strikingly handsome, Locky was always well groomed. He had short spiky hair, neatly cut clothes, and a fit body supplied gratis as part of his management contract. He spoke with a corporate accent, a homogenous international intonation self-consciously developed by mimicking his superiors. In contrast, Dan1 had maintained the flat Melbourne brogue that tied him to his city, and his place in society.

"Sit down and have a drink with us," offered Locky.

"Nah—I'm whacked."

"No please," insisted Locky.

Dan1 knew his part: make Locky look hospitable in front of his guest while quickly getting the hell out of the way.

"Nah…" sighed Dan1.

His voice trailed off when he noticed something on the table. Spread in front of Locky was a series of Dan1's gladiorg designs.

"I'm just showing Lijia some of *my* designs," said Locky.

Some months beforehand, Dan1 had entered into a lightweight gladiorg competition. He'd been working on it when he could—using the odd spare moment at work to hash together some designs. Locky had promised to help, but hadn't done a thing. Now he was using Dan1's work to impress a girl. It was pathetic.

It was moments like these Dan1 reminded himself that although Locky looked after him, although he let him stay in his apartment and paid the rent without complaint, he was still a complete asshole.

"Did you see the riot at the arena tonight?" asked Locky, clumsily changing the topic.

Dan1 was tempted to say that because of his brother he was *in* the riot. "Nah, I musta missed it. I'm gonna crash," he said. "I'm *really* whacked."

"Okay," said Locky in an annoying singsong meant to convey kindness, "well get a good sleep then."

"Thanks bro." Dan1 climbed the steps to his room. "Goodnight," he said to the girl, whose name he had already forgotten. Behind him he could hear Locky falsely boasting about his talent for gladiorg design. The door at the top of the stairs retracted.

Dan1's pad was a small elevated section separate from the rest of the apartment; not really a room, more like an enclosed balcony about eight meters square with just enough room for his coverall and a small shelf. The transparent pocket hung over the edge of the city on the western slope with an outer-membrane that was a clear film at night, but shaded itself with pigment during the heat of the day.

Dan1 opened his pouch and removed the small piece of coral that had fallen from the girl's armband on the train. He carefully wrapped it in chitin.

His only possession was a music box that he was told belonged to his biological mother. He opened the tiny theater and ran his hand over the red velvet carpet; clam shaped footlights spread delicate oval patterns onto the stage and arched over the gold gilt proscenium were glittering lights that spelled *Dancing Adeona*, the name of the tiny ballerina who came out and pirouetted to a set of melodic chimes. Dan1 had always found it comforting; Locky said it was creepy. He lifted a small compartment at the front and tucked the coral inside.

The moon was not bright but he could just make out a train

slipping away towards the northwest. The city seemed to be slowly teetering over, as if about to collapse like a tower of jelly, toppling into the suburbs below, dissolving back into the earth.

Lying on his bed he nestled into the coverall—the coverall nestled back. The flat insulation wrapped around him, embracing his legs, slipping under his arms, offering his head and neck support, and finally curling over the ends of his feet to keep them warm and protected from the cold perspiration forming on the inner-membrane of his room. Inside his coverall he was safe from the world.

Dan1 could hear the girl downstairs laughing cynically as Locky lured her back into the boudoir. He threaded a neuroline into the fleshy wall, helping it find the familiar path through the ceiling, then took the other end between thumb and forefinger and tucked the opalescent cell into his epicanthic fold; it wormed in behind his eye to the nerve, attached, then resolved the image of Locky's room onto a disused patch of neurons in his frontal lobe.

Through the inner eye Dan1 watched his brother slowly peel back the girl's integuments. He suddenly felt a sting; someone had sent out receptors to detect the neuroline, either Locky or the girl, most likely the girl. It was sophisticated stuff, seriously creamed his eye. He rubbed away the neuroline and fell back into his coverall, his eye stinging.

An update to his perineural BIOS pinged across his vision, but he brushed it away—didn't have the memory—his BIOS was shareware and last time he'd updated he'd forgotten large patches of his childhood. Locky had a better BIOS—more stable, proprietary, and too expensive on Dan1's wage. He wondered what it must be like to get what you want.

He wasn't thinking of Locky, he was thinking of those designers on the monitor at the arena, gazing down at their creation marching into battle. He was thinking of how to escape Locky—to get a job and afford his own apartment. If he could win the lightweight gladiorg comp, maybe he could get that job—as a designer instead of a shitty technician—and get that apartment. It would all come together.

These thoughts curled into him—he smiled and switched off.

A dead bird on the doorstep; sending Dex a message.
The morning sun had already risen over his dirty shack when Dex opened the door to let Dogbat, his dim-witted helper, scamper inside.

"A message for you Sir," said Dogbat sprightly, dropping the wet feathers and blood onto the rug. Dogbat's smooth round back had a small groove designed to safely hold messenger birds, but some early trauma scrambled his genes, causing him to express violent behaviour towards smaller organisms. His curious button nose sniffed the dead bird.

Dex sighed. Lesson learned: never buy the cheapest auxiliorg on the market. He should have guessed from the name—*The Biota Butlorg*—that Dogbat would be a disaster. The little freak was heavily discounted—for obvious reasons a talking dog/wombat gen-splice was never going to be a consumer favourite. At least Dogbat was too stupid to be disloyal.

"May I serve at your assistance this morning, Sir?" The little ball of brown fur was still bouncing on his stumpy legs.

"Scram," grunted Dex, picking up the murdered bird.

"Yes Sir!" Dogbat scuttled to his favourite spot under the couch, tucked his legs away, and promptly fell asleep.

Dex placed the bird in his scanner and extracted the animal's sequence. Somewhere in amongst the junk DNA was a message from a client. Lines of As, Gs, Ts, and Cs filled the screen. He ran the sequence and the four variables resolved into one line:

I HAVE AN URGENT JOB.

MEET ME IN MY OFFICE. PROF STERLING.

Followed by coordinates at the university.

He threw on some clothes, smiling. Urgent jobs meant quick cash. He walked from his shack, slamming the brittle bone door, waking Dogbat, who sprang from under the couch and barrelled after him.

"Where are we going Sir?" the butlorg yipped excitedly.

"Nowhere."

Dogbat furrowed his furry face, pushing his eyes even closer together, trying to work out how he could follow Dex to Nowhere. Dogbat suffered from severe separation anxiety, another curious quirk that was never programmed into his genome but somehow managed to express itself in his behaviour.

"Goodbye." Dex kicked his cat to life.

She was cold, even for the morning, and they moved slowly along the dilapidated streets of West Boons, Dogbat scrambling frantically behind, trying to keep up. His hind legs moved slightly faster than his forelimbs, an unfortunate disparity that meant after a certain distance he was inevitably running sideways.

"Where is Nowhere, Sir?" he asked from the corner of his mouth.

The cat accelerated away and Dogbat's legs collapsed, sending him rolling inelegantly into a pothole.

Driving through the city; finding the odd professor

Dex lived in West Boons, a community half-formed, a place of utter hopelessness, populated by the desperate and the lonely, the forgotten and those trying to forget. Patrolled during the day by an under-resourced police force, at night the main strip became a battleground of alleycat whores and knife-edge boondogs scrapping over the black market dollars that trickled in from wealthier parts of the city. It was an unplanned tangle of lanes, potholed roads and dirt tracks, far from a perfect place to live, but an obvious choice for those without options. Dex liked it because the rent was cheap and it was on the edge of the city, close to his hunting grounds.

He steered his cat towards the on-ramp and merged with the easy morning traffic on 3rd Arterial, which wrapped around the edge of West Boons as if afraid to enter, then connected with 1st, taking Dex to the northeast of the city.

As Central Melbourne grew it was supposed to absorb the inhabitants of the old camps, draw them in so their makeshift homes could be replaced by parkland. But the lure of the inner city was never so strong. People were happy to work there, but at night they preferred to escape to the open air, so the shantytowns on the edge of the city became suburbs, and the city grew out rather than up.

The university, nestled in an expanse of parkland known as Wurundjeri, was built around the remnants of the old university with newer buildings littered throughout the grounds. At the centre of campus an enormous angel gently wafted its wings, providing a light breeze and shade over the gardens stretching east and west. Dex's sat-map led him towards a honeycombed structure adjacent to the front gate, the old Political Science faculty, now called Behaviour and Organization.

He stretched his back as the panther came to a rest underneath him. It was Sunday and there were no students on campus; the place had an unsettling feeling of abandonment as wind pushed through large archways and over plazas that would normally have been swarming with kids on vespas and professors running late.

Dex walked along the confusing hallways that threaded through the old poli-sci building, following his sat-map to the professor's door. He pressed his palm to the fleshy welcome pad.

A man answered and immediately disappeared back into the clutter of the tiny office. The professor was speaking in a detached tone that didn't seem to involve Dex, evidently having a conversation in the hydra. It took Dex a moment to realise that the professor was, in fact, addressing him.

"Yeah, I'm here for the job," said Dex, still standing in the doorway.

"Excellent." The professor took his seat behind a desk piled with junk.

"Please come in and sit down."

Dex scanned along the shelves full of crap-knacks, tchotchkes, and other detritus. There was a series of figurines roughly sculpted from earthen clay, an empty bottle of South Australian Shiraz with scratchy signatures on the label, and a cabinet full of ancient taxidermy. Dex looked pointedly at the cabinet; the professor pointedly ignored him.

The professor was a tall, thin man with shiny black hair skirting a glabrous scalp, which was pinched in the middle so it looked like an arse poking through a grass skirt. He had a long face with aquiline features, a thin nose, a curious jutting chin and a salt and pepper goatee (more pepper than salt).

"I'm Professor Wilson." His goatee seemed to slide from his chin as he spoke. "Please call me Nip, or Pin, that's what my students call me, because of, you know," he gestured as if drawing a halo around his head, "my pinhead."

Dex was a little surprised by the professor's affable nature—not what he expected—but he smiled at the man's pinhead.

"Nip is a nickname for Napier, that's my birth name, and Pin is Nip backwards—just in case you hadn't already made that connection, which I assume you had, given you're a detective."

"I'm not a detective," Dex replied coolly.

"No, no of course not. You're a hunter and collector, yes?"

"Yes."

"Well I have an urgent job for you. A collection job. I just need a sample, but it will be difficult to get."

Dex nodded. "Do you have a name or a description? Anything at all?"

"Yes, quite. But may I ask the same of you? What is your name?"

"You called me. I figured you knew. My name is Dex."

"Dex. Just Dex. Okay then." The professor's narrow eyes peered down his beak at the desk. "Well Dex, I need her sample." He flicked over a picture of a teenaged girl.

"How old is this pic?" asked Dex. The girl seemed familiar.

"About two years, I think. It could be more." The professor looked distracted. "Yes, taken two years ago."

"And all you want is a sample?" Dex tapped the desk and his forefinger reddened as the data went intravenous, the pic uploading to his perineural.

"Yes, just the sample," the professor nodded his balding head.

"How much?"

"This is a ten percent deposit." The professor flicked a figure across the desk—a large amount for a small job. "All I want is the sample."

Dex recognized the girl: the protestor from the gladiorg match. It was a coincidence, for sure, but hardly unusual for a professor of Behaviour and Organization to want a sample from a protestor. It was not Dex's business what the DNA would be used for, and he wouldn't ask, but he was nonetheless comforted by the logical chain of connections in his head.

"I'll do it," he said.

"But you don't know where she is."

Dex shrugged. "Doesn't matter."

"Well I can give you a hint." The professor's initial aloofness had shifted towards a condescending playfulness that Dex didn't like.

"A hint will make it easier," he replied flatly.

"This is not going to be easy." The professor shook his head, his long black hair wavering in the dim light. "She is in a well-guarded compound on the outskirts of the city, PETSO headquarters. It will be difficult to get in, and it will be difficult to do it without being detected."

Dex nodded.

"But that's what I need you to do. Above all, you must not be captured." Dex touched his bank account to the table—it immediately took on a healthier glow. For this pay his other job would have to wait. He eyed the professor, who leaned back in his chair and stroked his peppery goatee.

"Do you know the compound's co-ords?"

"No." The professor shook his head. "You will need to find that out for yourself."

Dex tucked his bulging account back into his waistline. He nodded at the professor and left through the office door.

The working week; wrong paws, sick auxiliorgs and a good carpenter

Dan1 pumped out the entrance duct and hurled his snakeboard towards Biota, riding the rim to work, his rippling board fleshing and whingeing the whole way down. He slipped in through the rear gate where a few Golgi Prime-Movers had returned early, parked in rows along the travelduct with their drivers snoozing quietly inside, the stevedores and dollies stacked at the back of the yard. Dan1 snaked between them, pulling the occasional trick along the elevated edges and rails. He hopped onto the back ramp and flicked the board up, stashing it in his pouch.

"Good morning Mr. Dan," said his short and cheery supervisor.

"Morn' Mr. Horst." Dan1 echoed the fat man's strange accent.

Horst responded with a rumbling laugh that started deep in his chest and stopped somewhere in his throat. Horst was a short man with a perfectly spherical abdomen, which he mostly blamed on his Teutonic haplotype. As a lowly manager on the manufacturing floor he didn't have access to the comprehensive health benefits Locky enjoyed—unfortunately he had to live with the body he was born with.

"We're ready to go, Dan1. I've started the incubators already."

"Righto Horst."

Dan1 grabbed at the banister and slid up the narrow stairway to his workstation. Just behind his station three incubators pinched the ceiling like giant cocoons.

Manufacturing was a simple process: clay was fed into the top of the incubator and vehicles were born through a thin orifice on the ground. Dan1 could already see a line of them between the diaphanous skins, half-formed and haunting. It was quiet when he arrived, but when the incubators started dumping five hundred pound babies onto the floor the place would get hectic.

Dan1's first job each morning was to clean up after Morris, his miniature pet elephant—a paedomorphic mutant of the classic African genome. Morris waddled over and sat at Dan1's feet.

"Morn' mate," Dan1 reached down and scratched him behind the ears. The tiny elephant had his own indoor savannah with a watering hole. After a happy ear scratching he lumbered back towards the miniature grassy plain and resumed his morning dirt bath.

"Danny boy," hollered Horst. "Did you get a chance to look at the V5.3 Moto-Leopard?"

"Found it Friday afternoon. It was a marker slip in gene M5, 03. They sequenced it all ass backwards."

"Aaah, mein wunderkind." This was Horst's favorite expression—it really shat Dan1 for some reason. "I'll hold off incubating the V5.3s until you've updated the genome."

"Righto," replied Dan1.

He wiped his hand across his monitor to access the display then drew a rough cross, quickly dropping data into each quartile. There was not a lot to do as he had dealt with most of the crap on Friday.

Dan1 had an intuitive understanding of sequencing, a unique and unlearned ability to peer into the reams of chemical markers and catch defective patterns. He could read the raw data, predicting the outcome of gene-cascading to make a minute alteration to the concentration of an enzyme or a subtle change in feedback inhibition. The results of hugely complex data flows came to him as naturally and unconsciously as walking or breathing. This was a talent that some designers developed over years, perhaps decades—for most it never came. Dan1, who had never been formally trained in design, had mastered it in just a couple of years.

Everyday Dan1 got dumped with new sequences and upgrades from the designers upstairs. These completed genomes were uploaded into a totipotent cell—one with an ability to produce all the differentiated cells in an organism—and injected into blocks built from a composite of proteins, called clay. Theoretically, all Dan1 and Horst had to do was place the clay in the incubators where the cells fed on the proteins and developed according to their genomic design. If all went well, several hours later, a vehicle emerged and the auxiliorgs dealt with it from there. But things rarely went well.

Deformities were supposed to be ironed out by the designers, but every version invariably contained defects, mutations, and other screw-ups that only became apparent at the mass-production stage. Rather than sending it back to the design team, Horst let Dan1 retro-engineer and resequence the genomes on the manufacturing floor.

He took the revised sequence for the V5.3 Moto-Leopard and ran it through a simple debugger—it moved across his vision like coiling snakes. The sequence was pushed through a proteomic compiler and uploaded to the production system.

"V5.3 is done," he shouted at the cavernous roof.

"Thank you, thank you." Horst was crouched behind an incubator with his hands deep in its bowels.

At first Dan1 did the resequencing work because he could, because it broke the repetitive grind of the manufacturing floor, he was grateful for it. But then the design team upstairs got lazy and came to rely on him to fix their bugs, so he ended up doing their job for his wage. He still enjoyed it, but he wanted recognition. He wanted people to understand what he was doing. That's why he was working hard to get things done for the day, to find a moment to work on his designs for the lightweight gladiorg comp.

Vehicles were beginning to emerge on the production floor—the auxiliorgs standing around waiting to begin. First births of the day were often deformed, so Dan1 jogged down the gangway to check on them. The first out was a panther-cycle. It stood unsteadily on its paws. An auxiliorg approached with a delicate brush and cleared the mess from the panther's ocular units. The green eyes focused for the first time. The beast calibrated. It crouched slightly as its musculature rippled and contracted. It was tethered and led towards the cleaning pit.

Later that morning some of the auxiliorgs were starting to stagger on their feet. Both Horst and Dan1 noticed the disruption in the production line and met near the birthing pit. Horst put a mask over one of the affected auxiliorgs to test its respiratory system.

"Looks like a virus." His expression was grave as he removed the mask.

"Where would that have come from?"

"I borrowed some of these from M-Gee over in Domestic Products. They must have brought in viruses the others aren't immune to."

"I'll check the net."

Dan1 spread his perineural into the greater Biota network searching for unlogged bugs. Auxiliorgs could be trained to perform complex tasks but they were basic organisms with simple immune systems. Horst should have screened the newcomers before allowing them to mix. Dan1 found two viruses unique to M-Gee's manufacturing floor and uploaded a fix.

The fix was quickly distributed but the old man still looked miserable—he took a personal interest in his auxiliorgs.

"They're looking better already."

"Poor little buggers." Horst shook his head.

Company policy prohibited the removal of auxiliorgs from the manufacturing floor; even if they were sick they had to work until they died. Luckily the fix worked quickly and all symptoms of the virus had passed from the group by lunchtime.

In the afternoon there was a problem with the jackal-scooters—a V3,05 found with two left paws on its hind limbs. Dan1 tagged the scooter for destruction and returned to his workstation, loading a line of the jackal's genome into transcriptomic software to begin sequencing a plasmid for a patch. It took a while to sequence and by the time Dan1 had uploaded it the day was gone.

Horst, somberly watching the last of the machines emerge into the birthing pit, began to shut down the manufacturing floor.

"I'm stayin' late," said Dan1, trying to get it out casually. "I c'n look after the wind up."

Horst sighed. "I can't let you Dan1. Ya gotta clear out."

Dan1 fixed his pose on the gangway and stared down at his supervisor. He got it, Horst knew about the gladiorg comp. Dan1 wasn't allowed to use the machines for hobby work. If he let him stay he could lose his job.

"These machines aren't good anyway, Dan1. Go find yourself something decent to code on."

"This is th' best I got. This is me best shot." Dan1 gestured back at the monitor in his cramped workstation. "The comp starts this weekend and I ain't had a chance. Nothing decent to sequence, no incubator time, nuttin'."

The auxiliorgs finished their nightly cleaning ritual and filed silently past Horst. "You gotta clear outta here Dan1. It's now or in ten minutes when security blows through."

Dan1 leant down and scratched Morris behind the ears, patting his leathery head. He paused for a moment then threw his pouch over his shoulder and strode down the gangway. "See ya in the morn', Horst."

"See you in the morning, Mr. Dan1."

Life at the franchise; the spoiled brats; in her generous folds
Melbourne's mid-tier management and professional service providers had offered the most fervent support to the Circle of Seven, back when it was prosaically named The Committee for Public Safety. High morals and confected outrage sang through the hydra, praising the work of the Committee, pressing parliament to enforce tougher standards. Leviathan was seen as a sensible solution, an ever-vigilant organism that could stamp out the smallest transgression, and a replacement for an ineffectual and unpopular regulatory system that was considered past its usefulness.

Of course, as soon as Leviathan emerged on Black Saturday

the same mid-tier managers and professional services providers were the first to hop onto planes and flee the continent to watch the disaster unfold from a safe distance. After Leviathan was subdued they were slowly tempted back by a rising economy and promises of biosecurity. For Mother Umami it all reeked of opportunity—she was not the type to hold a grudge, not when there was a chance to fatten her account. By the time the boys settled in, she was building her third franchise, this time catering to a burgeoning middle class.

Dan1 and Locky, at just five and fourteen, were easily Mother's best employees. Dan1 shucked soup for customers while Locky played gregarious host for the bland dyspersonal progeny of stable corporate homes. Mostly they catered working lunches and family dinners, although there was always a brief period in the afternoons when Dan1 dispensed ladles of syrupy meat-flavoured soupiness to trans-fatty adolescents who crammed into the place after school.

After she franchised, Mother Umami stopped personally performing the magic shows and licensed her shtick to other overweight mamushkas who would perform for tips and often to fill a parenting void left after Black Saturday.

There was no early show, but Locky began entertaining the privileged school kids with tricks of his own—sometimes made up, sometimes learned on the street. Slowly this became a show in its own right, and frequently Dan1 was drafted to play some role, which he hated.

Locky seemed to genuinely enjoy hanging around these kids. Dan1 couldn't understand what he could possibly have in common with them. They talked about holidays and homework, they played sports and went hiking. Worst of all, they chose to eat at Mother Umami's, which as far as Dan1 was concerned was merely to spite him and Locky who were forced to eat there every day. Dan1 wasn't one of them and they weren't a part of his city or his life.

He didn't like seeing Locky so eager to please them. He would tuck his chin into his chest and sloppily ladle soup, trying to splash a little onto their pristine white shirts, until Mother's avatar approached with a stiff slap, which always made the school kids laugh. It's easy to laugh when you've never been slapped yourself.

Slowly, Locky made friends with them, while Dan1 withdrew. Locky was invited on ski trips and weekends at the beach. Sometimes Mother would let him go, offering Dan1 a break too. "Not while there's soup to ladle," Dan1 would joke. And Mother Umami would bellow with laughter at her diligent little worker.

Those weekends, when Locky was away, Mother would invite Dan1 back to her studio to play canasta and eat Turkish delight. She taught him to play well and he was quickly competitive. Some nights they'd play so late he was allowed to stay, curled into the massive folds of flesh and silk sheets in Mother's giant circular bed.

Locky the Unhelpful; an unexpected and generous offer
Locky had been complaining about work all week. Work might well have been busy, but it was unlikely Locky was busy doing anything about it. Locky hated numbers. He was not particularly adept at even the most basic arithmetic. This would present a problem for most accountants, but not for Locky, who had managed to advance through his department at Biota by force of charm and some lithe political moves. At just twenty-four he was in charge of the Accounts Integrity Group, which was undoubtedly kept busy by their leader's incompetence.

Locky did not usually complain about work, mainly because his work was a series of lunches interspersed with genial chats to the diligent members of his group and the occasional firing to keep them all working hard. His complaints were starting to aggravate Dan1, who knew exactly what was intended by them—namely that Dan1 should not expect any last minute help in designing their gladiorg. And that meant there was no way it would be finished in time for the competition.

Dan1 spent the day trying not to think of various ways to kill Locky. Most of the ways he avoided thinking about were devilishly ingenious, designed to inflict unbearable pain and humiliation. The rest just involved a swift kick to the nuts. He was angry with Horst too. He was angry with the designers upstairs and he was angry with M-Gee for infecting the auxiliorgs.

He looked out from his workstation at Horst and M-Gee discussing the recent virus. And then through the clouds of rage and frustration appeared a simple idea: blackmail. He ran down the gangway and over to the supervisors.

"Greetings Dan1." M-Gee was a lanky Anglo with a slightly cock eye and a severely cock brain. "Tough tits about those sick auxiliorgs, ol' chap."

"No M-Gee," said Dan1 slightly out of breath and eager to get to his plan. "No tough tits. I patched 'em, ya' owe me."

"Yes, Horst told me you nipped it all in the bud. Jolly good work." The genial man bounced on his toes and grinned broadly.

"I know ya' got a sweet lab over there and I know ya'd get in a whole hell'a trouble if upstairs found out about that virus. Both o' ya' would." He looked pointedly at Horst and M-Gee. "I wan' access t' th' lab. Only til the lightweight gladiorg comp in four days. Jus' so I can get somethin' ready. Somethin' t' enter."

The two men shuffled their feet, gripped their chins and studied their shoes. Eventually M-Gee came up for air.

"No, no, no, that ain't gonna fly laddie." M-Gee shook his head. "Ya can't go throwin' around accusations and tryin' it on wit me. No, no, no."

He turned and walked away. Horst just shrugged.

"Ya tried Danny," said Horst.

Dan1 was fuming. They both owed him one and they couldn't even do the smallest favor. He put down a detailed account of the virus incident, pulling records from the floor and compiling it into a comprehensive report. He sent a ping out to Horst and M-Gee, making sure to use the company network and official IDs. The reply from M-Gee was measured but hinted to Dan1 that maybe he could turn him.

Let's chat o'er this face to face, Laddie

M-Gee looked angry, maybe even a little hurt. Unfortunately, this was Dan1's only hope of getting something into the competition. This was his only way off the manufacturing floor, out of Locky's apartment, into his own life. He was determined to force this through.

"I don't like tha way ya gone about this," said Horst. M-Gee nodded.

"You is the only one t'give me access to a lab," pleaded Dan1. "I need this."

"If they catch you they'll destroy your designs as a start, likely fire you too." M-Gee looked as grave as a lanky Anglo could.

Dan1 nodded.

"This is all on you."

Dan1 nodded. "It's on me."

The two men pivoted and walked stiffly away, muttering between themselves as old colleagues do. As soon as their voices had disappeared behind the giant central incubator, Dan1 picked up his things and headed for the laboratory.

A life from clay

Dan1 couldn't believe it, M-Gee's lab was a playground: sequencing software, a full suite of proteomic design tools, a genomic compiler and a massive transcriptomic database. He had full access to Biota's library, the largest in the world, containing the DNA sequence of every evolved organism. It was the ultimate reference manual—God's playbook.

Dan1 sat at the monitor and placed his hands across the cortex. A deep vortex resolved around his field. When he threw out <webbed AND feet>, thousands of search results poured into his system, elegantly sorted under headings. He selected *amphibian* and worked through to FROG-GENUS. Long sequences of DNA scrolled across his vision. It would still take work to order the sequences in the chromosomes and properly compile them, but it made making life a lot easier.

Dan1 didn't have the time to design a gladiorg with multiple transgenic qualities, instead he was looking for a simple animal to be the foundation for a battle-ready beast. He figured he'd go for something defensive, so he pulled a proto-map of a generic crustacean designed in the 21st century, taxonomic designation:

Kingdom:	*Animalia*
Phylum:	*Arthropoda*
Subphylum:	*Crustacea*
Class:	*Malacostraca*
Order:	*Decapoda*
Suborder:	*Pleocyemata*
Infraorder:	*Anomura*
Superfamily:	*Paguroidea*
Family:	*Lithodidae*
Genus:	*Paralithodes*
Species:	*Chalabiens*
Patent:	Expired

It needed to be larger for the competition's weight range, but it was a perfect template.

After he had enlarged the creature and re-compiled the gene cascading he loaded the new model into his perineural and lightly spun it with his index finger. The beast was low and flat—likely to get hammered in the arena, there was no way around that. So he decided to harden the shell and focus on increasing speed and agility across the ground. It was time to get down to the source code.

He started with the shell, browsing the transcriptomic database for sequences. He isolated segments controlling growth patterns, using restriction enzymes to separate them and polymerase to form a complementary copy. He stayed late every night, working on the gladiorg until his perineurals ached.

Dan1 loved working with raw DNA, getting amongst the base pairs, past the chromosomes, past the genes, right down to the basic chemical interactions at the most elemental level. After spending the week working well past midnight he had nearly completed his beast.

It was Thursday night and Dan1 was lost in code. Locky called, warning him to knock before entering the apartment. He was completely consumed—the walls of his workstation covered in rough sketchings, indecipherable scrawl and arithmetic. He was working on a crucial stretch of DNA, trying to perfect a set of pincers (technically known as chelipeds) to serve as weapons and a defensive shield.

He had discarded the model—perineurals were no help at this level of detail—and had a series of DNA strands under the scope, adding ligase enzyme to glue the ends of the DNA molecules together, creating the related gene sequences that needed to be inserted into the chromosomes. He pulled up the chromosomes one by one, manually inserting the new genes, then ran them through a genomic compiler, which spat out a single celled zygote captured in protein rich clay. He placed the clay into an incubator and prayed to some higher power for it to work.

It didn't.

He started again, taking more time to identify the required sections of DNA, meticulously isolating the sequences and making sure the polymerase had created an identical copy.

The calendar slipped slowly over to Friday as he passed the chromosomes through a compiler—confident it would work this time. He uploaded the completed genome into a zygote and injected the totipotent cell into clay.

The cell divided to form two cells. The two cells divided. The process repeated. There was still work to do, but finally he had life.

An old farming community; taking off for PETSO

Dex was on a train heading northwest, hooked into the hydra, a dossier on PETSO drifting across his vision.

They were formed after Leviathan, an attempt to fully enforce the Charter after the Circle of Seven were pushed from power. The file outlined their rise as a bullying political action group; their use of mass protests and targeted corporate assault. The fact that the group had been founded in Melbourne, the very heartland of bio-industrialism, was indicative of its style. It had become an increasingly aggressive operation, its interventions executed with military precision. Biota was blindsided by the discipline of its command structure.

After a disaster like Leviathan things should have settled down, but instead people just took more extremist positions. PETSO wanted an end to bio-industrialism entirely. Biota wanted to make its own rules about what could and couldn't be manufactured. As far as Dex was concerned both groups were wrong, but the political stalemate metastasized and suddenly everyone in Melbourne had an absolute belief one way or the other. A reasonable society was suddenly split by a bitter political war.

After a prolonged operation to destroy PETSO's political infrastructure, Biota called a truce and PETSO set up headquarters in an isolated compound northwest of the city. It had not been easy for Dex to find the location. He had tracked down a few former members squatting in an abandoned warehouse and sniffed out a juicer who left the group after developing an addiction. She had been happy to cough up information after Dex caught her attention in a vial.

He unhooked from the hydra and stepped off the train at Orbdalak—surprised at how close PETSO was to the city limits. Orbdalak was an old cattle town sucked dry after the bio-industrial revolution and decimated by Leviathan. It catered to bio-prospectors seeking their fortune in the old growth forest, or just as often tourist groups out for something authentic.

Dex wandered down the main street—the only street—and approached a geezer sitting in shade outside a stable.

"These for hire?"

The old man studied him from beneath a broad-brimmed hat—Dex wearing black boots and dark clothes with a pouch slung from his hip. To the old man's eyes the spikes on his forehead marked him as just another untrustworthy punk. The stable owner rocked back on his chair and spat into the middle of the road.

"Sorry cobber, they're only for tour groups. I don't lend my girls to strangers." He tilted his hat and resumed staring into the middle distance.

Dex fingered the spider web on his neck, used to this kind of attitude.

Older folk didn't take to splitters.

"Well sir, mind if I share some of your shade?"

The old man didn't respond. Dex squatted in the shade by the stable's open door and took a deep breath of the stale air wafting from the pens.

"You feeding them oatniks?" he asked, staring into the same middle distance that had captivated the old man, who did not directly respond, just subtly changed the pattern of breathing through his nose.

"I fed my Gracey oatniks when I was with the force," reminisced Dex. The old man altered his breathing again. "She was a fine mare, my Gracey."

Dex squatted for a minute longer and drew his fingers in circles through the dusty ground. Finally the old man sat forward in his chair.

"Come in," he said, without looking at Dex.

The two of them walked into the cool and cavernous stables where more than a dozen pegasuses lined the pens on either side, their wings tied back with aged leather straps.

The old man pulled a harness from the wall and threw it over a mare who whinnied and kicked a cloud of dust with her hooves. He patiently strapped her saddle.

"So you ran with the bulls, eh?" he croaked. "Which division?"

"I started in the 16thmounted. Then I transferred to homicide."

The man screwed up his face and scrutinized Dex. "You look like a punk to me. You undercover?" Dex shook his head. "Oh well, if you're not telling the truth she'll soon discover. She can be a tough ride, a bit flighty, but if you've ridden for the force then you'll be a match."

He led her outside into the sunshine.

"You got some kind of account?"

Dex nodded. The man pulled a surprisingly sophisticated bank-nex from his back pocket.

"Press your thumb on there."

Dex pressed into the nex. His account, which had been surprisingly healthy of late, suddenly looked a little wan.

"That's a deposit," growled the old man. "You'll get it back when you return her." He tucked the machine into his back pocket. "Where you planning on going?"

"Thought I'd go look at the camps in the old growth forest." Dex shoved the contents of his pouch into the panniers on the pegasus's rump and pulled himself up onto her back. "Should be back in two days."

The old man nodded and looked down at his shoes. "Just steer clear of the sawgrass forest," he said. "It's dangerous in there." He unclipped the leather strap holding the mare's wings. She whinnied and flapped, pig-rooting and bucking slightly—Dex tightened the reins and drew her head into line.

The old man shook his head and spat on the ground, patting the bank-nex in his back pocket before returning to his seat in the shade.

Dex moved at a trot down the main street until he was clear of the town, then built to a canter and kicked the mare with his heels. She spread her wings and took them airborne with a powerful flap.

Flying over the sawgrass forest; respect giant rabbits
In the middle of the barren saline scrub was a dense forest of giant sawgrass, the blades of grass razor sharp and serrated near their tip, shimmering and waving through the air, slicing the breeze in scissor-like movements. Dex gained altitude.

The pegasus was happy to ride the updrafts coming from the sunbaked dirt of the plains, but she was struggling in the more unpredictable breezes above the sawgrass. He thought about landing and camping, but wanted to get the job done quickly.

He kept a safe distance above the cuspidate grasses, listening to their edges singing in the wind, beneath that the stirring of the forest floor, the occasional birdcall, and the constant *whump* of his pegasus's wings.

After nearly an hour's flying he could see no end to the forest. His informant had only known that PETSO was located at the center of the sawgrass. By his sat-map he was barely a quarter of the way. He was not concerned about the mare—she was showing no signs of tiring—but he was becoming acutely aware of the approaching point-of-no-return. He wondered about the reliability of his information. Perhaps the junky squealer had sold him a lie just to get a hit on the vial.

A quarter hour later Dex noticed a movement in the sawgrass. It was not the wind. Whatever was moving below him had direction and purpose. It was a line—two lines—of rustling grass beneath him. He steered his mare to the right. The lines followed.

After another ten minutes the two lines had multiplied to five and it was obvious he was being pursued by a group of large creatures. Their powerful hind limbs, covered in a rough reptilian hide, sprang through the tall grass, their heads flattened by a thick bone plate that protected their faces. They were not following his path, but anticipating it, like dolphins at the prow of a ship.

The longer these strange beasts were with him, the higher they jumped. He could clearly see their faded, cracking skin as they leaped through the grass like rabbits—rabbits the size of bull elephants. Suddenly one of them came dangerously close, its updraft enough to make his mare dip and slide. She stalled and reared at the air, nearly throwing Dex off. He steadied her and turned back, gliding for a few meters towards the sawgrass.

The animals disappeared into the forest cover and he quickly gained altitude, circling back, heading for the center of the forest.

This time two beasts rose directly to confront him, approaching from either side, pinning his mare in the collision of their bodies. As they dropped they dragged Dex and the pegasus with them. She flapped her wings, desperately trying to free her crushed legs and at the last moment they gently rolled away from each other, releasing the pegasus, allowing her to take to the air and escape.

She climbed for a few beats of her wings as Dex recovered from the sudden fall. He had no intention of abandoning his journey—he just wanted to avoid these animals. He dug in his heels and pushed the pegasus higher.

There was the briefest moment when he thought he could fly above them. Then, in the periphery of his vision, he saw the dark mass rising. It crashed into the pegasus, throwing Dex from the saddle. The pegasus tipped, her wings twisting in the wind, falling fast towards the sawgrass with Dex clinging to the reins. She tucked her wings into her flanks, slowly bringing her nose around to pull from the dive.

The sudden change of momentum tossed Dex violently at the end of the reins and his shoulder rolled awkwardly, dislocating. His hand slipped from the leather.

He fell for several meters and landed on the fleshy curve at the center of a giant blade of grass, bouncing twice, jarring his back, before sliding completely out of control towards the forest floor. He crash-landed onto a bundle of pointed blades, all as sharp as spears. One pierced clean through his shoulder, the others snapped against his heavy leather jacket.

He was unconscious and hanging face down about a meter from the ground—his pannier fell nearby.

Working the well; oil, muscle and fat
The windmill had stopped turning about halfway through

the autumn, mainly because Brother Sampson had stopped oiling it, which he blamed on a lack of castor oil in the store. Oil wasn't usually a problem on the compound; they had access to plenty of vegetable oils, but they preferred to use castor oil on the windmill because it didn't dissolve the natural-rubber seal in the hub. While they waited for more castor beans from the compound up north, it was Sister Lickety-Split's job to pump the ground water into Percy's tank.

She figured it was a good way to build muscle bulk in her arms and leaned enthusiastically towards the spigot, pumping laterally to work her bicep. She had started to chafe under her armpits—her tits didn't used to get in the way like this—when her dad appeared at the edge of the clearing beneath the tank.

"Working up a sweat there, E19." He always called her by her real name when they were alone. She had been allowed to choose her compound name when she was five, which he had never approved of, preferring instead her birth name, the name he had chosen. "Must be looking forward to getting the windmill back up and running again."

"What? And miss out on my morning workout, hell no!" She switched biceps and doubled the rate, showing off to her dad.

"Well then maybe we don't need those castor beans from the North, always pushed our terroir protocols," he winked cheerfully at his daughter. "Good of you to ease my conscience. Anyway, I was just dropping by to check Percy's—Brother Tao thought he noticed a leak."

"Nothing here Dad, wouldn't be putting all this work in if it was just coming straight out again, would I?"

"No, I guess not." He smiled gently at her feisty retort.

"Go check someone else, Dad. I got things here."

He nodded and then looked lost. She noticed his eye linger

on her coral bracelet, a memento of her mother. She knew he didn't like her wearing it anymore.

"Well it's past sunrise, you should be out in the orchard by now," he sounded hurt, not by the tardiness, she knew, by the bracelet.

"I know Dad."

"You tell me you want to do more than just organize protests, but you don't show me the dedication."

"Yes Dad."

He tramped off, leaving her to finish filling the tank. She threw her weight harder into every stroke, despite the chafing. If she just kept working the well, eventually that soft fat on her chest would turn into muscled pectorals. The first water gushed from the overflow and she fell back from the pump, dusting her calloused hands, breathing heavily from the final effort.

Recovering from the fall; continuing towards the center
A blade of dried grass, brown and brittle but brutally sharp, had pierced through his shoulder. He needed to reach his pannier to dose himself with enough anesthetic to remove the blade.

Lightly, with his toes, he pushed away from the fleshy stalk. The broken blades moved slightly. The pain in his shoulder was intense. He rocked forward, teetered, and then the pile collapsed, sending him face first into the ground. His pierced shoulder slipped further down the blade, leaving streaks of dark blood on the brown shaft. He lost consciousness.

He awoke with his face in the dust, spitting muddy slag onto the ground. He rolled his head around and felt the electric pain in his shoulder. Looking up, he could see the pannier just in front of him.

He reached around and opened the bag, awkwardly emptying its contents until his medikit slipped out. Across the top, tiny vials filled with enough tranquilizer to kill a car were temptingly close, but the flap had fallen so that it was just out of reach. He shifted the kit on the dirt, drawing it closer to his face. He could feel the spear twist in his shoulder as he breathed in dust through his nostrils. With a final effort he threw his hand forward. The vial pierced his skin and emptied into his system.

His body relaxed.

He snapped the brittle spear from its stalk, then reached around and broke the top, leaving just a short column inside. His body shuddered and spasmed. He rolled over onto the dirt.

With his uninjured arm he searched inside the medikit for some ready-aid, sitting up to place the tube against the shaft of grass still penetrating his shoulder. He pushed it inside, slowly expelling the broken spear out his back. Blood surged out the wound. The pain wafted over the anesthetic. He swayed slightly and fainted.

The local anesthetic in the ready-aid worked slowly, but the coagulates were almost instantaneous. The bleeding stopped and the tube formed to match the tissues in his shoulder. He slept deeply for an hour while his body healed.

When he woke it was mid-afternoon. He rubbed ointment into his scratches and bruises. His shoulder was stiff, but he slowly rotated it to loosen up. He put his supplies back into the pannier, enough equipment to take samples, but all his weapons were in the other bag. His pegasus had fled—as loyal as any other woman in his life.

He set off into the forest where the vegetation grew in clumps: dense in some places, easily passable in others. The giant sawgrass cast undulating shadows across the dirt, hard packed and sucked dry by a complex root system reaching deep into the earth.

It was nearly dusk when he came across a cleared space in the sawgrass. There was a large watering hole about one hundred meters wide, surrounded by a muddy bank. He was thirsty, but also wary of the large footprints on the opposite side.

He crouched behind a copse of brown sticks. He would need water before he left the forest. He could catch enough condensation during the night to slake him, but he would prefer to take a deep gulp from the lake right now. He waited and watched.

There was a rustle on the other side of the watering hole. An enormous creature bent towards the water and flapped open its mouth from beneath the bone plate covering its head. Its dry, lizard-like tongue lapped at the water. Dex wished he had his rifle. He retreated slowly from the watering hole, marked the place on his sat-map, and resumed his hike.

It was dark by the time he reached the center of the forest. The moon was shining brightly enough for Dex to see clear across a vast field of crops. He skirted around the edge of the settlement and discovered an orchard extending inward. He used the fruit trees as cover, setting off quietly through the bright night. At the end of the orchard he paused, climbing a tree so he could see the rest of the way into the compound. In the center was a large building, scarcely lit, with a series of small cabins surrounding it. In front was a fire pit, burning low in the ground. Silhouettes passed before the red glow. On the far side were three enormous warehouses. Dex marked all the structures on his sat-map.

He climbed down from the tree and retreated back into the forest. That night he circled the whole perimeter, finding a handy observation point in a stack of fallen sawgrass at the edge of the clearing. His perch was nearly ten meters in the air with a clear line of sight to the camp. He activated the binocular function in his perineural system. The eagle-eye was disorienting at first. He slowly adjusted to the vertiginous viewfinder. He scanned through the figures sitting around the fire. He could not see his target, but his job was never that easy. He decided to wait until morning, making himself a nest out of softer grass and lying back, his body torn and exhausted. The night rolled over.

Putting away childish things

The sun had dropped behind the long blades of the sawgrass forest, making it difficult for Sister Lickety-Split to distinguish between knotted clumps of leaves and bunches of fruit. She climbed down from the tree and packed her stuff into her fruit laden dray, picking a choice peach from the top of the pile. She was always the last one to leave the orchard during the season, always the last one to finish sowing or pruning, always the hardest worker, the most diligent, making up for her position as the leader's daughter, wary of everyone looking for any sign of favoritism. They needn't look—it wasn't there. Her dad had always expected more from her than any other brother or sister on the compound.

"Nice cart, eh Splits?" said Brother Umwelt as she carefully poured the peaches onto his scales. "You know they've been making cobbler in the kitchens all day? How's that for bounty then?"

Brother Umwelt phrased every sentence as a question, which, surprisingly, made conversation easy. But Sister Lickety-Split wasn't in the mood; she was too exhausted after a day in the trees. She smiled wanly and staggered towards bed, hoping to get in a few hours before the others returned to the sleeping quarters hyped-up on cobbler and schnapps.

She found her father waiting outside, puffing on a meerschaum pipe. They were both silent, apart from the *puh-*

puh of his pipe smoking. When she fiddled with the hemp twine on her mother's coral bracelet he stopped puffing and met her gaze. Her fingers were numb and rubbery from picking and climbing all day—it was difficult for them to understand the knot securing the bracelet. Eventually she simply tugged at the cord until it snapped, sending tiny twists of coral scattering across the floor. She unwound the leather strap that separated the rough coral from her skin, gathered up the fallen pieces, and threw it all into the bin.

"That leather can be used again," said her father, lips still firmly wrapped on the pipe.

She was close to crying for a moment, but this banality brought her back. "I'm ready for a big project now, Brother," she said, stooping for the leather cord. "I want to organize something more than just a protest, something more substantial. I want to smash them."

"We'll see," he said, shifting his weight so he turned away from her, staring out across the fields surrounding the compound.

"Night Brother."

"Goodnight Sister," he said, still staring resolutely into the nightscape.

Down from the nest; a handy bug helper

Dex woke with a dream still lingering—the image of his mother in the morning, eye blackened, cheekbones unevenly healed after the night's beating—and the sense of his father nearby, menacing.

He punctured a vial into the skin behind his ear, felt the pseudopodial sucker worm inwards and connect to his carotid artery. The vial disgorged a cocktail of doctor-approved good feelings. Neuro-chemistry took over and the memories bled away.

Despite the dream he had slept surprisingly well, waking after dawn. He drank some of the condensation collected during the night and stored the rest in his pouch.

Climbing from his nest, he scanned across the fields. Dozens of people were scattered across rows of crops, ducking and extending, chopping and digging, hoeing and raking. Their movements were deliberate and repetitive—like machines. He trained his eagle-eye to check they were human.

He couldn't see his target so he skirted the clearing, careful to keep himself in the cover. He eventually found the young woman sitting in the orchard beneath an irregularly shaped tree, its branches heavy with strange looking fruit. She reached up with deliberate poise, like a ballerina stretching to that impossible point just beyond the fingertips. Despite the sun, she was wearing thick woolen leggings and rainbow colored socks. She had a knitted headband and copper leaves woven through her dread locked hair.

Dex licked his lips. She was cocky, sixteen or seventeen, physically fit and happy to be outdoors. Every part of her body was smiling—he imagined even her puckered mut was stretched in a self-satisfied vertical grin. He was once sleeping with an organik just like her—ended in tears; hers not his. Still, he winced at the memory of bitter fruit.

He took an ovum containing a tiny insect and plugged it into his perineural system. Using the eagle-eye he established the exact coordinates of his target and released the bug.

The insect zipped over the grassy field until it reached the fruit trees, its minute wings flapping furiously. It reached the girl and buzzed around her, but she took no notice. It swung in towards her exposed neck and without a sound, without her noticing, ingested a slither of skin into its hollow body.

Dex was pleased; he had the sample. He placed the ovum

back inside the pannier and waited for his bug to return. As he lifted the pouch of water to his lips he heard a soft grunting from behind. Something left moist breath on his shoulder. He turned and stared straight into the eyes of a giant, bone-faced beast.

The rise and rise of Mother Umami's empire; a concomitant expansion of her waistline

Mother Umami began her career as a magician in a traveling circus before meeting and falling in love with the creep she called a husband for seven years. Aside from creep and husband, he was also called Frank. She performed her magic show at his restaurant five times a week, drawing in crowds despite the repulsive menu and oleaginous host. Then, after a particularly successful week and a rave review from *Shazam Bulletins*, she found her husband under a double-breasted burlesque player in the back room.

Following Frank's mysterious death she inherited his hangnail establishment and despite the fact that it was on the outer orbit of town, filled with festering bar flies and at the mercy of braying creditors who were ready to collect a return on their investment and never believed she could rescue the accounts from the deeply stained red Frank had left them in, she made a go of it. When Leviathan struck, most people in the hospitality business shut up shop and got the hell out of town. Mother Umami expanded.

She started by selling basic foodstuffs to the desperadoes in the outer camps, but her first real customers were Biota employees bored with the office canteen's daily fare. As the city got safer they started drifting out to see the local colour beyond the citadel. Mother Umami's reputation went viral and soon everyone wanted to slurp up her addictive magic soup.

Mother Umami's Magic Show and Lucky Protein Carvery du

Jour quickly became the first successful business on the outside. She expanded rapidly, opening new franchises every year, two of them inside the citadel. She was a well-known figure in Melbourne, publicly acknowledged as the inamorata of a very senior and very married Biota executive with a predilection for chubby girls. This relationship ended famously after she bridled at having to play the mistress and was ultimately dumped for a woman twice voted "Most Likely Mistaken for a Bus" by the gentlemen subscribers of *Pushin' Cushions*.

The end of this relationship was the beginning of an even bigger corporate expansion. She took a more detached management position, controlling avatars from her studio apartment: a gang of slim, young hotties embedded in every store as proxy managers, always vigilant for any slackening in the supply chain or word from a dissatisfied customer. Mother never left her giant circular bed, constantly hooked in, perineurals feeding sensory data from avatars while tracking inventories, customer volume and spend per head. Her empire lay at her fingertips—quite literally.

She developed a penchant for legacy meats—the exotic and the extinct. Illegal be damned. Melbourne had discarded all semblance of traditional governance; the corporates were the only trusted institutions remaining. Biota controlled the city proper—it had designed and seeded Central Melbourne, it felt natural for the corporation to run the city too. Outside of Biota there were a few thriving businesses, predominantly hospitals and hospitality. This corporate oligarchy was a loose arrangement, a temporary measure while the memory of Leviathan prowled. They funded the police force and kept the courts open, gradually restoring order and cleaning up the mess.

All this gave Mother Umami the cover she needed to indulge in unrestrained hedonism, becoming Queen of the Boons, stretching her great girth across the slums as if they were her personal chaise-lounge.

The morning after; a visit from Mother Umami; getting on with it

Dan1 stumbled from his room after a shocking night's sleep. Locky had invited friends around and what started as a quiet get together to watch the Friday night gladiorgs ended as a full-scale fiesta. The noise had kept Dan1 awake for most of the night.

Mother Umami announced herself at the door, but Dan1 was pretty sure Locky would ignore her. He walked through the living room, where the audio system was still playing Nor-hemi Ribofunk and the walls were a thumping swirl. He turned off the system and opened the door to find a slim, blond avatar wearing short-shorts and a halter-top. He gave the mindless twenty-one-year-old a lackluster hug.

"Hullo Mother."

"Hello dear," the avatar's voice was chirpy, not a match for Mother's weary cynicism.

"I see ya wore short-shorts."

"Their legs distract from the ugly truth, dear boy. Is Lock about?"

Dan1 glanced back at their chaotic apartment. "He's in, but he ain't up yet."

"What a pity. I thought I'd pop by t'say that I can't make it to ya gladiorg competition tomorrow. You know how it is, no avatars in public buildings and all that."

"Ya could always just come in the flesh, ya know."

"I could, but that would involve gettin' up, and that ain't gonna happen."

"Well thanks for tellin' me."

"Think nothing of it deary."

"I better..." Dan1 gestured back inside and made a cleaning motion with his hand.

"Oh of course, I'll let you get back to it." As Mother's avatar leaned in to kiss him Dan1 reached around and cupped her ass.

"Deary me...."

He smirked and shrugged, gently sliding the door behind him.

The apartment was a disaster. It didn't just need a superficial clean—it required major surgery. The whole place was trashed: goldfish in the sink; the answering machine had laryngitis; a toilet with gastroenteritis; and someone had infected the walls with a strange psychotropic virus. Even the appliances that could sanitize themselves were struggling to look presentable. The self-grooming carpet choked on a mysterious coagulate of food and booze. The oven tried cleaning itself, with all the hope of a penguin in an oil slick. It must've been a hell of a party.

Locky emerged from his bedroom, half-dressed, with a coverall wrapped about his legs.

"Good morning my brother." He strained to sound happy but his larynx was tired and croaky. He staggered unevenly towards the bathroom.

"I wouldn't go in there," warned Dan1.

Locky shook his head. "I need the cure..."

He opened the door and staggered back as the toilet vomited across the floor—the smell gushed out. He held his nose and stepped in carefully, reaching for the bathroom cabinet to take a handful of vials.

"My god that stinks." He was already stumbling back towards his room.

"You gonna help me with the gladiorg t'day?"

"I need to take care of this hangover first and...," he pointed at his bedroom and mouthed the words *I have company*. "But later for sure," he said confidently.

"Uh huh. Mother just come past t'tell us she ain't comin' to...." Locky's door sealed shut before Dan1 could finish. He tensed and crouched, his fists drawn up to his ears—for a moment he just held the anger inside—then he shot forward so his body was long and taught with his arms straight by his side, like an Olympic skier launching into the air. Inside his mind screamed, "I gotta get outta heeeeeerrrrreeee," but the apartment was perfectly silent, apart from the soft gurgling of the carpet.

Incubation; the final push

Dan1 headed back to the lab on his snakeboard. Stashed in his pouch were six translucent films each containing a single totipotent cell. He slipped one of the cells into the drive and the crab-like gladiorg resolved in his vision.

She had a thick shell, just over two meters wide, midnight blue at the high arch of the back but lighter towards the outer edge. He had designed her this way to confuse competitors with poor eyesight. There were two pincers at her front and eight sandy colored legs along the side, bristling with spikes. The right pincer was large enough to protect her; the left pincer had a thin, sharp edge that moved with a quick stabbing motion. Towards the front of her carapace were four long-stalked eyes that articulated 360 degrees.

Dan1 was concerned that the cortex was inappropriately constructed. Designing the brain was the most complex element of building a gladiorg. He double-checked the nervous system coding.

Slowly, carefully, he placed the cell into a slide at the back of the incubator, lowered a block of clay into the machine and attached four nerve endings to the top corners. He checked the various protein packs, making sure the cartridges were full and ready.

At his direction a large needle extended towards the block of clay, penetrating to the middle. After a moment's pause the needle retracted, the monitor on the incubator telling Dan1 that the totipotent cell had been successfully injected.

He watched the cell on the monitor—dividing and dividing again. The tiny organism moved quickly from zygotic through the embryonic stages, starting to fill out the block of clay, replacing the uniform lines of protein with more complex patterns.

Halfway through the process the bicoid levels spiked catastrophically and the imbalance cascaded, causing massive malformation. He quickly destroyed the beast and recycled the carcass.

It was early evening and Dan1 wondered whether it was still possible to get another beast ready for the competition. He carefully examined the DNA sequences in all the chromosomes and realized that the problem was not genetic—it was the incubator. He removed the cartridges and cleaned their heads, flushing the machine, then fed another totipotent cell into the slide and prepared a block of clay.

The incubator shuddered as the process began. Dan1 tracked the cell development on his perineurals, which displayed the critical concentrations of the growing organism, monitoring every catalyzing chemical, every protein, every tissue, every organ. He sifted through the information, searching for a potential problem.

Just past 3am Dan1's body was saturated with exhaustion, but the beast was ready for birthing. He prepared a mat on the floor in front of the incubator and made a tiny incision through the thick tissues that had built up along the inside wall. Floating in the semiotic fluids was the tranquil beast, more than two meters across and nearly a meter high. She had been given a sedative to ease her through the harrowing birth.

With a concerted effort he pulled on the tissue sitting on the floor of the incubator. Slowly at first, and then in a sudden whoosh, the animal slid from her womb and onto the mat. He quickly cleaned the fluids from her body, wanting to have her secured as quickly as possible, before the sedatives wore off.

He attached a collar and placed a powerful electromagnet on a rolling jack beneath her, locking her into place, although she could still freely move her limbs.

Her rapid movement surprised Dan1. When he lunged she lowered a giant limb in defence. When he retreated she jumped forward, thrusting with her pointed pincer.

Dan1 could barely keep his eyes open, but finally his beast was fully formed and ready for battle. It was after four in the morning and he needed to get his gladiorg to the competition for registration by seven. He caught the Metro back up to the second level—even in Melbourne people were shocked to see a boy dragging a caged gladiorg, they kept well away from him.

He arrived at the apartment and left the cage in the corner of the living room. He had managed less than four hour's rest out of the last forty-eight. He staggered up the stairs and into bed.

Waking up in crap town on the big day
Dan1 woke with a jolt.

His faulty system had failed to wake him and it was already past 9am. He sprang from bed and hurtled down the stairs, bursting into the living room. His gladiorg was gone. He jumped the coffee table and searched the apartment, wildly flinging furniture. His gladiorg was gone and Locky's room was empty.

"Fuck you Locky!" he screamed, connecting to his system.

"Hey bro," came a cheery voice over his perineural, "we've already won the first round!"

Dan1 gritted his teeth.

"I didn't want to wake you so I brought her down myself. She's a beauty mate! I named her Beesk. You coming?"

Dan1 simmered on the line.

"You better hurry, the second round is about to start."

"I'll hurry."

Dan1 ran from the apartment and caught the Metroduct back to the atrium. Sun poured through the city's eye as he approached the exhibition hall. The light was gently diffused, covering the building and her surrounding grounds in a warm golden mist, the magnificent hall capped by a large domed roof that rose into the middle of the city like an enormous bald head. Out the front was a sweeping semi-circular driveway where a queue formed a snake stretching down and along the street.

Dan1 stood at the back of the crowd feeling simultaneously restless and dispirited. The lightweight gladiorg competition was popular. The event drew scouts looking for new recruits, and the winner of the final, which took place on the following Sunday, was always head-hunted by one of the major bio-industrials.

Dan1 writhed with impatience. A queue is a curious organism—it houses hope in its tail and relief in its head—the exact opposite of the human arrangement. To settle his frustration Dan1 studied the building's fascia, adorned with metope panels that recounted the history of bio-industrialism in a series of interlinked dioramas. Beginning on the left, Gregor Mendel was growing beans to prove his theory of genetic inheritance; in the middle Crick and Watson were building a model of the double helix; and the final panel depicted the legendary Kueper and Lysenko—giants of bio-industrialism.

By the time Dan1 entered the hall he had watched all four

rounds through the hydra—four convincing victories for his gladiorg—but was still keen to see her in the flesh. The crustacean, which Locky had inexplicably named Beesk, was ferociously snapping at the bars of her cage.

Locky, standing next to her looking smug, was wearing a sharkskin suit and alligator shoes—a sharp cut, even for Locky. His hair was immaculately styled into short spikes that sprang at surprising angles from his head.

"Can you believe how well we're doing?" Locky slapped his brother on the back.

"Nah mate, can't believe it."

Locky grinned at Dan1 and raised himself on the balls of his feet, obviously looking for a compliment.

"Real stylish, Lock."

"Thank you my brother. I sense good things, big things for us, Danny Boy. And I promise, mate, if we win I'll give you full credit for the design of this baby."

"You mean you won't lie?" snapped Dan1.

Dan1 saw his foster brother stumble back a little, obviously caught off guard in his sharkskin suit. Locky had always carried a certain momentum, an overwhelming self-assurance that swept up those close to him. Dan1 felt the current waning.

"If we win one more round, we're in the semi-finals!" Locky tried again.

"Yep," said Dan1 sourly.

"Come on, mate, this is exciting!"

Locky passed him the event biometrix and the word TECHNICIAN appeared across Dan1's wrist, just below a lion-headed human fighting a human-headed lion. Locky's wrist designated him DESIGNER.

"Sorry about that," said Locky. "That's just the way it happened."

"We'll have to fix it," replied Dan1 curtly. "I designed her."

He wanted to punch his foster brother, but more than that he wanted to win the competition. He tried to stay focused on what mattered.

"Yeah," said Locky. "I'll get onto that."

Dan1 looked over the battlefield. They were one round away from a place in the semi-finals and their gladiorg was pretty much unscathed. Their next competitor was an armoured worm with large branching horns protruding from either end of its tubular body. Locky waved at friends as the gladiorgs were led onto the battlefield and the crowd settled into the seating. Beesk scuttled along the sand, her eyes rotating around the crowd; the worm squirmed along the ground, moving awkwardly, keeping its horns from catching in the sand.

The judges gave the final signal and the magnets were released. The worm reared up. Once upright it could move with surprising agility, digging a set of horns into the ground and flipping itself over until the horns at its other end dug in. It was a graceful and acrobatic motion. Bone plating meshed around the beast so that when it moved it only revealed tiny strips of exposed flesh on the outside arc of its body. Beesk scurried sideways to avoid the somersaulting worm.

The worm attacked with deadly precision, its horns crashing into the sand. It could twist in any direction, so Beesk's sideways retreat was not particularly effective. The horns rammed down, glancing off Beesk's shell and damaging one of her legs. It arched up for the deathblow, but Beesk dodged away and the worm came crashing down, firmly planting its horns in the sand, leaving soft flesh exposed on the arched side of its body. The worm had indeed turned. The crab sank its pincer between the plates and with a swift sawing action cut the worm in half. The beast stood twitching in two pieces, each section of its body resting on a set of horns buried deep in the sand. It was still alive, but totally immobile.

The crowd cheered loudly as Beesk sliced the worm to pieces. It was a decisive result, sending the brothers through to the semi-finals.

Run; just run

It sniffed him.

Dex sprinted along the edge of the clearing as the beast reared on its hind legs and leaped into the air. He could hear the whooshing sound as it passed through the sawgrass. A giant paw crashed down within meters, bending the grass and knocking him over, pressing him to the ground.

As he staggered from the ground the beast paused, jutting its giant nostrils in his direction to sniff him out again. Dex seized his only chance and sprinted into the orchard.

The beast turned its back, bounding away into the forest, but the people in the orchard had noticed the commotion and were calling to each other, quickly collecting their things and fleeing towards the compound. Dex knew he didn't have long before the orchard would be as dangerous as the forest. He sprinted through the fruit trees, trying to make it to the other side, away from the beast and away from the people.

He noticed a bright pink spot in his peripheral vision: the tiny bug containing the girl's DNA sample was desperately trying to catch up with him, its energy fading fast. As he turned back towards the bug he heard the baying of dogs—a pack of twenty—sprinting through the trees in a strategic v-shaped phalanx, snarling and howling, mouths fresh with froth.

The tiny bug groggily wended its way towards him, dipping and hovering. He ran towards it, watching its life-force fading—he lunged forward as the bug fell to the ground. It dropped lightly into his hand.

He picked himself up from the ground and sealed the bug in his pouch. The dogs were fast approaching, not the quickest he had seen, but nasty looking. He charged into the forest, bashing his way through the grass, slicing his arms and face as he crashed through.

He ran for nearly an hour, the bawling dogs dropping further and further behind. Finally, he stopped to rest and rub his wounds with ointment. As he crouched down a sling of vomit fell from his mouth and across his shirt. He was exhausted and needed to stop for a longer break, but the renewed howling spurred him on. He wiped the bile from his lips, slung his pouch onto his back, and resumed running.

After half an hour he came to the bank of a watering hole, his tired feet slipping in the oily mud. He knelt and took deep gulps of water, abandoning his pannier to begin a slow freestyle stroke across the water.

He was exhausted, but the swimming offered him some relief—at least he was using different muscles. He was halfway across before the effort became too much; his clothes difficult to drag through the water, his heavy boots attracted with a seemingly magnetic force to the bottom of the lake. His arms were leaden and he could barely raise himself for breath, but he struggled on.

The final meters were torturous, the slippery bottom gradually rose beneath him. He was so exhausted it was difficult even to wade. He wanted to collapse on the bank, but forced himself to trudge the few extra meters into the forest cover where he fell down to rest under a sloping blade of grass. The water had thrown the dogs off his scent and he lay on his back, panting at the sky.

Getting paid; the professor digs out some old news

Dex swung his leg off the cat and laid it down to rest. The university was so full of students that it had taken some time to find a park. He made his way towards the professor's hexagonal building. Students were buzzing back and forth inside the crowded hive. He pushed his way to the professor's door and announced himself.

"Come in," called the professor's kindly voice.

The door retracted and Dex stepped into the cramped office.

"Aaaah," sighed the professor. "I did not expect you so soon."

"It wasn't difficult," grumbled Dex.

"So you have the sample?"

"Of course. Why else would I be here?"

"Good, good."

The professor stood and walked around the desk towards his tiny hexagonal window, staring mindlessly at students across the square. Dex took the sample from his pouch, laid it on the table and cleared his throat.

"Take a seat."

"I'd rather not," replied Dex gruffly.

"Well, I will." The professor stepped back around his desk. "You know, I already have her sample." He tented his fingers and slipped his sharp goatee inside, rubbing the edges of his chin with his forefingers.

"You'll still have to pay me," replied Dex sharply, unhappy about where this was going.

"Oh, of course." The professor tossed a figure onto the desk. "But don't you want to know what it was all about?"

"Is it my business?"

"Yes, indeed it is Dex. You make a living from this sort of thing now, don't you?"

Dex noticed the way the professor had stressed the word

now. He stared down into the man's bright eyes.

"You see," continued Professor Wilson, "I just wanted to see if you'd lost your touch."

"Well I'm glad you've found me satisfactory," sneered Dex, ignoring the inference. "Thanks." He picked up the pay, his account swelling with a pinkish glow. "Please don't waste my time."

"I want to hire you for a job," said the professor directly.

"Another job," Dex corrected him.

"Yes, another job."

"Well, what is it?"

"It starts here."

The professor pulled an article onto the cluttered desk. The headline read: FAMILY ATTACKED IN MUTANT SLAUGHTER. Dex didn't bother reading the rest. He knew the story very well.

"I remember," said Dex. "They called it the woodland killing."

"Yes," breathed the professor, "but do you know the whole story?"

Another headline washed across the desk: 1 KILLED, 2 MISSING, BOY MIRACULOUSLY SURVIVES! Dex shifted uncomfortably and looked up at the grinning professor.

"Are you interested?"

"I don't know what you want," growled Dex. "But if I wanted to play games I would've married an actress."

He walked towards the door.

"So am I to understand that you are refusing the job?"

"Yes." Dex stepped out of the cramped office.

"The way I see it you are already involved, so you may as well get paid for your efforts."

"Screw you." He stalked off down the corridor.

An impressive competitor; the semi-final battle
Locky and Dan1 were checking out the most successful
gladiorg of the day, a strange fusion of dog and snail, perfectly
designed and flawlessly incubated, a very impressive piece of
transgenics. He was lying in a cage languidly wrapped around
a water bowl, his long canine body extending from a durable
snail shell. He yawned, revealing a set of vicious teeth, then
retracted slightly into his shell and resumed resting.

"That's Freyja von Bremen." Locky gestured towards a tall
girl standing next to the snail-dog. She was in her early twenties
with straight shiny black hair, clear fresh skin, perfectly trimmed
eyebrows, one emerald eye and the other completely black—
pupil, cornea, everything black—like a large dark marble. "She
works in the design team at Biota."

"She designs for the major league?"

Locky nodded. "She helped create Rex Australis."

"No shit."

Dan1 was suddenly aware of spending too much time
observing her. He looked away, but Locky had already noticed.

"You like her, eh?"

Dan1 rubbed his nose.

"Trust me, that bitch is a moo short of a cow," snorted
Locky—which was his way of saying she had refused to sleep
with him.

Dan1 sighed as his brother turned away from Freyja and her
snail-dog. He had gotten off pretty lightly that time. Locky had
a reflexive habit of putting down anything or anyone that Dan1
showed an interest in. Locky had always discouraged him from
joining sports clubs or belief circles or even having friends outside
Locky's own select group. At some point, Dan1 had gotten used
to the idea that things were easier if they were pre-approved. It
wasn't something that sat easily with him that day.

"I don't reckon she should be allowed into the competition."
Locky shrugged. "Let's just hope we don't come up against
her until the final."

"I wanna watch her fight." Dan1 turned to Locky. "We got
enough time before the next round?"

In silence, the brothers watched Freyja's snail-dog tear
hellish shit through a reptile. The sturdy canine forelimbs
ripped over the sand dragging a fortress shell, a very effective
defense mechanism: when the fierce jaws and razor claws failed
to supplicate his opponent, he retreated into his impenetrable
shell and waited for the reptile to expose a weak point—then
suddenly pounced and snapped his jaws around its neck.

A short man walked over to congratulate Freyja.

"Holy shit," sighed Dan1. "Theodor Slit."

"The man himself," Locky beamed.

Theodor Slit, the Melbourne legend, head of the gladiorg
design team at Biota and worshiped by gladiorg fans around the
world. He was wearing a neatly fitted dark suit, accentuating the
sharp angles of his body, which were overly rigid and correct,
like a high-tension fencepost. He had black hair slickened over
to one side and eyes so sharp they could clip tin. He smiled
tightly as Freyja's gladiorg continued to demolish its opponent.

Dan1 began to prepare Beesk for her semifinal fight against
a fierce triceratops. Freyja von Bremen and Theodor Slit sat
down at reserved seats in the bleachers, keen to see who would
be the snail-dog's final competitor. Dan1 wore their presence
on his back—all he wanted was a chance to show people like
this his design skills. He had the chance. He felt the pressure.

Beesk and the triceratops were led into the center of the
battlefield, the triceratops nearly three times as tall as Beesk,
but not as wide on the ground. Its hind legs were badly injured
from the previous round, so it did not move well, but its body

was heavy and its hide thick. The judges gave their signal and the beasts were released.

Instantaneous action.

The triceratops charged, lowering its front horn to the ground. Beesk was caught off guard and couldn't get out of the way. The horn slipped under her large pincer and the triceratops lifted its powerful head, flicking her up and over its body. She crashed onto her back in the center of the battlefield, her broken leg snapping off in the fall.

The triceratops turned slowly, giving Beesk time to recover, then charged again. This time Beesk scuttled out of the way, turned and jabbed her left pincer into the dinosaur's soft belly. The triceratops twisted and trumpeted in pain, throwing its horns in the air and thumping down on the crab's back. There was a horrible cracking sound.

The triceratops was groggy. It staggered around the battlefield in a clumsy, wobbling trot, reaching the other side and turning to face Beesk. The crowd was on its feet as the triceratops charged, completely removing Beesk's large right pincer. Its massive body collapsed on top of her shell. There was a splintering crack, and then both animals were still.

Beesk was pinned under the triceratops, the life slowly being crushed out of her. Locky was screaming, but Dan1 was calculating. Judging from what he had seen, the triceratops would win on points. He was suspended in agony as the clock counted out. The crowd fell silent, waiting for the judges to signal the end of the round.

A ripple of movement flowed through the remaining legs on Beesk's right side, like fingers drumming on a table. The triceratops groaned but could not get up. The three legs dug deep into the ground and strained against the crushing weight. The cracked shell began to move, giving Beesk enough room to free her remaining pincer. Awkwardly, she raised her left pincer and drove it into the triceratops' neck. The massive gladiorg shuddered and died.

The crowd was screaming. Locky was screaming. Dan1 collapsed back onto the bench in the bunker, people rushing around him. He saw Locky hoisted above a throng of friends, but remained in his chair, staggered at the outcome. They had made it. They were through to the final round.

He looked up and saw Freyja slowly closing her notebook. She had a faint smile on her face, perhaps a look of confidence. Dan1 placed his head in his hands and fanned out his fingers. He was already thinking of a way to beat her in the final fight.

A new job turns into an old job; he'd rather forget

Dex walked in and shooed a swarm of barflies from his regular stool. He sat and coolly watched them re-settle by an ugly pack of Boondogs in the corner. Rhonda Le Guin, owner of The Hoary Blandishment, slipped down the bar towards him.

"You, hun, are the only customer I got that can scatter the trash like that. How d'ya do it?"

"I got the devil's eyes, Rhon."

"That the same as deviled eggs?"

"Yep—hardboiled with a sprinkle of curry dust."

Dex liked Rhonda's place because she put up with Dogbat. She was open to all comers, much like the group holding its regular meeting in the corner of her establishment, The Lonely Hearts Existential Society, a strange cabal of hydra philosophers, Theolotricians, Alu proselytizers and a single pious Jew still waiting for the Messiah.

"Dark and Stormy?" Rhonda was already rinsing the ginger.

"Drop a vial of something happy in there for me, Rhon. I

got a healthy account and some things to forget."

Dex had not liked the professor. He was happy to take his money, but not his shit. He didn't want to be reminded of his days running with the bulls. He had never joined the force to become a part of society; he had joined to elevate himself above it—an effort at control. The effort had failed.

Dex had been a lieutenant at the time of the woodland killing, in charge of the investigation. All his energy had gone into it, but he never got close to finding the killer. The animal force he found in the woodland that day, the sheer destruction of the brutalized mother, had made him realize he could never right wrongs, only chase shadows while trying to stay busy. There was no point in trying to control the uncontrollable— those things at the fringes, the things he saw in glimpses: the fear, the frightening things, the old memories.

He had obsessed over the killing, so desperate to find the killer that he neglected his other work, spending months interviewing, scouring the crime scene for evidence, compiling pages and pages of reports.

It all felt too personal. Who else would have recognized the silver cross? No one else would have appreciated its significance. Dex was last in a long line of preachers, his father a violent Calvinist whose fierce sermons on predestination and total depravity had scorched his childhood memories with the same force as the physical beatings handed out to his mother. He knew the power of the church—its catechisms and contradictions. His mother had escaped to the safety of a convent. And somehow the woodland killing had pierced that sanctuary, leaving him with the brutalized corpse of a mother and a nun.

Even after his captain press-ganged him into giving up on the case, he persisted, staying back late to work in secret. He pulled double shifts, smoothing himself out with endo, found leads where no leads existed, then the paranoia took over. The drug took over.

Leviathan struck and the whole world fell apart, but Dex barely noticed from his own fractured vantage. He quit the force and drifted away—then spiraled down.

After the binges, the rages, the all-night fighting, he found himself broke and homeless. He wandered for a while, living in the town camps, sharing a square of dirt sometimes with a scrap of iron for a roof. As Melbourne slowly recovered, so did he, gradually rebuilding his life.

The camp councils put bounties on the murderous mutants that patrolled the fringes, so Dex took up hunting. Later he started collecting for clients, his old police creds getting him plenty of jobs. It had taken a lot of persistence to kick endo, but he had managed to control it. He set up in a neat little shack at the edge of town and stitched his life back together—now the professor wanted to pick the scab.

He shot the Dark and Stormy, the vial bled into his system— Biota approved, controlled and relaxing, strong enough to contain time. He floated in the moment, a cleared mind.

He got home and slumped in front of his desk, pulling El9's sample from his pouch and plugging it into the board. He had filed a sample of every sequence he collected, dating right back to his final job on the force, the mother and son from the woodland killing. He patted his bulging account, reminding himself that the day hadn't been wasted—the professor might've been a maggot, but he was a generous client.

It was time to refocus on work for his other client, the famous gladiorg designer, Theodor Slit. He turned back to the hunt for Dan1 Kallikak.

The Sermon

The fire pits were burning reddy-orange as Sister Lickety-Split emerged from her sleeping quarters, tired and hungry. The rest of the compound had been feasting for the full moon since late afternoon. It was one of those perfect feast evenings when the clouds were dispersed and the air had settled at a comfortable temperature.

El9 sat down by one of the pits and picked over the food arranged in wooden bowls. She hadn't been seated long when her father stood up before the compound to speak. Torches around the low wooden stage were stoked, sending curls of bright flame into the evening. The congregation fell silent.

"Dearest brothers and sisters," he began, raising his arms gently to embrace the evening air, "I hope you have enjoyed our full moon feast."

The congregation responded with a sharp cry of "Ha-lah!"

"Brothers and Sisters, we came here because we had no choice. We looked at that mess in there," he pointed towards the city, "and we demanded justification. We searched for an overarching reason, but found that none existed. That city is no longer a society! It is so riven by the force of its own contradictions it shall not stand."

Again, the congregation responded, "Ha-lah!"

"We stand here in solidarity! We stand in solidarity because we have found justification. We know that a good life, an ethical life, is predicated on consuming that which cannot feel pain. Our dedication to this cause is defined by what we consume. People, we don't *practice* our beliefs, we *consume* them."

"Ha-lah! Ha-lah!"

"We know and we understand that true happiness cannot be founded on another's pain. We understand that we are morally required to forgo a small pleasure to relieve another's immense pain. That's why we left our old lives, abandoned the city, and came here to build afresh. Any house built on a rotten foundation will inevitably collapse, no matter how we buttress her supports. We must start anew, building from a moral core, beginning again from a position of strength, not compromise.

"And here we are: comfortable, learning new skills and abilities, providing food and shelter for our loved ones, able to bask in the warmth of these deep personal relationships, yet free to pursue our own projects without interference."

El9 rolled her eyes at this last one, but the rest of the crowd enthusiastically shouted "Ha-lah!"

"Some of us chose to leave our mothers, our fathers, our children even, because from our beliefs we have forged a new family, a greater family, a better version of ourselves. We intuitively understand the rightness of our cause. We have joined together on this journey to create a fresh vision, a moral society, an ethical family."

"Ha-lah! Ha-lah!"

"Everything we are is a product of our consumption. The partners we choose, the lovers we take, this is just another form of consumption. How so? Because sex is consumption. Because in sexual relations we are consuming a part of another's body. That is why it is so important that our relationships are with someone on the same ethical journey, of the same pure spirit. There's no need to be ashamed when we are all pure! Only those who are tainted should feel shame. People, be proud of your purity!"

"Ha-lah! Ha-lah! Ha-lah!"

"Lovers, demonstrate your purity tonight! Understand that freedom is the gift of your purity. And remember, above all else, to retain that purity in all things you consume. Goodnight and enjoy!"

Ushers poured oils across the fire pits, sending roaring yellow conflagrations into the night sky. The congregation cheered and embraced their leader as he stepped down from the rickety stage.

Preparing for the final; a surprising picture
Beesk never made it from the battlefield. Her exoskeleton had been smashed by the triceratops and much of her neural network badly damaged. Although still technically alive, Dan1 decided to retire her. He wanted to review the DNA and incubate a new version for the final.

"Well done, my boy!" Horst slapped Dan1 around the shoulder. "It is good news for you, no?"

"I'm pretty amped." Dan1 lowered his voice, "Think M-Gee has cancelled me access t' 'is lab?"

The older man shrugged and grinned. "It's good to see one of us from the floor out there winning. Very good."

Horst wandered away to begin repairs on the central incubator. Dan1 ran to his workstation, greeting Morris with a customary ear scratch, then sitting down to work. There were a few things he needed to catch up on—things he had put off from last week—but after that he would begin his review of Beesk.

Freyja had finished the day with her snail-dog completely unscathed. With such a perfect record it was unlikely she would alter her gladiorg before the final. The competition rules allowed for minor modifications to the exonic genome, and Dan1 planned a rewrite.

He spent the week redesigning Beesk's shell. It was difficult to reinforce her armour without making it too cumbersome. He altered the legs to give them more protection. She would not be as quick on her feet, but would be better in defense.

The night before the competition he was sitting in bed with

his mother's music box on his lap, staring into the matte black evening, a thick cloud shrouding the moon. The city belched excess water trapped after an unusually humid day, covering the outer membrane of Dan1's room in a film of moisture.

He opened the music box and gently thumbed the weary red carpet, wanting to find the piece of coral he'd hidden in there—he planned on taking it to the battle for good luck.

A corner of the carpet rode up under his thumb, slipping from the skirting to reveal the box's underlay. There was something there, trapped between the underlay and the carpet. He raised it slightly with his fingernail, gently levering the surrounding red velvet. It was some kind of card. He pinched the card between his thumbnail and his forefinger, extracting it from under the carpet.

It was a pic—an old one, slightly embossed, but motionless and faded—two people, arms slung casually around each other, caught in a happy moment. The woman was bright and pretty, the man darkly intense, despite his smile. It took Dan1 a moment to recognize him. It was Theodor Slit.

What is a pic of Theodor Slit doing in here?

Unconsciously his finger pressed the woman in the picture. She had short-cropped brown hair and a button nose. It dawned on him slowly. It was difficult to believe, but it was the only answer that made sense. This was his mother's music box. *Who else could it be?*

The musical chimes started to play and the tiny dancer, Adeona, emerged from backstage and pirouetted, her delicate limbs flicking and prancing across the stage in time to Tchaikovsky's ancient dance. Dan1 ignored the tiny ballet recital, dumbstruck by the pic.

"Me mum," he mouthed the words quietly under his breath. "And…" The tiny dancer stumbled slightly, distracting Dan1 enough to look up. *Did Adeona just look at him?*

The dancer finished her dance and glided backstage. Dan1 tucked the pic back into the music box, quickly closing the lid.

A moment of enlightenment for Dex; getting tickets for himself

"Get me a beer."

After a hurried scurrying, Dogbat emerged from underneath the couch, brushing short hairs from his face with a stumpy, unarticulated limb.

"Yes Sir. Absolutely immediately Sir."

"Just get it and stop crapping on."

Dogbat scampered into the kitchen to fetch a beer as Dex reclined back into the couch, watching a bulletin scroll across the wall—a story about the lightweight gladiorg final. A light breeze stirred the thin curtains draped over his windows; the setting sun pierced his eyes, making him squint. A face Dex recognized flashed across the wall. He skipped back through the bulletin to make sure it was his target.

A frustrating job had just become very simple. Another logical chain formed in his head: Dan1 Kallikak was part of a champion gladiorg team; no wonder the crazy bat from Biota wanted his sample, probably trying to draft a new recruit.

Dex heaved himself from the couch and tapped into his landline—cheaper than connecting through his perineural system. He connected to his scalper.

"Yeah, this is Dex."

There was a brief pause while the man remembered he owed Dex a favor. "Yeah, I need a pass for tomorrow's gladiorg final." A muffled response.

"No, the lightweight gladiorg final. The one that's on tomorrow."

The man protested. It was too difficult to get Dex a pass in such a short time.

"Well I'm sure you've got a pass for yourself. I'll use that one." The man refused to budge.

"Here's the thing." Dex lowered his tone to ensure the man understood. "I am a hunter and a collector. You owe me a favor. If I don't collect from you by tomorrow, then I will hunt you. Do you understand?"

Dex returned to the couch as Dogbat arrived with his beer.

"I need you to pick up a biometrix pass for me."

"Yes Sir." During the short trip to the fridge Dogbat had lost control of his right eye, which was focusing on the end of his nose, completely independently of the left. Dex tried to ignore it—these things will happen to discount assistants.

"You'll find him here." Dex passed the coordinates. "He'll be expecting you."

"Yes Sir." Dogbat's right eye twitched.

"Well off ya go."

The brown ball scurried away. Temporarily lacking depth perception he crashed spectacularly into the leg of the kitchen table, which instinctively kicked back. A little concussed he staggered into reverse, then took another run at the door, this time clearing the opening and arriving on the front porch, skidding across the dusty yard and out into the street.

Dex heard a yelp and a screech. He resumed watching the news, slowly swigging at his beer. A half hour later Dogbat returned and spat something onto the carpet.

"There you are Master."

Dex sighed and gave his chemically imbalanced butlorg a long-suffering stare.

"Is there something the matter, Sir?"

Dex picked up the severed thumb and examined the fleshy sample. It was definitely still bio-vital.

"There are easier ways, Dogbat, there are much easier ways."

The butlorg looked hurt. Dex sighed. "This should work fine. Thanks."

Dogbat perked up immediately and retreated to his burrow under the couch.

The empty hall; a first glimpse at giants

The day of the big fight. Dan1 and Locky entered the exhibition hall through the grand arches. In the middle of the hall enough seating for thousands of spectators surrounded a circular battlefield, like an indoor coliseum. Dan1 took a deep breath.

The spectators hadn't arrived yet. A janitorial crew of auxiliorgs was sweeping around the base of the seating while an officious man with a clipboard bellowed instructions at various people around the hall.

"Are you the Kallikak brothers?" he asked in a supercilious tone.

"Yes we are!" said Locky. "And who the hell are you?"

Dan1 noticed the hairs bristle on the prim little man's neck.

"I am the event organizer. Please gentlemen, bring your competitor this way," he said, leading them to a well-appointed dugout. "If there is anything else, just ask."

Locky strode into the dugout and examined the buffet. "Mmmmm," he hummed, skipping up and down the table, "this all looks pretty good."

Dan1 wandered down the pitway and out towards the battlefield. He pushed the mesh door aside and walked onto the sandy surface, the vast expanse of tiered seating towering above him—intimidating even when it was empty. He reached down and took a handful of coarse sand.

"What the hell are you doing?" shouted Locky, slightly muffled by a mouthful of lobster buttersteak. "Get over here and eat this with me."

Dan1 meandered back towards the pit.

"Check this out." Locky shoved half the lobster into his mouth.

"Why're ya eatin' that?" asked Dan1.

"Because it's all for us."

"Nah, I mean eatin' crab before Beesk fights. Ain't that bad luck?"

"Oh come on Dan1. Relax."

Locky put down the buttersteak and took a handful of oyster nuts. "Is there some kind of break in the middle of this thing?"

"Nup."

"So there's no half-time show or anything like that?"

"Nope. It's a straight fight to the death." Dan1 quivered at this thought, reconsidering the generous buffet spread in front of him. "Maybe I should eat somethink."

The brothers were eating in silence when they noticed a movement in the opposite pit. Freyja had arrived, talking loudly about the fight.

"I knew it would be impossible to penetrate that shell and I figured, why try? The triceratops really rattled her with body blows, so I trained Pavlov to smash open doggy treats with his...." Her voice trailed off when she noticed them watching. "Well, you'll see."

She flicked her straight black hair and bent down to tend to her gladiorg. She was accompanied by things that might have been men, each with a boulderous head, a bulbous nose, and tiny eyes set at bovine positions on their broad, flat faces.

"Luke Fafner and Regin Redstone," said Locky under his breath, pointing at the things that might have been men. "Slit's assistants. Thick as two fat dwarves."

"Are they human?"

"I have no idea," responded Locky. "But I never want to fight them."

The two sacks of human body parts stood at the front of the pit staring across at the brothers. Even from a distance Dan1 could see the veins laced through their bulging and disfigured noses. "Why they starin' at us?" asked Dan1.

"I think they're trying to intimidate us."

"It's workin'."

"Let's get back to the food."

The two brothers returned to their buffet table. The crowd began filing in through the arches, taking their seats. A judge came down to the pit and inspected Beesk's modifications. She was sampled, measured and weighed, the information taken back for confirmation. The judge returned and placed a magnet around Beesk's neck, removing the jack and the cage. There was a brief moment when she shuffled towards an invisible spot on the floor as the electromagnet took hold.

Dan1 could not believe how quickly everything was happening. The arena was filled with spectators. Locky was waving to friends in the crowd.

The two gladiorgs faced each other across the center of the field. The judges conferred and flashed the signal to begin. The roar of the crowd was deafening.

The final battle began slowly, the beasts stalking each other, inching their way around the edge of the field, the cheering of the crowd swelling and falling with every step.

On the opposite side of the pitch, Freyja's snail-dog inexplicably retreated into his armored home. The crowd was quiet. Suddenly the snail-dog launched across the sand with his paws inched out of his shell, scampering along on his slippery behind. Beesk raised her large right pincer in defense.

Moments before the snail-dog arrived he turned sharply and rolled onto his side like a jack-knifing truck. All his forward momentum transferred into his tipping shell, crashing spectacularly on top of the crab's back. There was a sharp crack.

Beesk reeled from the blow. She staggered to the right then recovered, lashing out with her left claw but failing to connect.

Quickly her opponent was at it again, running in a circle and returning to roll his heavy shell with enormous force onto Beesk's flat back.

The coliseum shook as the crowd rose.

"Cut him," called Locky over the noise of the crowd, "Cut him while he's outta the shell."

But the snail-dog had been carefully trained to remain protected. He charged again, executing the same rolling blow as before, slamming onto Beesk's back like a hammer. The tactic was devastating.

The brothers' gladiorg was severely stunned. The snail-dog ran another lap of the arena, building speed for a final attack. Beesk tried to scuttle out of the way but she was mildly concussed. The tall snailshell crashed down, flattening her against the sandy floor. Beesk heaved herself from the ground, then collapsed.

The snail-dog paused at a safe distance from the collapsed crab. His inquisitive canine face turned to examine his opponent. The crustacean had not moved, her pincers lying on the floor, her legs collapsed. The stalks that held her eyes were drooped and motionless. It was obvious, after only a few moments of observation, that Beesk was immobilized.

Locky was distraught, screaming at Beesk to get up. He had not expected the fight to end so quickly and decisively.

For Dan1, everything seemed to have slowed. His eyes lost focus, distracted by a tiny fleck catching the light in the air above him. He followed its meandering path out of the dugout. When his eyes refocused on the crowd he was staring at a man that he recognized—the punk from the riot—and Dan1 had a strange feeling the man was trying to ignore him.

Freyja's snail-dog emerged from his shell on the other side of the pitch. Sensing victory, he ran at full pace towards Beesk. Instead of jack-knifing, he dove forward with his claws outstretched, intending to flip the helpless crab.

He slid like a baseballer coming home, his weight driving his momentum, his sharp claws ready to dig under the unconscious crab's defenses, his serrated teeth fully exposed.

At the very last moment, when the snail-dog was stretched from his shell and skidding unstoppably towards the crab, Beesk lifted her eyes.

Chasing down Dan1; *front row seats; the final movement*
Dex had no intention of letting his target slip through his fingers again. He woke early, packed his sampling gear, and headed for the citadel.

He arrived far too early—if he was first inside he would be noticed—so he stepped into a Mother Umami's franchise, the warm oily air lingering on his skin and smooching his clothing, the familiar clammy coziness immediately making him crave dumplings and pats and other vessels for triglycerides. Instead, he ate an easy breakfast—eggs and hamspinach—while nervously checking over his gear.

When the exhibition hall opened and people started walking through the arches, Dex joined the crowd and found his seat. It was in the front row at the midway mark between the two dugouts—way too far from his target.

He walked over towards Dan1's dugout and took a seat a few rows from the front. From there his bug would be able take the sample and return unscathed. A teenage kid approached and double checked his bio-pass.

"Excuse me," said the kid nervously, "but I think you're in my seat."

Dex held out the severed thumb. "It's for one of the best seats in the house, kid. Enjoy."

The kid looked horrified as Dex tossed over the thumb.

"Now give me your pass," insisted Dex. "I want to sit here."

The kid transferred his bio-pass and scurried off. Dex was not the type of person people argued with, especially when he looked stressed. He was finding it difficult to get a lock on his target, who was skulking at the back of the dugout, and the gladiorgs had already been led onto the field—the battle was beginning.

In the first minute of fighting it looked like Dan1's gladiorg was going to be decisively beaten. Dex quickly prepared a bug, assessed the boy's position, and locked it in—the insect flew off.

Dex was trying to keep an eye on his target while tracking the bug with his sat-map. The bug swooped in for the sample. Dex was so overjoyed he looked directly into the dugout, almost catching the boy's eye.

He quickly turned back to the battlefield where, with only seconds left in the fight, the boy's gladiorg was totally immobilized, barely conscious. The crab's eyes were badly damaged. It looked like most of its higher neural functions had shut down completely. The snail-dog was charging towards the motionless crustacean, ready for the deathblow.

At the last moment, hundreds of quills bristled through the crustacean's shell, so it suddenly resembled a transgenic porcupine. The snail-dog turned his head and threw out his paws, but his shell was too heavy and the momentum hurled him straight into the waiting trap. The first spike pierced the canine's chest, the second hit his neck and before he could yelp in pain a third quill impaled him through the eye, severing his central cortex.

Dex's target was victorious—good for him. Dex had his sample and it was definitely bio-vital, so everybody had won a prize.

The crowd was on its feet, applauding the surprise victory. Dex pushed through to the exit, the bug stashed deep in his pocket. As he passed the judges' table he noticed a familiar figure watching from the shadows—it was his diminutive client, Theodor Slit.

The medal ceremony; a reward for effort

The brothers were handed the trophy: a lion-headed human fighting a human-headed lion. The two golden-skinned figures faced each other—kicking, scratching, howling, punching. Around the base was a thick coil of snakes, their headless bodies seamlessly braided, writhing about as Dan1 and Locky each took hold of one side and lifted the trophy above their heads—Locky's grin broad as a keyboard on a cathedral organ. The crowd cheered the new champions.

The brothers were walking from the dais when they came face-to-face with Freyja von Bremen.

"Congratulations," she said primly, offering the boys her hand. Locky shook it vigorously.

"Thank you Freyja." He was grinning like a crocodile. "You were a worthy opponent to beat."

Freyja looked slightly pained.

Dan1, attempting to shake her hand, became lost in her one black eyeball. At first it appeared completely black, but on closer inspection he could see lighter gray clouds drifting through the inky sphere. He was mesmerized by her.

"Congratulations Dan1." She grabbed his hand and shook.

"Yeah," he drawled. "Ya gladiorg was a hell of a beast. Real well bred."

"Thank you," she said, looking genuinely complimented.

She moved aside to reveal Theodor Slit, standing perfectly straight in his trim suit, flanked by Regin and Fafner, the giants who had earlier escorted Freyja to the arena. Slit smiled tightly and approached the brothers, keeping his hands clamped behind his back.

"Quite a show." Slit spoke in the clipped tones of a military barber, his sentences all short-back-and-sides. "I'm impressed."

"Thank you," said Locky.

Slit looked the brothers up and down with a curt nod. Dan1 got the feeling he was being subjected to a significant judgment and braced for a bald-headed observation.

"She was very well designed." Slit directed this comment at Locky, glancing at his wrist that designated him DESIGNER. "The low-lying beast was a sensible choice and the hidden spikes were a neat trick."

"Thank you, Mr. Slit. That is a huge compliment coming from..."

"I designed her," said Dan1 flatly. "I knew there was no way to beat the snail-dog in its shell. I had to catch it attacking."

Slit took a moment to examine Dan1. "A neat trick," he repeated.

"Are you looking for someone to join your team?" asked Dan1 directly.

"A neat trick," repeated Slit again, softer but more deliberately, as he walked a pace towards Dan1 and bobbed on the balls of his feet. "What really impressed me was the breeding. What model incubator was that?"

"A Tri-Womb," said Dan1. He could feel Slit surveying him again, carefully studying his oversized shoes and working up to his birds nest haircut.

"So you were the designer and the technician?"

"Yes."

"We're looking for a junior laboratory technician. Are you interested?"

Dan1 eased into his chest slightly. "I'm looking for a design position."

"What we have is a junior laboratory technician position,"

said Slit coolly.

"I'll take it."

Slit turned sharply on his heels and disappeared into the crowd with the giants on either side.

"Come to the reception desk at the gladiorg design lab," said Freyja, holding out a Biota notebook. "It's on the fifth floor."

"I know where it is," said Dan1.

"Welcome aboard," said Freyja. "I'll see you tomorrow." The clouds in her dark eye shifted and swirled as she turned away from the brothers and hurried to catch up with Theodor Slit.

BetaMax; catching up

Brother Bassblow lifted the heavy television onto its pedestal and pushed the BetaMax tape into the player.

"I was testing the museum's system out by Ying's Mound, near where the intruder crossed into the orchard," explained Brother Bassblow. "It's a bit blurry because of the magnetic tape."

An image flickered on the screen and then resolved: the orchard in the morning, just near the edge of the sawgrass forest. A few gray lines slashed across the screen, hovering while it was paused, then disappeared as the tape scrolled through the heads.

"Can we zoom in?" asked the leader.

"Unfortunately no," said Brother Bassblow, "we'd need more sophisticated equipment."

It didn't matter. He recognized Lieutenant Declan immediately, despite the remodeling. It wasn't a face he would forget. Sometimes it took a long time for the past to catch up, but it always did, it was always there, nipping at the heels.

"Leave me with this," said the leader. "And fetch Sister Lickety-Split," he added, as Brother Bassblow headed for the door. "I think I may have a project for her."

The final word from his client; why not just give it all away?
Dex contacted Slit on his personal line.

"I have the sample."

"I no longer require your services."

"That's not the way it works, Mr. Slit."

"You may keep the deposit."

"That is not the way it works," breathed Dex.

"It was a generous deposit. I think the deal is fair."

"That was not the deal we agreed upon, Mr. Slit."

"We are in business Mr. Declan. In business, circumstances change. We must be flexible. My offer is reasonable in the circumstances. You may keep the deposit. Goodbye."

The line died.

Dex was tense with anger. It wasn't the money—the professor's pay would keep him for a while—it was the way Slit had spoken to him. He was being treated like a child. First the professor with his inexplicable taunts, then Slit refusing to pay. It had been a frustrating week.

He walked into his office and turned on the lamp. A jaundiced light settled on the desk. He swept his files aside and opened a drawer, removing a small pouch containing a row of hypodermic vials, all but the last one empty. He plucked the vial from the stitching and held it up to the light. The endo inside glowed with a greenish tinge. He flicked his finger on the hollow spine and considered pressing it to his finger.

Instead, he put it down on the desk and took out Dan1's DNA sample. Reaching over he placed the sample onto his board, turning back to the desk to make a label for his files. Out of the corner of his eye he noticed the board respond, a blood-red line extending across it, searching out a match for Dan1's DNA.

Dex spun in his chair and watched the progress of the line. It turned and moved slowly between the hundreds of collected samples. Row by row it passed through the years until it reached the top, stopping just short of the mother, connecting with the young boy's DNA.

1 KILLED; 2 MISSING;
BOY MIRACULOUSLY SURVIVES

Without even knowing it he'd returned to the woodland killing. The professor was warning him: the old job was back.

Dex turned to his desk and picked up the tiny vial of endo, slowly raising it to his quivering finger.

PART TWO

THE SPIRALING BIND

Invisible threads are the strongest ties.
—Friedrich Nietzsche

A familiar killer

The head was faceless. The skin had been torn from the bone leaving rough junks of meat where cheeks once flanked a nose, now just a thin strip of cartilage extending up the middle of the head. The exposed forehead slipped back to a beige skull where clumps of hair and blood stuck together in irregular patterns.

It was perched on the edge of a dumpster looking over the alleyway. In front of it, spread across the ground and up the walls, were the shredded remains of its torso, blood and splinters of bone daubed high across the walls of the alleyway, more than three meters from the ground in some places. The stench was overwhelming.

"I've never seen anything like it," said the young lieutenant, shaking his head and holding his nose.

His captain stood quietly, hand covering his mouth, eyes shifting uneasily over the corpse in front of them. He had seen this modus operandi before. Many years ago in the woodlands, high in the hills behind the city, there had been a murder like this one.

"How could such a large mutant get into the city undetected?" asked the lieutenant.

The captain observed the body for a long time. "Wait to hear from forensics before calling a bounty hunt."

"Why wait? This is clearly a mutant kill, there's no way it's homicide."

The captain looked back over the alleyway, remembering a time as a young bull when he had thought the same thing. It was curious the way the killer thoroughly mutilated the body but left the victim's head mostly intact, leaving it to survey the ruin of its own corpse. Perhaps it had been deliberately left that way to delight the killer's macabre sense of humor. If so, the killer was not a mutant—only a human could be that sadistic.

By mid-morning forensics had cleared away most of the body. The stench drifting from what remained was thick and pungent. The young lieutenant and the captain were standing at the mouth of the alleyway when a figure in a dark coat pulled up on a black panther-cycle. The cat heaved and sighed, sinking gracefully onto the pavement. Dex squinted into the shadowy alley. He walked towards the two police officers, keeping his hands deep in his pockets.

"Morning, Warren."

"Morning, Declan," sighed the Captain. He gestured at the corpse spread about the alleyway. "So, you think it's back?"

Making Brains

"Good morning," said a spectral voice through the system. "Please come through."

The door retracted to reveal Slit's personal secretary, Ms.. Sundew, standing on the other side. Dan1 attempted to shake her hand but seemed to slip right through; the woman had no substance, barely a person—more the suggestion of a person, as if her parents had agreed to have a child but didn't pull it off with much conviction.

"You have been assigned to the neuro-design team as an assistant technician." There was a hint of disdain in her voice, as if the word *technician* had no right being part of her vocabulary. She swished off down the corridor.

They moved quickly through bright white halls lined with various labs—*The Ocular Group, Haemalogics and Cytoarchitectonics, Ossific Testing Facility*—the names washed across Dan1's perineural. The gladiorg department was the elite, drawn from outstanding employees and the best new graduates, divided into specialist groups working on research and design projects. It functioned has Biota's R&D hub, engineering the next generation of bioindustrial technologies.

Dan1 peered through an orifice at several workers hunched over an enormous jade green iris spliced vertically by a distinctly feline pupil. Dan1 smiled at the idea of designers and technicians working together in the same lab, producing machines that were both manmade and organic, unseating the Creator, *walking hand in hand with God*, as they said.

Ms.. Sundew whisked down the halls as if she were caught in a draft, shifting and disappearing in front of Dan1's eyes, slipping into fissures of air, emerging from cracks in the background and weightlessly whisking away again. She stopped in front of an office door, which sensed her arrival.

"Miklos Pohl is your supervisor and will show you to your workspace." She lightly touched the back of his hand so the metrix bled into his system—the design lab acknowledged his superior clearance and augmented his perineurals with richer data. "There will be no formal induction program because you are already an employee." She turned suddenly and slipped away, without saying goodbye.

Here he was, standing at the threshold of his new career. This was, literally, the Major Leagues. Somehow they had let some street kid into the citadel, allowing him access to the loftiest heights of gladiorg competition without a degree, without pedigree, and with no network helping him out. Suddenly he had arrived.

Miklos Pohl, a man in his late fifties, emerged wearing a long tatty lab coat that at some point had been white but had turned liverish gray. He was tall and nervous with a thin face and a red rash running along his hairline. As chief laboratory technician, Pohl was in charge of preparing gladiorgs for the battlefield.

"Dan1 Kallikak." He stared blankly for a moment, as if he had forgotten his own name, then something appeared to click in the old man's head and he gestured for Dan1 to follow him.

Dan1 hurried after, down the endless white corridor, suddenly a little unsure in his steps. He was streetwise and sly, he was talented at sequencing and would pit his engineering against anyone's—in fact, he had done just that in the lightweight comp and won—in some ways his life had prepared him for the battle, but he'd also missed some steps. He was never schooled and never had the luxury of an adolescence. He was a boy operating in a man's body, borrowing an adult's voice to fake his way through conversation. His remote control limbs followed Pohl through a door marked *Neural Development*.

"You'll be making the brains," said the old man.

The Major Leagues

"Your job is to incubate the prototype neuro-units for testing." The words echoed from Pohl's hollow cheeks. "Things are fairly calm around here at the moment. But it will get more hectic as we approach the Grand Final." Even delivering this urgent warning his speech was low and eerily disembodied. He opened the door and ushered Dan1 into a dark room. It took a moment for their eyes to adjust.

"These are the prototypes we're currently working on." Pohl gestured towards a line of ungainly organisms floating in transparent cubes. "One of these neural units will be used in the Grand Final. Apparently Slit feels that Dear Rex could do with a more sophisticated brain," he said, referring to Rex Australis, the gladiorg design team's greatest achievement. "After you have incubated a brain you need to bring it here for training."

"Trainin'?" Dan1 had never worked with such sophisticated organisms and was unsure of their regime.

"These neuro-units," began Pohl, tapping lightly on one of the tanks, "have fully functional ocular, aural and olfactory units."

"So they c'n see and 'ear us?" asked Dan1.

"And smell us," replied Pohl sourly. "Your job as a technical assistant is to incubate the brains; one of my jobs is to ensure they are trained correctly." He gestured towards a monitor at the front of the room. "We have a very specific input regime that teaches them to be aggressive."

"Of course," said Dan1. "You need t'teach 'em."

"The way the brain develops is critical to its effectiveness in battle. Manufacturing neural systems is not just about sequencing DNA, the genetics of neurology are only half the story. You cannot design a brain to be violent; you must *train* it to be violent." Pohl hunched and vigorously scratched at his arm. "We should leave these in peace," he said quietly. "I'll show you to the incubators."

Dan1 was led into his new lab, a pristine white cube with several high-end incubators spread along two walls and an opalescent monitor covering a third. He was disappointed to discover that the orders were processed remotely from the neuro-design lab upstairs.

Pohl showed him how to access the orders and briefly tested his knowledge of the incubators. Dan1 had spent his first year with Horst learning the ins and outs of maintaining temperamental incubators, understanding their moods, playing the good shepherd. Pohl quickly realized that Dan1 was an excellent technician and left the boy to work alone in the small, silent laboratory.

The pathways of the brain; a small promotion
For his first month in the gladiorg design team Dan1 did nothing but incubate brains. There was none of the problem solving he had enjoyed on the manufacturing floor and at first he wondered whether it had been a good move. His new

laboratory was a sterile place—no audio system, no pictures, no mini-elephants. Not even a window. Just the glaring whiteness of the lab.

His perineurals pinged with a request and a DNA sequence scrolled across his vision. He uploaded the sequence into a totipotent cell, injected the cell into clay and incubated the block. After incubation he checked for defects (there were rarely any) then immersed the finished organism in cerebrospinal fluids, wired up its sensory systems and sent it to Mikos Pohl for "education".

It was repetitive work—skull transcending boredom—and he felt like he had incubated the same brain a billion times. The brainstem and cerebellum rarely changed at all, but the designers often made subtle alterations to the bulbous cortex surrounding the brain. At first, Dan1 only knew the basic architecture, the two hemispheres—left and right—and the four lobes: *frontal*, *parietal*, *temporal* and *occipital*. Then he started to notice differences in the little wrinkles that covered the brain like hills and valleys, the gyri and sulci.

He worked with a Hydrapedia feed in his periphery, familiarizing himself with the geography of the cerebral cortex, like a cabbie learning the streets of a new city. He got to know the main thoroughfares, from the post parietal sulcus up to the post central gyrus and then all the way down to the lateral cerebral sulcus, and he learned the Brodmann areas, small neighbourhoods in the brain that specialize in particular neuronal functions.

The designers were constantly sending down DNA sequences with minor edits to improve the cytoarchitecture of their neuro units or augment the retinotopic maps. As far as Dan1 could see, too much time was spent obsessing over small changes in the physical structure of the brain instead of focusing on the development of the mind. He should have been working with Miklos Pohl to train minds—not stuck in the lab making brains.

It was a particularly frustrating Friday when he received a sequence from Fuego Wing, a designer on the team. The code streamed through Dan1's eyes on its way to the incubator. He spotted an error and instinctively paused the transfer. Back on the manufacturing floor Dan1 would've quickly rectified the issue but here he had to send it back to the designers for them to review and fix. He turned the code around quickly.

You sure you want to query this?

Wing's message flashed across his perineurals. It seemed a little menacing and more than a little patronising. It irked him. He decided the best response was just to show Wing how good he was with code. He made the fix and sent it back with the corrected sequence highlighted and circled. His response was pretty aggressive, but it had been a very frustrating Friday.

Yikes.

Wing slowly withdrew from Dan1's perineurals, leaving only the threatening presence of Theodor Slit. Dan1 suddenly noticed the log line—it wasn't Wing's code, it was Slit's. Panic rushed through his brain and he tried to prevent it spilling into his perineurals. His fingertips pulsed with electric fear. He could feel Slit reviewing the code, line by line. He felt the wash of indignation across his perineurals—Slit was not trying to mask his feelings.

Then suddenly, nothing. Slit was gone, the patch was approved, and Dan1 was alone in the crisp whiteness of his lab, waiting for the adrenaline to subside.

As he incubated the sequence he wondered if there would be repercussions. He thought he was being insubordinate to Wing, which was probably bad enough, but directly challenging Slit was… unthinkable. He felt it all slipping away—the Major

Leagues, the job, the money—before he'd even had a chance to save bond for a new apartment.

He was dreading the weekly review meeting. He felt sure Slit would humiliate him in front of the gladiorg department and its entire technical staff. The whole week he felt he was slowly being pushed towards this horrible moment. The hours were long but the days rushed by. Suddenly it was Friday and the whole department had assembled under Slit's gaze. The slim man was flanked by his neuro-design team—Freyja von Bremen, Fuego Wing, and Donny Chan—while the designers and technicians from all the other departments gathered in front. Dan1 hadn't heard a word from Slit since correcting his code. He tried to find a place in the crowd well away from the neuro team—perhaps the distance could save him. At the very least it minimized the chance of any eye contact with Slit.

Slit called the meeting to order simply by standing and looking expectantly at the crowd. "Rex Australis did it again," he began smoothly. "Our gladiorg is performing well. We should be proud." He continued with his speech before any real sense of achievement could set in. "I am concerned by an apparent weakness in his left knee, severe enough for all relevant teams to review their sequencing. I want full reports by tomorrow. Make sure you send a copy to Miklos Pohl. If we need to incubate another version of Rex Australis then we must give our technicians as much time as possible. Re-breeding a gladiorg in the middle of a season has its disadvantages, but by the end of this year Rex Australis will be the most successful gladiorg in the history of the sport. We must give him every chance to succeed. Pohl, I want you to be prepared for any contingency."

"Yes sir," said Pohl.

"I don't want to keep you any longer," said Slit. "We have much to do."

He tucked his head into his chin and stepped away from an imaginary stage. The group immediately began to file away, breaking into smaller clusters and dissolving away.

Dan1 let the air from his chest. It was almost the weekend. He felt like if he could just get to that safe zone he would be fine. Everything would be reset by Monday. Sure, he'd have to see Slit again, but maybe the great man just never noticed his insolence. Maybe he was just a fly buzzing around an elephant's ear—annoying, sure, but not something Slit would even be conscious of.

"Kallikak." The word cut into Dan1's thoughts like scalpel through a brain.

He looked up and found Slit's laser-like gaze boring into his face. Total mental shutdown.

He walked over to Slit, basically lobotomized. His gait was that of a zombie, uneven and unsure but unstoppable. Wing and Chan, standing slightly behind Slit, exchanged surreptitious smirks. Freya watched his approach directly. He tried to ignore them all.

"You had a problem with my code?"

"I noticed a small error."

"You applied a very quick fix."

"I'm sorry, Mr. Slit."

"I'll be keeping a close eye on you." Slit's eyes narrowed and darkened.

Dan1 just nodded. Horrified and terrified.

"You'll be working in my lab now," hissed Slit. He turned and walked away.

Dan1 was completely unsure how to respond. Wing mouthed, "What?" to Chan, but kept his back turned and his head down. Freya was still looking straight at him, her eyes had never left him. She smiled gently and flicked her eyebrows.

It was only that almost imperceptible movement that made Dan1 realise he had just received a promotion.

Getting to know his boss; the question of mind and matter
A group of young corporates were laughing and chatting near the entrance to the gladiorg design department. He could feel them tracking his approach. He knew they were wondering what someone like him was doing in their sector. Their eyes were judging him; their expensive ostrich, snake and shark skin integuments were judging him too. He tilted his head so his wiry birdnest blocked their line of sight and flicked his snakeboard into his hand. Skipping lightly up the steps, the entrance recognized his clearance and retracted. He glanced back at the group of mid-twenties, who quickly averted their gaze.

Dan1 was in an awkward moment. He had skipped from the bottom, from the depths of the manufacturing floor, to the absolute pinnacle, the top of the top. Yet his clothes, his body, his BIOS and his whole understanding of who he was as a person had not yet updated. Locky pushed him to "get himself improved", but for some reason Dan1 was hesitating. He was keen to get an apartment and was quickly saving the bond required for the move, but he wasn't yet ready to become corporate.

Instead he was focusing on the work, which had suddenly become challenging. The team was developing a new cerebellum for a sophisticated neuro-unit and Dan1 had been placed in charge of incubating the prototypes. It was tough work, with significant responsibilities, but it also meant being shoulder to shoulder with the legendary Theodor Slit. The man was a demanding boss, a hardworking genius who lived his life in fast-forward; he had graduated early from high school and went straight to university, where he quickly distinguished himself, then quit before receiving his degree to take charge of gladiorg design at Biota.

The pace at which he worked tested the limits of Dan1's newly acquired skills. He had moments of shuddering doubt. Incubating such subtle organisms took time and a considerable amount of technical expertise. Dan1 consulted regularly with Miklos Pohl, drawing on the older man's experience and encyclopedic knowledge of incubating neuro-units.

He could tell Slit was pleased with the progress of his new protégé. The two of them spent all day together in the antiseptic design laboratory listening to Slit's favorite music, *The Ring Cycle* by Richard Wagner. The ancient opera soared from a hidden speaker system, building in the back of Dan1's consciousness, affecting his mood to such an extent that he wondered what affect it was having on the neurological units.

"Aren't ya worried that this music will mess with the brains?"

"Pardon?" Slit was examining an intricate formation of axons clustered near the front of the cerebellum.

"I'm just wonderin' 'bout the music," continued Dan1, suddenly unsure of himself. "Won't the music affect the development of the brains?"

Slit grimaced. "Are you talking about Miklos Pohl's little project?"

"Yeah," replied Dan1, "the neuro units in that dark room."

"It is nonsense," said Slit. "I let him continue simply because he is so convinced it works. I indulge him. Yet it is strange that a man who knows so much about neurological incubation should be so misguided about neurological design."

"Doesn't make no difference then?" asked Dan1.

"Pohl's aim is to train a brain to be violent, but when you saturate an intelligent neural system with violent images on a screen, all it will learn is that screens are violent. It will not affect its perceptions of the real world."

"But then how do ya design a brain to be violent like?"

Slit laughed at the rawness of Dan1's question.

"That is the question, my boy." He waved his scalpel in the air. "First you must learn the *craft* of making a brain; then you can learn the *art* of making a mind."

"I guess I always reckoned a brain was like any other neuro unit, ya know? A blank slate ya can fill with data, just like programmin' an auxiliorg."

Slit laughed. "If we sent an auxiliorg's brain into battle it would be slaughtered!" He jabbed the air with his scalpel to make the point.

"So how does a gladiorg win then?" Dan1 had stopped his work and was looking at Slit. It was a question that had been at the edge of his mind for weeks. He had learned the basic architecture of neurology, but he was no closer to understanding the dynamics of the mind.

"A gladiorg needs cunning and aggression, but above all it needs the *desire* to win," explained Slit. "That is the aim of our design, to implement neuronal networks that release the chemicals that give our gladiorg the desire to kill."

"Are you saying desire is a chemical?"

"Of course desire is a chemical. Everything we are is chemical. We are material beings. We are chemistry. We do what we do because we are programmed to do it—simple as that. Everything we are is a result of genetic inheritance, so if you are disappointed with your life then blame your parents, they wrote the code that has led to your misery." Slit laughed and resumed his work. "The sins of the father are the sins of the son, Dan1."

Dan1 looked down at the lumps of meat on the table. He had spent weeks assembling brains. Initially he had assumed that a brain was a separate entity from the mind; now he realized that the architecture of a brain is reflected in the temperament of the mind. Brains are not *trained* to perform a task, they are *pre-programmed*.

If his biological parents provided him with his genetic roadmap, that could explain his design abilities. They had always felt innate, perhaps they were inherited—his mind flicked to the photo of Slit he had found in his mother's music box.

He watched Slit pick up a neuro-unit and carry it over to the trash, flinging it in with a casual flick of the wrist. As Slit turned back to the bench and washed his hands Dan1 noticed a small hair resting on his shoulder; a perfect DNA sample, definitely bio-vital. He plucked it from his boss's back.

"What did you just do?" snapped Slit.

"There was something on your shoulder."

"Well don't groom me boy, I'm not an oran-u-tang." Slit grinned at his attempted humor. "I am having a dinner tonight at my house. The other members of the neuro-design group will be there. It will be an opportunity to get to know each other."

"Sure," said Dan1, aware that it was never put to him as a choice.

"Excellent." Slit spun sharply on his heels and walked from the lab.

An offer from the old precinct

Dex eyed the police captain from across the desk. He was a lumpy man with a broad gut and a strange growth below his lower lip that looked like a stray piece of food. Occasionally he flicked at it with his tongue, as if trying to draw it back into his mouth and devour it.

"It's not an easy case, Declan." His tongue flicked along his lip and paused at the growth. "We might need your help."

It was the first time Dex had returned to his old station since leaving the force. Captain Warren had been a young bull back then; they had never got on well—Dex's hypodermic personality made relationships difficult. He grunted at Warren's request.

"No one knows more about this case than you, Declan. We can't even figure out if the killer is human or mutant. So do we bring you in as a bounty hunter or do we hand it over to homicide?"

"You don't even know if it's the same case." Dex stared levelly at the captain—unsure whether he wanted the case. If he did, it would not be as a favor to Captain Warren.

"No," said Warren. "We don't know if it's the same killer. The boys in forensics haven't been able to compare samples yet. We're having trouble locating the file."

The edge of Dex's lip turned but he quickly stifled the smile. Warren leaned over the desk so his gut pressed into his shirt.

"Declan, it's the same MO. How many times in your life have you seen a corpse spread out like that? I'm betting the answer is once. It's gotta be the same killer. And if it's not, after they dig out the file and test it, then you can tell us you're not interested. But for the moment, I'm asking you, will you take the case?"

"What's the pay?"

"A full lieutenant's wage."

Dex looked up at the ceiling and breathed through his nose. It was an attractive offer. He could do with the extra cash. He rocked back slightly and stared at a point just above Warren's head.

"Officially you will be commissioned as a special consultant. That means you can work on your own if you like." Warren was desperately pimping the deal—he wanted this case off his books and Declan was the perfect subcontractor. "You will have access to all our facilities—anything you want."

Dex smiled and rose from his chair. "This organization can't even find the file, why would I want access to your facilities?"

"It's only an offer, Declan," said the captain, edging forward in his chair. "Just think about it…"

Dex turned at the door. "I'm taking the case, but I won't need your help. I'll start as soon as you fatten my account."

The door retracted behind him and he padded off down the corridor.

The dinner party; Schrodinger's hair

Slit lived in Swanston Heights, a wealthy suburb to the northwest of the city. His house was a sprawling gothic-styled mansion with a pitched roof drawn in tight sweeping lines to the guttering, where gargoyles mouthed a silent howl. Set into the second story were three gables, hunched and menacing, sheltering opal black windows. Below that was a hooded balcony and a blood-red Japanese maple dripping over the front steps.

Dan1 walked along a path lined with prim box hedges and up the steps to a heavy wooden door. The door swung open revealing an elaborate foyer with a large tiger pelt stretching its paws to the four corners, its head propped awkwardly on its chin. An elephant foot stamped twice as he crossed the threshold.

"Welcome," growled the tiger head. "Please state your name."

"Dan1 Kallikak," he announced too loudly, a little unhinged by the talking head.

"I will inform them of your arrival." The elephant foot stamped again and a tiny shadow scurried into the house. The door swung closed behind him.

Dan1 stepped through the foyer into a large entrance hall. Snake skin banisters wound their way up a grand staircase; the floors were covered in deep maroon carpet; twisted ivory light-fittings grew from the heavy oak paneling covering the walls; diaphanous skin lamps, set at regular distances, somehow cast more shadow than light, leaving deeper corners unexplored. The house was silent.

"My boy," said Slit, suddenly emerging from the shadows with his hand extended. "Please, come in. Welcome to the family home."

"Thanks," replied Dan1 quietly, unfamiliar with this hospitable and amiable version of Theodor Slit. "She's a beautiful home."

"Please, come through, come through. The house is called New Swanston, it was the first in the area," boasted Slit as he led Dan1 down the hall. "In fact, the suburb was named after the house."

Slit motioned him into the drawing room. Perched inside were the two giants, Fafner and Regin, seated on dainty sofas, each holding a highball glass filled with something blue, looking as comfortable as a couple of buffalo brought in from the savannah to sip mixed drinks and make polite conversation. They smiled awkwardly.

Dan1 had not yet spent time with the other members of the neural-design group. He rarely saw Fuego Wing or Donny Chan in person and had not spoken a word with Freyja or the giants since the lightweight gladiorg final.

"Hello," said Regin.

Fafner got up and lumbered over to greet Dan1. Upon arriving he was unsure what to do with his drink. He tried shaking hands without putting it down, then withdrew awkwardly, rubbed his other palm against his expansive forehead, and sighed.

Regin was definitely stupid, but Fafner was so dim you could hear the spelling mistakes in his speech. He removed his palm from his forehead, looked slightly stunned and said, "Hello."

"Hey guys." Dan1 grinned and bowed slightly.

"Would you like a drink?" offered Slit.

"Yeah, that'd be sweet."

Slit left Dan1 to make conversation with the meatbox morons. Every great duo has a straight man, the fall guy for the zany antics of the *agent provocateur*. Unfortunately, Regin and Fafner were both straight as rods—a severe restriction on their ability to maintain interesting conversation. The best they could come up with was a kind of mono-directional patter, where a listener became increasingly frustrated waiting for two parallel lines to meet.

Thankfully Slit returned with a glass of the same strange bluish liquid the giants were drinking. Dan1 took a generous swig—it tasted like the dentist. He stumbled onto the sofa and sipped quietly.

"The others should be here soon," said Slit, "but until then I guess it's just us." He chuckled. The giants chuckled too. "Dan1 and I have made some significant progress on the N106," commented Slit, referring to the neural-unit they were currently testing. "This should interest you, Regin."

Slit expertly lariated Regin into conversation, careful not to spook him, like a cowboy leading cattle through a run. The slightly brighter of the two giants grunted and sat forward in his chair.

While Regin and Slit discussed the N106, Dan1 was left to make small talk with Fafner. Luckily this was the only size of conversation that Fafner's brain could compute.

"So what do you do in the neuro-design team?" asked Dan1.

Fafner shrugged. "Mosdly lifft hevy stuf."

"I see."

Fafner nodded.

Dan1 grinned awkwardly.

Fafner nodded.

"I see."

Like many before him, Dan1 was discovering that Fafner had a mind like a steel trap—only those who have attempted conversation with a steel trap could appreciate what is meant by this. Just in time, the elephant foot stamped and Freyja slipped into the room wrapped in black bear fur.

"Exquisite timing my dear." Slit kissed her cheek.

A short time later Wing and Chan arrived in well-cut evening wear. Slit clapped sharply, causing hidden things to scamper; the door to the dining room opened and they moved through.

A long table was set with elegant cutlery lined on a white tablecloth. Slit, who was still discussing the N106, reached casually for some bread and dipped it into a small serving dish made from bone china. Dan1 did the same. The flavor was incredible—a meaty and aromatic fungus. The rest of the meal was similarly spectacular. First course was caviar the size of quail eggs, followed by quail eggs the size of pinheads. The main course was abalone steak on a bed of saltwater lamb—*gastronomique surreal* at its finest—not that Dan1 recognized it as such.

In fact, he was having a hard time distinguishing the food from the decoration and had to take cues from Freyja, who was sitting opposite. She had shed her bear fur to reveal a snugly fitted dress covered in inky scales. It showed off her incredible figure—a supple and muscular torso, like a wild salmon. Dan1 spent most of the evening avoiding the gaze of her dark, glassy eye.

A troupe of sophisticated auxiliorgs emerged to collect their empty plates.

Over dessert the conversation again turned to Slit's spectacular house.

"Yes," said Slit as he swilled the remnants of red wine from his glass, "it was seeded by my great-grandfather, left to me by my parents when I was twenty-five. Very lucky to have survived

Leviathan. They moved to Queensland—too humid up there for me. Anyway, the house is larger than one person really needs, but I can't sell it—too much a part of the family. Of course I don't have my own family," he grinned at his nervous guests, "apart from you people."

They all laughed at this comment. Dan1 tittered, then worried it sounded contrived, so he stopped and made a strange high-pitched gurgle.

"I decided a long time ago that work was the only thing that could truly satisfy me. And it does. Just look at our Dear Rex, eh?" There was a murmur of approval at Slit's observation.

"By the way Dan1, next week you are invited to my private box for the game."

"Cool. Where's the box?"

"The best position in the arena," enthused Freyja, her dark eye glinting. "You'll love the view."

"Nod too menshion tha buffay," grunted Fafner.

The evening concluded with a small glass of sauterne. The guests thanked their host and left through the massive wooden door. Freyja offered Dan1 a lift home but he refused, telling her he had arranged his own transport. He found his snakeboard, stashed in a nearby garden, and headed for the nearest train station.

On the way home he took the hair he had found on Slit's suit and sequenced it—the spiralling base pairs moved across his vision. He pulled up his own sequence and spun it gingerly with his finger. He went through a brief period when he first arrived at Biota of looking over his sequence, initially hoping he could see his parents in there, but quickly realising the fruitlessness of that hope.

He now had a picture of someone he presumed was his mother. And she was standing next to Slit. It was impossible to avoid the implications.

He isolated his paternal copy of chromosome 7. He knew that on chromosome 7 there is a stretch of DNA, known as D7S820, prone to a harmless mutation, a short tandem repeat of A-G-A-T occurring between 7 and 14 times. He pulled the same stretch of Slit's DNA. The mutations in D7S820 were a match, meaning Dan1 and Slit were of a similar haplotype, not a huge coincidence given they had both emerged from the same genetic pool.

He leaned back in his chair and watched the travelduct wash past the translucent membrane of the train. The sequences were still sitting in his perineurals, drifting in and out of his peripheral vision. He wiped them away.

The unstable killer

Dex spread the monitor on his desk and uploaded the file. After leaving the force, a parting gift to himself had been a copy of the woodland killer's file. It was an enormous work. At the time he had considered it his *magnum opus*, now he saw it as testament to his unstable mental state in those days, full of endo induced fantasies and paranoid theories. The thing that frustrated him most about the woodland case— apart from the sheer brutality of the killing—was that for all the time and energy he had poured into the investigation, he had never made any progress.

The killer's DNA, too unstable for the board, was stored in a hard sealed cryo-pac in the file. He slipped it into his scanner to refamiliarize himself. It was a nice piece of splitting, like looking through a kaleidoscope—every time Dex shifted the sample it changed slightly, constantly mutating to adjust to the environment.

It was definitely a human haplotype, but one that had been synthetically transformed—a rare human gen-mod. Animal mutants were commonplace—any fool with an incubator and a devious mind could breed their own mutant—but few people had the technical capacity, or the moral iniquity, to incubate a mutant human—especially one as sophisticated as this. It could have been some smartarse chromo cowboy from Wurundjeri. That kind of thing was in breach of the Charter, but it happened. Dex had a bigger theory.

The way he saw it, the killer's DNA was a decoy. It had been built by someone as an elaborate puzzle to throw investigators off the scent. Someone had left this DNA at the scene to make it look like a mutant killer, when in fact the case was a lot simpler.

When Dex was in the force he had always tried to keep perspective on the human drama of homicides, without getting lost in forensics. A murder is made up of actors, not sequences of DNA. From this angle, there were two big questions: Why had the boy been left completely unharmed? What had happened to the father? Dex was sure the answers were related—and it all came down to the father. Yet for all his effort, he had never found much information on the man, a well-respected theolotrician who simply disappeared without a trace.

And now there was this mess in the alleyway—Captain Warren had been right, it was exactly the same method of mutilation. If there was a connection between the killings Dex wouldn't be surprised.

He loaded the swatch of samples collected from the alleyway and isolated the victim's, placing it on his board, then slipped the rest of the samples into his scanner—more than thirty distinct sequences from people whose DNA had been found at the scene, most of them random passers-by and police officers. One of them would be the killer's.

He flicked through the cells under the microscope, watching for the familiar sequence. Inside a cell is a chromosome, a continuous loop of DNA, a chemical fingerprint, a unique identifier. He found a possible match. Strings of letters fell across his periphery. Dex watched the probability narrow. The sequences were compared and probability stopped short of 100%.

He examined the two samples in the scanner—they were both highly unstable. Yet there were subtle differences: small stretches of genetic information in the most recent sample were not present in the one collected from the woodlands. Given the inherent instability of the killer's DNA, it was hardly surprising that small mutations had occurred over time. Dex returned the DNA back to the cryopac and stashed it away.

He had spent a long time running from his addiction, a long time hiding from history. Now the woodland killer was back and hiding somewhere in the city. Dex worked late into the night reviewing the old file, removing anything useful and storing the rest separately. He wanted to write a report on the original murder so he could begin research on the most recent killing as soon as possible. It was well past midnight. He leaned back in his chair, closing his eyes and pinching the blade of his nose.

At this point endo was the only thing that would keep him awake. He took the last vial from the leather pouch in his drawer and walked into the kitchenette. He placed it in the sink and with the bone handle of a knife, smashed it. Greenish fluid poured away down the drain.

He walked towards the bedroom, desperately needing to rest. Tomorrow he would begin again.

Ratboy and the incident at Mother Umami's

The matinees were Locky's idea, of course, it was hardly Dan1's choice to parade in front of the privileged little prats that drifted through Mother Umami's in the early afternoon. The school kids would crowd into the booths and feast on plates of carbo pats covered in powdery sucrose and sip milksteaks while Locky, dressed in a red cape and top hat, opened with his easy after school shtick, a custom blend of the carnal and the scatological. After a decent serve of prurience they moved on to the magic.

Their most popular act was called *The Mystery of the Amazing Ratboy*, a title scrawled in silvery lettering across the side of a large red box handmade by Locky. The act began with Dan1 crawling into the top of the box while Locky explained to the crowd that a magical force existed that would cause organisms to combine once sealed together inside. Locky would then produce a cage full of rats, always guaranteed to prompt howls from the audience, and shake it in front of the kids who looked most fearful, the ones most likely to squeal.

Locky slowly and dramatically poured the rats into the box, seemingly onto Dan1's legs. In fact they fell through the floor and into a special compartment sealed in the trolley below. Dan1 would writhe and scream as if the rats were crawling over his legs and up his torso. The top of the box was then sealed.

While the crowd was imagining Dan1 trapped in a box full of rats he was supposed to reach into a separate compartment in the trolley to fetch a rat costume: tail, whiskers, nose and yellow contacts for his eyes. The idea was that he would then emerge as The Amazing Ratboy, to the relief and applause of the audience. Unfortunately Locky's handmade box hadn't survived the rigors of five shows a week.

Locky knew as soon as he shut the lid that something had gone wrong. Either Dan1's acting skills had improved immeasurably or the rats had escaped from their sealed compartment. With the professional indifference usually found in seasoned showmen, he pushed on regardless, confidently following his usual shtick, dragging it out even longer, dreading the moment when he would be forced to reveal the failed trick to the audience. As

Locky prevaricated, Dan1 remained trapped in the box, wildly screaming and kicking.

By the time Locky had finished his usual patter about The Amazing Ratboy the box had gone curiously quiet. He slowly peeled back the lid, steadily eyeing the audience, trying not to look inside the horrible box. He saw it first on the expressions of the boys in the front row. Absolute terror. Screams erupted as kids scrambled from the booths.

Dan1 emerged, a dead rat in his mouth, looking more rat-like than ever. Locky grinned, why did he doubt his little brother? A natural born sidekick. Dan1 launched from the box and scampered around the restaurant, blood dripping from his mouth. Locky laughed, wondering whether this was brilliant improvisation or an ingenious addition to the act that Dan1 had devised on his own. The whole place was quickly cleared of customers, but Locky remained, cackling to himself. He took a generous bow to the empty booths and went off in search of his sidekick.

"That was genius!" He found Dan1 in the back pantry sobbing over a sack of protein pats. "You really got back today, eh bro?" He laughed and clasped a hand around Dan1's shoulder. "Did ya see how frightened the lil' fellas were? You seriously scared shit through 'em. Don't figure we'll be allowed to do that act no more, but it was worth it, eh?"

He looked down at Dan1, now without his costume, and stroked his hair kindly. Dan1's body shuddered and a tuft of rat fur fell from his mouth. He let out another loud sob.

"Went a little far today, eh bro?"

Of course, the whole incident was captured and fed to the hungry mob in the hydra. People were outraged. Mother Umami flew off the handle, the incident had touched a raw nerve. She claimed it made them look like another savage business from the Boons. "We was getting a reputation in the citadel!" she screamed from her circular bed, cramming unidentified meats into her maw to punctuate her outbursts. "Now that reputation's gone to hell!"

The boys bowed their heads in front of her. Dan1 looked particularly upset, Locky may have been secretly proud. It wasn't long after that they received a visit Jimmy Bex, offering to open a new chapter in their lives—an opportunity that Locky enthusiastically seized.

Novel consciousness; God gets nervous

Final testing on the N106 was scheduled for mid-week. Dan1 was expected to debug the sequence and have it ready for incubation by Friday. After attending the gladiorg battle on Saturday night with the other members of the design team, he headed into work on Sunday to clean and prep the lab for Monday morning, happy to keep himself busy. He had not told Locky about the pic or his thoughts about his paternity and he had no intention of approaching Slit about it. He buried himself in work and resolved to deal with his personal matters later.

The N106 was a stunning piece of neurological design, a re-creation of nature's greatest achievement—not just conscious; it was the world's first artificial form of conscious*ness*. The N106 existed beyond a state of mere being, it was aware that reality was a construct, and as reality could be constructed, it could also be manipulated. And yet, staggeringly, no part of the N106 was the same as a human brain, keeping it within the Charter. Somehow, Theodor Slit had managed to design an entirely new form of hyper-sentient organism.

Trying to understand the N106, Dan1 studied its inspiration, the most powerful neuro-unit on the planet: the human brain.

There are three tiers—the cortex, the cerebellum and the brain stem—and it is the sympathetic relationship between these tiers that creates a connate union of perception, emotion and action.

While working with Slit, the master designer explained that beneath the valleys and ridges of the brain flow rivers of chemical messengers, pulses of neurotransmitters released by tiny electrical charges in the cells, passing from neuron to neuron, moving in complex patterns through the cortex. It is the co-transmission of these neurochemicals, the way they trace the ancient pathways, and the synchronous systems of the mind, the complex interplay of the bicameral brain, that coruscates into consciousness.

Slit understood the awesome complex of circuits and networks, built on a neuronal syntax that forms learning algorithms, the processes that lead to awareness and, more important, awareness of their awareness, *the relation that relates itself to itself or is the relation relating itself to itself in the relation*, as Kierkegaard so bafflingly put it. Where that put Slit's level of consciousness is a sublime mystery.

When Dan1 began work on N106 he had been unaware of the purpose and intent of the project. He was not comfortable with the notion of a fabricated consciousness, but it was not his biggest concern at that time. He worked diligently throughout the week and by Friday the N106 was ready for incubation.

The project had been conducted largely in secret; only the neuro-design team was aware of its implications. The group met on Friday afternoon to discuss their progress. Freyja, Wing and Chan had been resourced to an unrelated project called Menos. When Slit explained that the N106 was complete they were stunned. In little more than a month Slit and Dan1, working together, had managed to come up with a solution to an age-old problem. No aspect of the N106 was a direct replica of the human brain, yet it clearly demonstrated consciousness. The N106 was an entirely novel form of intelligent being.

"God must be feeling nervous," joked Fuego Wing.

"Well, I am exhausted," replied Slit. "Now I can see why God rested on the seventh day." He snickered and looked at Dan1. "I think we should leave the final incubation for Monday. Let's have a rest; it's been a big week."

Slit walked from the lab with Wing and Chan following, excitedly discussing the N106. Freyja took Dan1 by the arm and led him into the hall, the giants following close behind.

"Slit has ordered us to take you out," she chirped. "He even left us his car."

"No shit," said Dan1, flattered and surprised.

"So the boys and I have planned quite an evening. Have you ever seen a real fight?"

Dan1 looked confused. She laughed and tossed her head so that her hair fell prettily onto one shoulder.

"Have you ever seen a no rules, no police, no-way-they-can-stop-us fight?" Dan1 had absolutely no idea what she was talking about.

"I can see that this evening is going to be your first time. Prepare yourself." She raised a perfectly trimmed eyebrow above her emerald eye. "We better line your stomach. Let's stop for a meal on the way."

Of cats and men; the second time he saved her
Slit's black limousine slithered through the streets of West Boons to the very edge of the suburb, sliding up a mud embankment and onto a vacant lot on the far side of a makeshift housing estate. In the middle of the lot was a circular building patched together with scraps of steel and rusted corrugated iron.

"Is that thing metal?" asked Dan1, squinting through the darkened window of Slit's enormous limousine.

"Oh that's not even the interesting part," said Freyja. The giants grunted and harrumphed respectively.

Through the holes and gaps in the shell of the building Dan1 could see hundreds of naked flames. The headlights of the limousine animated the cold steel gray and damp rusted orange of the entranceway. Inside, past the falling girders and pieces of iron, was a warm rich light crossed by a frenzy of shadows. The music was high and loud.

"What the hell is this place?" asked Dan1.

Freyja smiled and went to open the door of the limousine.

"Nah seriously." Dan1 grabbed her hand.

"It's perfectly safe." Freyja's voice was smooth and soothing. "We wouldn't bring a friend anywhere he could get into trouble. Just trust me Dan1, you're going to love this."

Dan1 was a little surprised by the news that Freyja and the giants were now his friends. Even so, he was not going to argue. He stepped from the limousine, following the elegant curve of Freyja's leg into the crisp evening.

Standing in the open air, the music inside the metal hall sounded even louder, the beat was incredibly fast and aggressive. It shivered through Dan1's body.

"Don't wurry my frend," growled Fafner, throwing an enormous arm around Dan1's shoulder. "No wun wil giv us eny trubbell."

Dan1, buried inside Fafner's armpit, felt safe and strangely comforted—probably because his brain was running out of oxygen. Fafner and Dan1 walked together towards the entrance.

The four of them were waved through after being scanned for weapons by an angular punk doorbitch.

Inside the metal building the atmosphere was heavy with sweat, dust and cigar smoke choked Dan1's lungs. The place was full of splitters in dark coats, big boots and scraps of black material held together with studs. Blur-drum beats with a screeching undersong blared from every direction. The only light was coming from fires burning in steel drums. A crowd of dryads—tiny girls with dark hoods and ashen faces—swarmed around a concrete table drinking something that looked like petrol. Cracked cups of violet liquid were passed from hand to hand.

"The first time you come here it's pretty intense." Freyja had to shout above the music, but from the flare in her eyes and the nod of her head Dan1 could tell it was a question as much as a statement.

"Yeah, intense," he shouted back.

In the center of the room was a concrete pit with walls built up to about chest height and a sheet of wire mesh stretching to the ceiling. Splitters were crowded around it; some scaling up the mesh and hurling themselves back into the crowd, others perched on the concrete wall clinging to the wire. Around the outside of the room was a circle of rough wooden planks, intended as tiered seating.

Dan1 pointed at the splitters gathered around the pit. "What're they lookin at?" he asked.

"They're waiting," called back Freyja.

"For what?"

"Just watch those two over there in the corner." Freyja gestured towards two dark figures huddled in a corner on the far side of the room. "They're the ones who organized today's fight. Do you want a drink?"

Dan1 nodded nervously.

While Freyja was at the bar he gazed over at the men in the corner. One was a thin, malicious looking bloke covered in amateurish tattoos—definitely not done by a tattoo artist. Tattoo hobbyist, maybe. More likely a sadistic blind man with Parkinsons. Next to the little guy with tats was a much larger man wearing a black sleeveless tanktop and black pants. Growing from his forehead was a short silvery spike, which twisted and writhed, anticipating the man's head movements before they occurred. The thin man with the tattoos muttered something to his neighbor, got up from his chair, and disappeared into a back room.

Moments later he returned, wheeling a large cage covered with thick matting into the middle of the pit. The crowd gathered expectantly. The man threw his tattooed hands towards the crowd. There was a roar around the room. People ran towards the wire mesh or gathered at the top of the seating. Dan1 was shoved and squashed in the sudden frenzy.

Fafner yanked Dan1 by the collar and dragged him into a clear space where Regin and Freyja were waiting with drinks.

"Here ya go," called Freyja. "My shout!" She winked her dark eye and passed the drink. "Let's go up further so we can see."

The four stood on the wooden benches and looked down into the sandy pit. The thin man with tattoos whipped the cover off the cage and threw a latch, allowing the animal trapped inside to escape. He left the pit through a rear door, dragging the cage and its cover with him.

The beast in the pit was clearly distressed. It rose to its full height—nearly two and a half meters—and scratched the ground with clawed feet. It was screaming a strange tormented whine. It had long limbs with sinewy muscles woven through taught sallow skin, standing on two legs but hunched, as if it would have been more comfortable on four. Its narrow eyes gave it a distinctly feline appearance—yet the beast was obviously humanoid.

The thin man moved around the outside of the pit taking clutches of dollar bills. There was a frenzy of bidding and betting. He tallied the amounts in a notebook. The creature's screaming grew louder and it agitatedly clawed at the ground in the sandy pit.

The giants were too involved in the build-up to the fight, but Freyja was staring straight across, her dark eye fixed on Dan1. He tried to remain expressionless. He had realized that the beast in the pit was an illegal gladiorg—a human gen-mod bred for fights. He turned slowly towards Freyja, scrunched up his face and nodded at her. The gesture was noncommittal. She seemed pleased nonetheless.

The roar of the crowd built as the feline-humanoid snarled and bashed itself against the mesh. The crowd was jostling for position. Some of the splitters were being torn from the fence, others pulled themselves up onto it. No one wanted to miss out.

The large man with the silvery spike entered the pit wearing only his black sleeveless top and pants. The feline-humanoid turned to face him, baring fangs and extending its claws. The creature launched forward with extraordinary speed and swiped. The man leaped back to avoid the attack, briefly dropping his arms by his side, as if relaxed. The humanoid looked puzzled. The man seized his moment, stepping to his front foot and delivering a solid punch to the skull. The creature collapsed back into the mesh. He leaped forward again and smashed the humanoid in the sternum with a sound like wet newspaper slapping cement. The gen-mod buckled and rolled into the corner.

The crowd seethed and roared. Spittle and sweat rained into the pit.

The creature recovered, rolling onto all fours and leaping onto the mesh. It raced to the ceiling, scurrying out of its opponent's sight, hanging upside down for a moment, before dropping back into the pit.

Savage claws tore down the man's back. Five bloody gashes bloomed through his black shirt. He twisted and screamed, throwing a wild fist into the air. His fist collected the humanoid under its jaw. It fell to the sandy floor, blood leaking from its mouth. Its body quivered and its eyes turned back in its head. As suddenly as it began, the fight was over.

The crowd cheered and hissed in equal measure.

The man with the spiked forehead had retreated from the pit and was healing the wounds on his back. His wiry little associate appeared again, dispensing wads of cash from tattoo-stained hands.

Someone in the crowd poured drink on the unconscious feline-humanoid. Soon the rest of the crowd followed suit, showering the brute with alcohol. The wiry man egged them on.

"Time to destroy the evidence," said Freyja into Dan1's ear.

A drum of accelerant was brought out, the humanoid doused. The creature twitched and shifted as the pungent fuel was poured onto it.

The wiry man stalked around the pit, throwing his hands in the air, agitating the crowd. Finally he drew a lighter from his pocket.

"What the hell is goin' on?" Dan1 could not control himself. He didn't want to lose face in front of his Biota colleagues, but he couldn't stand by and watch this humanoid be incinerated. "What the hell is this?" he called again. He was furious. But Freyja and the giants couldn't hear him. They were standing on the benches hurling encouragement into the pit.

The wiry man narrowed his eyes and held the lighter above the cowering creature. He called something to the crowd and dropped the lighter.

Fire engulfed the humanoid. It sprang into brief consciousness and wrestled, squealing and snarling, throwing itself around the pit, flames searing its skin. The crowd roared with delight. Crackling fire consumed the flesh. Finally the charred figure slumped into the corner as the dying embers licked its body.

After a few minutes the smoldering corpse was pulled from the pit and lifted into a drum.

The wiry little man with the prison tattoos settled himself back into the corner. His large collaborator, wearing a new black tanktop, had healed his wounds and was ready for the next fight.

Dan1 wanted to leave but Freyja, who had no inkling of his discomfort, had gone to fetch another drink. He was planning on making an excuse: it had been a very long week and he was exhausted; dinner was not sitting well in his stomach. Anything that would get him out of there. He was absolutely disgusted by the whole show.

When Freyja returned her skirt seemed shorter. As she sat down next to him her bare legs twisted together, like eels embracing.

"Fun, isn't it?" she called over the blaring music.

Dan1 smiled, accepting the drink. "Thing is, I'm feelin a bit crook."

"Sorry?"

"I'm feelin a bit ill," he shouted.

"Oh." Freyja looked disappointed.

"I'm real sorry. It musta been dinner."

"Oh okay," she said. "Well, you can take the limousine back. Do you want me to come home with you? I mean to make sure you get home alright."

"Nah s'okay. I'll be chipper. I'm jus' real sorry," he reiterated.

He slapped Regin on the shoulder to say goodbye, but both giants were distracted by something across the room.

There was a girl standing in the top row of seating carrying a small machine, which she slowly panned in front of her, some kind of recording device. She was wearing thick black boots, torn black stockings and a dress that was mostly black with scraps of hot pink patched above the sleeves. Dan1 immediately recognized Sister Lickety-Split.

He scuttled towards the door—all he wanted to do was get home. The heat, the smell and the noise were making him dizzy. He looked up at the PETSO girl, still recording with her camera, oblivious. Over his shoulder Freyja was talking to a tall splitter who immediately started shoving his way through the crowd.

Dan1 stopped in front of the door. He was less than ten meters from Sister Lickety-Split, staring straight at her. Eventually she looked down.

At first she avoided direct eye contact, but then she noticed the bouncer forcing his way towards her. She understood at once and slipped the camera behind her back. Dan1 gestured at her to meet him outside.

As he walked through the door and past the doorbitch, he looked back across the searing pit and saw Freyja standing on the other side staring straight at him, her eyes hard as bone.

By the time Sister Lickety-Split reached the exit she was running. The huge splitter that Freyja tipped off was close at her heels. Dan1 retracted the door of the limousine and prepared it for a quick getaway, watching as the PETSO girl fled across the open ground, the splitter less than a meter behind. The huge man lunged forward and snatched at her camera. She stumbled and fell to the ground. He lunged again, this time for her ankle. She kicked him sharply in the face.

She got up and sprinted towards Dan1 in the limousine, the splitter stumbling after her, blood running over his eyes. She dived into the limousine and the slick black machine slipped off into the night, leaving the bloodied splitter crouched and panting in the vacant lot.

"I can't believe I lost my cam," is all she said, as she collapsed into the fatty folds of upholstery.

The professor's bright eye

A winged eyeball flew through a hexagonal window into the office of Professor Nip Wilson, landing on his desk. The Professor quickly shut the window on the cold evening.

He picked up a framed copy of his favorite poem, *The Road Not Taken* by Robert Frost, his bright eyes scanning over it, thin lips curling into a smile. He placed the poem onto the cabinet and shuffled back to his desk.

"What have we here?" he asked the empty room.

He picked up the eye and gently massaged its wings between forefingers and thumbs. The tiny ocular unit drooped and relaxed.

The Professor raised his upturned palms and stared straight into the eye. With a sudden movement he deftly thrust it onto a nerve spike. The shocked pupil rapidly dilated. Images flashed across his perineurals.

A boy on a snakeboard.

A crowd at the arena.

A metal hall lit by fires.

The boy and an organik in a limo.

The images slow.

The Professor removed the i-bird from the nerve spike and gently patted it. He opened the window, allowing the chilly night air to rush through the office, and heaved the i-bird skyward.

Sitting down, he puffed out his chest and ruffled his shoulders, like a bird drying itself in the wind. His stopped shivering and rubbed his hands together.

"Our boy is making decisions," he whispered. He would need to report this to the Circle.

The obvious implications; a call from outside the hydra

Dan1 flipped his snakeboard into his hand and walked

through the large archway of writhing beasts that curved above the main entrance to the design labs. Freyja, hurrying with her head down, obviously late for an appointment, ran straight into him, jarring her hip against the strip of cartilage at the edge of the board.

Dan1 turned to apologize. There was a very awkward pause.

"I wasn't looking where I was going." She put her head down and continued walking, glancing back with her black eye, her countenance cutting: blade-like lips and slicing cheekbones. She was clearly furious about Friday night.

Dan1 didn't care. What he had seen disgusted him. The image of the feline humanoid writhing on fire burned deep in his conscience. He wasn't just disgusted at Freya and the others for thinking that was entertainment, he was angry that they thought he would like it too. He didn't for a moment doubt his decision to help El9, but he knew it was going to stir shit at work. PETSO was Biota's enemy. He'd just helped them. But he also felt like they were in the right on this one—the image of the humanoid pushed into his mind again.

When he arrived in the lab Slit didn't ask any questions about the weekend. Freyja must have stayed silent about the incident at the fight, which was half-decent of her. Slit and Dan1 launched straight into work, spending the first part of the week focused on incubating the N106. After the second day, Slit's frustration was building. He stormed about the laboratory slapping things closed with unnecessary force. Dan1 was pleased when Ms.. Sundew arrived to remind Slit of his other commitments.

On Wednesday, Dan1 consulted with Miklos Pohl and the two of them discussed the N106. After a lengthy meeting— nearly three hours—they arrived at a solution. Dan1 successfully modeled a functioning prototype on his monitor and called Slit into the laboratory.

That night, well after ten, Slit and Dan1 stood by as the N106 was born. It was the first form of consciousness created entirely independently of evolution, an alien way of understanding, sharing no direct physical link to the human brain; not a single line of DNA in the N106 neural unit was homologous to *homo sapiens*. It was an artificial form of enlightenment. Slit was astonished by his own success.

"We must keep it… um, we must keep *him* in a secure tank for the evening," said Slit excitedly. "No impurities can be allowed in, must be completely bio-secure."

"Of course," replied Dan1. He stepped forward and took the neural unit in his hand. "A brain," he said under his breath.

"Pardon?" Slit was excited and every word he spoke was overly sharp.

"A brain. Miklos Pohl said I'd be making brains."

"And indeed you are, completely new forms of brain. It is done. It is finally done."

As Dan1 immersed the N106 he couldn't push the thought away, "This is *someone's brain*." Something that had seemed normal, everyday, completely unremarkable, suddenly sickened him.

Slit carefully locked the transparent cube with an encrypted code, leaving it on the laboratory bench, and the two of them walked from the silent laboratories into the empty city.

The next morning Dan1 arrived at half-past eight to a laboratory filled with security. Slit was twitching his legs and talking rapidly at an officer.

"Well it must be returned," was all Dan1 caught him saying. Slit looked sharply away as he passed. Freyja and the two giants were in the corner talking amongst themselves. Dan1 bravely approached.

"What happened?" he asked.

Freyja looked at him with such intense hatred it almost

knocked him onto his back. "The N106 is gone," she snapped.

The giants looked at him expectantly, but there was nothing he could think to say. "So who stole it?"

"It wasn't stolen," she emphasized the word *stolen* to convey the stupidity of the idea. "It has been *confiscated*. Someone tipped off the board—they've confiscated it and now it's been sent back to Paris for clearance. It's only three weeks until the Grand Final. We'll *never* get it back by then."

"Nevva," growled Fafner.

"*Someone* is going to have to pay for this," commented Regin ominously. Dan1 did not like the emphases being placed on any of their words. There were obvious implications.

The rest of the week was a nightmare. Dan1 had been reassigned to the tiny, white incubation lab. Freyja was being a passive-aggressive super bitch. She sent him orders, then canceled them, then changed them, then demanded he fulfill the original orders within impossible time constraints.

Slit was obviously pissed. He didn't like the board, he didn't like the Charter, and he really hated Paris. Dan1 sensed that he was also furious at the apparent lack of discipline within the team. Slit immediately conducted a security review, and as the newest member of the team, Dan1 was the most obvious suspect. He was interviewed several times.

Working for Biota in the major leagues was every Melbourne kid's dream. Kids from the streets weren't even allowed to dream it—it was laughable to imagine. And here he was, a part of the team. And he was good enough to thrive—he was succeeding. He could see a path to him moving beyond technician, grabbing a spot as a designer. And suddenly the biggest obstacle to obtaining the impossible was himself. He was wondering if he wanted it, if he wanted to work with people like this. It was disorienting and depressing. It was hard to find the energy for even the most menial tasks.

On Friday afternoon Dan1 was counting down the hours before he could go home. Freyja had pushed through a few large orders that needed to be incubated before Monday, but Dan1 was over it—he figured he could come back in on Sunday to finish. He was dousing the lab and preparing to leave when a message flashed across his perineural, someone attempting to contact him from outside the hydra. He accepted the call.

"Hello Dan1." The voice was a little husky, but mellifluous and flirtatious. "I'm in the city for a while, wondering what you're up to"

The voice paused, waiting for Dan1 to speak.

"Not much, not up to much at all." Dan1 was dumbfounded by the sudden appearance of the PETSO girl in his system. "So… what are you doing here?" he asked lamely.

"Just working on a research project. I called because you're the only person I know in this city, so I was wondering if you want to hang out."

"Hmmn. Hang with an organik eh?"

"It's not all politics. We can have fun you know?"

Dan1 couldn't help but grin. He hadn't expected organiks to be so self-aware, so self-deprecating. From the moment they fell together the night of the protest she had been nothing but a train of surprises. And after the illegal fight, he was even kind of interested in her politics.

"Great. There's a party in the Boons tonight. You free?"

"Hmmm, lemme check my cal." Just to fill time, so she didn't think he was desperate, he slipped into his social calendar. A tumbleweed blew past. "Looks like I'm free tonight."

"Great! Meet me at… ummmm… let's see. Meet me at a city train station. Make it NW1. That blint?"

"Yep that's fine. What time?"

"How about an hour?"

Dan1's heart stopped. This was his first real date. He needed more time to prepare—three, maybe four years.

"Righto," he chortled.

Her real name; Brother Boom Box of the Boons

Dan1 hurried home from work and immediately began preparing for his date. Amazingly, two and a half hours later, he looked exactly the same. His hair was a messy bundle of string, his jacket and baggy pants looked exhausted, and the tongue on his left shoe hung listlessly to the side like a St Bernard's waiting for supper. Nonetheless, he set off for his date, his train worming towards the outer-ring of the Boons.

As Dan1 slid out of the city he thought about that moment we are first conceived, when we are just a single totipotent cell, a cell that divides and divides again into a tiny cluster of cells. Meeting this organik felt like that moment—where a tiny cell has the potential to develop into an entirely new and unique organism. His train staggered briefly, stopping just short of the end of the line.

"I've got a confession," she said, bounding up to him as soon as they spotted each other across the concourse. "My name isn't really Sister Lickety-Split." She extended her hand. "I'm El9, and it's very nice to meet you Dan1."

"Yeah, I gotta confession to make too," said Dan1 with mock embarrassment. "My name's really Brother Boom Box of the Forty Thousand Beats, so if ya wanna just call me that for the resta the night..." He trailed off with a cheeky grin.

She laughed and slapped her thigh. Literally, she slapped her thigh. Dan1 was filled with his own magnificence. He was on a date with an older girl and he was charming her. Cop that Locky.

The two of them wandered off down the main strip, with

El9 seemingly unaware that her white cotton dress was sharply incongruous with their seedy surroundings. Strip clubs, liquor stores and all night arms dealers filled both sides of the street, the facades of the buildings alive with solicitation. Hookers and boondogs plied their trade, standing over the gutters trying to scrape up business from passers-by. *And this girl*, thought Dan1, *floatin' above everything in her white cotton dress.*

They made their way past the main strip and headed towards the quiet end where the street was darker and the alleyways more menacing. The buildings offered wares that were completely unrecognizable to Dan1.

El9 stopped outside a dirty shop front and pushed through the rickety door. The air inside was bruised like the breath of a heavy animal. Women were bent over ancient wooden racks apparently making fabric, although it looked to Dan1 as if they were playing ancient instruments in some discordant orchestra. El9 led him out through the room to an open-air courtyard.

The spacious suburban backyard was strung with brightly colored lights and surrounded by a tall paling fence covered in vine; the ground, covered in red volcanic pebbles, crunched under Dan1's feet. In the center, four crowded wooden tables were arranged in a square. The diners passed around large bowls of strange looking food and pitchers of mead were being sloshed and spilled into large wooden goblets.

El9 smiled at Dan1, who was still anxious, even though the mood of the courtyard was soothing.

"Come on," she gestured, "let's take a quiet table in the corner."

Dan1 hadn't noticed the smaller tables stashed against the fence beneath the heavy growing vine. The two of them sat down and a waitress came over to light a tallow candle.

"The menu is on the board." The waitress casually pointed at a large blackboard covered in a messily scrawled writing. "Can

I get you something to drink?"

"We'll have a pitcher of mead," said El9 chirpily. "And let's order food too. I'm starving."

Dan1 looked over the board and ordered the only thing he recognized. El9 ordered a vegetable platter.

"Do you like it here?" El9 settled her eyes on him, her gaze soft, not studying, but sweet and engaged.

"Yeah," replied Dan1, beginning to relax. "Don't get out to the Boons much but."

"Oh, I like it here," she said airily.

"Why?" He wished he hadn't said that. "I mean…" He began to explain himself, but then realized it wasn't necessary. El9 was obviously not the overly-sensitive type. The waitress dropped a heavy pitcher of mead and two wooden goblets onto their table.

"I don't know why I like it here so much." El9 looked dreamily towards the colored lights while Dan1 picked up the pitcher and poured them both some mead. "I guess I just don't like the feeling of being trapped in the city."

"I don't like it here at all," admitted Dan1.

"Why?"

"I reckon it's a bit scary and… I guess I just don't like the feeling that I'm about to be killed."

El9 laughed and offered her goblet for a toast.

"Here's to not getting killed," she said.

They drank from their goblets. Afterwards there was a comfortable silence, which Dan1 managed to make awkward by launching into a pre-planned conversation.

"So you is all about the Charter, right?" El9 nodded curtly. "Well my bruvva reckons the Charter's just a hangover from back when th'Circle a' Seven ran stuff. Reckons we should get ridda it."

"Hmmm," she put a finger to her chin. "I've spent pretty much my whole life trying to enforce the Charter so, you know, I'm pretty against that idea."

"Why not?" So far the conversation was going exactly as Dan1 had planned.

"Well," she began, somewhat awkwardly, "like I said when we first met, if we allow corporations to manufacture machines that think like humans, what's to stop us from treating humans like machines?"

"Yeah but machines don' think like us people."

"Of course they do." She laughed at him mockingly. "They're conscious right? That's the point of a gladiorg battle: whoever is knocked unconscious loses. So if they can be beaten unconscious, then they must be conscious to begin with."

"Yeah but they don' 'ave conscious*ness*." Dan1 was drifting out of his depth— he had planned the conversation only to this point. "Only we got the conscious*ness*."

"Have you ever read the Second Statement?"

"Yeah, the Second Statement says ya can't make machines the same as human beings. Stops us from using all kinds of sequences just coz they're from people. It's a total pain in the ass."

She breathed in slowly. "The Second Statement says," she stressed the last word, then paused to let him know she was reciting from memory, "*Understanding that living machines may be created for the benefit of human beings, no technology shall be employed or otherwise manufactured that creates a conscious living being.*"

"Inn't that what I said?"

"But don't you see? It specifically prohibits the manufacture of anything conscious, anything that can think, anything that can feel pain. It's not just about stopping designers from using neural functions that are homologous to human beings."

"So ya reckon we can't make anything conscious, not even gladiorgs n'that?"

"Exactly!"

"But then everything would be illegal—including us!"

"Not us silly—just nothing manufactured should be conscious."

"Inn't that what the Circle of Seven reckoned?"

"Kind of. And they were right. They were trying to save us."

"Save us? Leviathan nearly capped us all."

"I think the Circle were protecting us from something so important that it was worth taking the risk," she said firmly.

"And what's that?"

"They were protecting us from ourselves."

This somewhat baffled Dan1, but luckily the waitress arrived with two enormous wooden platters piled with steaming food. El9 immediately began eating—Dan1 eyed his platter cautiously.

"What on Alu's tits is this? It ain't what I ordered." He laughed nervously. She covered her full mouth and laughed with him. "Of course! You've never had real food before, have you?"

A group of diners on the large central table turned and raised their glasses at him. Dan1 returned their cheers, leaning over the table so only El9 could hear. "Course I've eaten real food—how'd ya reckon I survive!"

"No, this is what you need to survive. This is real food. It's from strains before gen-mod."

"Yeah? It's *historical* food?"

El9 laughed. "Yeah, I guess you could call it that."

Dan1 peered down at the oddly shaped meat on his plate. "S'that thing's the steak?"

El9 stifled a laugh and nodded.

"So why's it all crooked and weird? The machine broken or

something?" El9 peered over at the meat on Dan1's plate. "Well, if I tell you now you probably won't want to eat anymore… It's pretty gross. That's why I don't eat meat. No one at PETSO does."

This left Dan1 feeling unsure about his meal and he only ate the vegetables from around the meat.

"This is tasty stuff." He leaned over to pick at the misshapen potatoes on El9's platter.

"This is how it's supposed to taste. Designed by Mother Earth, not by committee." She smiled, casually swatting his fork away from her plate.

"Mead's good too."

The two of them drank a lot more mead and laughed over the remnants of dinner. Apart from the food, it was the single most fantastic meal Dan1 had ever eaten.

Eating animals; party people; followed by the apple incident
"Really? An animal? With a brain? That's disgusting!"

El9 and Dan1 were giggling after the mead. He quickly promised he would never eat meat from an animal again. Their laughter settled and they strolled comfortably down the main strip of the Boons.

"So you've never eaten gen-mod food?" he asked.

"Never," she said, shaking her head. "I was raised on the compound. I've been in PETSO all my life."

"But what's wrong with gen-mod food? It was designed for us."

"But it's not what our body wants. It's not natural."

Dan1 waved his arm around at the gaudy suburban strip. "Nothing is natural! It's not natural to live in cities or drive panther-cycles or do any of this stuff, but we do it."

"Usually I don't." She grabbed his hand and pulled him along the pavement past the unconscious addicts and scanty-panted hookers.

"Where are we going?"

"It's a surprise. It's all going to be a big surprise!" she shouted and a pack of boondogs turned and scowled.

The two of them were running down the brightly lit street when El9 suddenly darted into a dark alleyway. As Dan1 rounded the corner he ran straight into her. She wrapped her arms around his waist and pulled his face close to hers.

"Are you ready?"

"Course."

At the end of the alley a door glowed faintly pink. She pressed her palm to the wall. The door peeled open like lips and an enormous doorbitch, three meters tall and ambisexual, stepped heavily into the alleyway. She was wearing a skimpy biopolymer leotard, stretched tight enough to advertise distinctly hermaphroditic tackle.

"Invite only," barked the gruff voice.

"El9 plus one." She smiled sweetly.

The behemoth checked a list in its head and looks disdainfully at Dan1 in his hooded top and snakeboard shoes.

"In ya' go."

They stepped from the alleyway into a vast open space, the roof an uneven dome of heavy rock, the floor covered in lush grasses, except for a circle of hard-packed earth in the center, where a crowd rhythmically swayed to the music. People were sitting and lying back on the grassy slope, chatting and drinking. The air was stirred by a gentle breeze that smelled sweetly and faintly fruity.

"It's amazing," said Dan1. "Seriously."

El9 squeezed his hand. "As soon as I saw you relax in the restaurant I knew you'd like this place. Let's get a drink."

They wandered across the rolling grasses. Bars serving drinks were carved into the rocky walls around the perimeter. They ducked into one of the grottos where small groups sat at tables set into the wall, the only light in the room emitted by the pure white of a crystal bar.

"Whatta ya drink?" asked Dan1.

"Whatever you're having. But make it organik," she added with a wink. Dan1 approached the bartender. "Something organik," he said, leaning on
the bar. "Make two o'em."

The bartender was wearing a neat black shirt, his four arms working quickly, crushing fresh fruit and mixing it into two glasses, then adding a shot of something red. Dan1 returned to El9, who was nestled into a mossy rock groove at the back of the grotto.

"The bartender has four arms."

"I have forearms too." She raised two fists in front of her.

"Oh no! Worst joke I ever 'eard!" Dan1 shook his head. "Seriously, didn't 'spect t'see a splitter 'ere."

"He's not gen-mod." El9 smiled. "He's a mutant."

"Oh." Dan1 sipped his at drink, which violently grabbed his lips and twisted back. He was briefly cross-eyed.

"He didn't choose to be like that," explained El9, "he was born like that, probably because of some batshit crazy experiment at Biota." She took a deep pull on her drink and looked at Dan1. "Let's not talk politics tonight." She dismissed the conversation with a wave of her arm. "Let's get dancing!"

She swilled the rest of her drink and pulled Dan1 down the sloping savannah towards the dance floor. They paused at the edge of the hard-packed earth. The crowd was stomping and swaying in front of a massive rock edifice, fifteen meters tall and ten wide. A waterfall tumbled from the rocks on the left hand side, collecting in a deep pool that had been obscured when Dan1 first entered the club. A cavernous booth was carved into the base of the rock filled by a morbidly obese dj who could barely move to his own music.

"The beats are kind of relaxed now," said El9, pulling Dan1 closer, "but Triam Twin is playing later on."

She winked at him and tugged at his sleeve, dragging him straight to the center of the crowd. The floor was congested, but she swirled across it, spinning and dancing towards the other side. Dan1 followed, never taking his eyes off her. She was wondrous, spinning in a fluid motion, like a graceful eddy. He had never felt so much like dancing.

They found themselves caught in the light spray coming from the waterfall, the mist settled on her face. She laughed and tilted her head back, opening her mouth.

"Wanna rest onna grass?"

She nodded and led them away from the dance floor. They found a place on the slope and lay back, gently kissing for a moment. She fell away from him and propped her elbows on the ground, smiling and chewing.

"What's that ya chewin?"

"Here take some," she passed him the small amber nugget. "It's tree sap." Dan1 took the sap in his mouth and chewed.

"It's tasteless," he noted.

"Keeps you interested though." El9 pulled another chunk from her purse. "I'll get us a drink."

Dan1 returned with drinks and they rested a little longer. The music had changed tempo. He noticed a three-headed person—or possible three people conjoined—swaying in the rock booth. Dan1 had heard of Triam Twin—everyone had— he would have been the single greatest dj ever, except for the fact that he was not single, he was triple. Such is the curse of being a triplet. And now he had taken the decks, was playing a set, right in front of them.

They ran back to the dance floor, Dan1 ecstatic. More so than he had ever been. He was dizzy with it. Everything started slipping, as if time was moving too fast. He had been dancing for a long time and felt drained—his chest tight, his heart beating fast.

"Here, take this," called El9 over the music. "It will help."

She passed him a strange reddish fruit with nicked skin. He took a bite—the flavor was overwhelming; powerfully sweet and crisp. Dan1 figured it for a legacy apple. He ate the whole thing greedily. El9 smiled at him. Only the swinging colored lights remained. He wondered how much time had passed. He swayed slightly on the dance floor. She took him around the waist and pulled closer. He almost fell.

Slaughter in the Boons

"We have to get homicide onto this." Captain Warren was standing on a dusty track at the back of West Boons, a large pool of blood coagulating at his feet.

"Should I draft a transfer order, sir?" asked the young lieutenant beside him.

Warren ignored the question and swung his foot at a loose stone on the road. He paused to trash some personal mail in his peripheral vision—all from his wife, all nagging him about their arrangements for the weekend. This made him feel momentarily better. "What the hell are we going to do?"

With Warren's approval, Dex had ordered a broad sweep of the area. The purpose of this search was not at all clear to the captain - hundreds of sequences of DNA had already been collected; the tiniest remnants were documented and stored. Warren had witnessed Dex's first mental breakdown—had even taken advantage of it, managing to leverage a promotion out of it. But if there was trouble this time, he'd own it, and he was worried that history had a tendency of repeating itself.

"We have to get homicide onto it," said the young lieutenant, parroting what his captain had just said.

Warren looked down at the blood and dust clinging to the edge of his shoe. "Jeez!" He stamped his foot. A small cloud of dry dust rose and settled in speckles on the darkening pool of blood. "Dammit! Dammit!" He stamped his foot twice.

"Where's Declan?"

"Over by the drain." The lieutenant nodded towards a water drain obscured behind thick lantana. "Collecting samples."

Warren stepped around the mutilated head of the victim, once again left to survey the remnants of the body, and walked towards the drain. Dex's first breakdown had manifested itself as an obsessive collecting of information, spending days camped in the woodland collecting samples. Now he was at it again: collecting, documenting and organizing vast amounts of information, most of it unnecessary. Same killer—same modus operandi—same crazy cop.

"Do you wish to speak with my master?" Dogbat sat in front of the bushes looking cross-eyed.

"Get out of the way." Captain Warren kicked Dogbat's flank, sending him scurrying to the far end of the bush but miraculously un-crossing his eyes. He pulled back the lantana to find Dex crouched in the ditch clutching a handful of swabs, henpecking the ground, picking up anything that might be bio-vital.

"What the hell are you doing Declan?" yapped Warren. "Let forensics do their job, you stick to your job: *find the killer*."

Dex ignored him. The Captain drew a tobacco stick from inside his coat and chewed it sourly. "Anyway, I didn't think forensics was your thing."

"I've been working as a collector." Dex looked up at the

Captain and gave him an even stare. "Picked up some new skills since I left the force."

Dex returned to his work in the drain. Warren huffed and walked away, letting the lantana slump back towards the ground. A shower of dried leaves and loose sticks fell from the heavy vine.

Dex brushed the debris from his hair and looked up into the lantana. The morning sun was barely above the rooftops. Something glistened on a thin spike of deadwood. Dex pushed back the vine. A branch had been snapped off. Someone had fallen into the bushes, leaving behind a sticky red smear. Dex scraped it with his swab, stashing it in his pouch.

"Forensics," he bellowed from behind the lantana. "Someone from forensics get over here. I want this greenery searched."

The head of the forensics team looked over at Dex, unsure whether to follow orders from the crazy splitter. Captain Warren angrily whipped a hand towards the bush and the forensics leader called to one of his officers. The lantana was dismantled and scoured.

Checking in

"I know how you are, I remember Brother Belltop."

She knew it had to come up eventually. There was no way she was going to make it through this project without her father raising it. As a twelve-year-old she had kissed Brother Belltop on All Hallow's Eve. The next day his entire family was expelled from the compound, sent away to the city for breaching PETSO protocols. At the time, El9 got it in her head that they were sent away to punish her. She had given her dad a hard time about it.

"I've grown up since then."

"We'll see," he said without conviction. "So how did you

make first contact?"

"Very subtle. Let him "save me" at an illegal fight."

"And then you took him out?"

"Yes. I did everything you said, everything in the brief."

"And he didn't come back with you?"

"No Dad—left him in West Boons."

"Good," sighed her father. "E19 this is not an easy project, especially for someone your age. It would be easy to develop feelings for the target, so just remember, keep physical contact to a minimum, never invite him back to your apartment and —"

"Dad, the little maggot is fifteen years old. It's not that hard—I've got a handle on it."

"Yes, well, I'm just concerned that..."

"I'm not going to fall in love with this kid, Dad. Don't worry. I'm not twelve—it's not all ponies and love hearts anymore. This is my project and I'm all over it, I own this boy."

Blood everywhere; the core problem

He woke up with blood on his shirt. He couldn't remember getting home. He was in bed, alone—no sign of E19. He looked over his sheets but there was nothing on them. Only his shirt was stained.

He stumbled down from his room and into the bathroom. The bottom part of his face was awash with blood, a red stain sweeping from his nose and down his chin onto his shirt.

He couldn't work out what the hell had happened. His nose burned like ice—painful, probably broken. He found the medikit and cleaned up his face, throwing his shirt into the laundry hamper.

Standing—swaying—in front of the mirror, he clutched his hungover head, wondering if he had gotten into a fight, which would explain not only the blood but also the bruises.

He wondered about El9, hoping she had made it home safely.

"Let's go Dan1!" Locky hollered from the other room.

Dan1 was too weak to resist. He hadn't exactly agreed to go shopping with Locky, but he hadn't forcefully opposed the idea either. He threw the cure down his throat and emerged from the apartment wearing last night's clothes.

"Late night huh?" Locky had a cheeky, almost proud look on his face. "Too much fun with the design geeks?"

"Somethin' like that." Dan1 was sheepish.

"How's it going with Freya?"

Dan1 shook his head. "Wasn't Freya," he said. "Went out wit' an organik."

"What?" Locky slapped him incredulously on the shoulder. "You stunning, kinky, crazy bastard! What the hell have you become Dan1?"

Dan1 shrugged and grinned a little. "Jus' kinda 'appened."

"So what's next then, Freya huh?"

"Ain't sure 'bout that." He quickly changed the topic. "Hey Locky, you ev'r 'eard a these illeg'l fights o'er in the Boons?"

"Yeah sure, some of the people from Accounts go over there sometimes… or they say they do. Pretty dangerous I've heard. You should stay away from that." Locky glanced at him. "You'll get fired if Biota hears about it. They can't have their elite hanging around places like that."

"Well they do. Freya 'n the whole team took me there th'other night."

"Huh." Locky nodded. Dan1 could feel his discomfort. He'd always been the one more knowledgeable of corporate life, of Biota, of the world in general.

"They took me there in Slit's limo."

"Woah," Locky threw his head back and kicked an imaginary stone with his foot. "What was it like?"

"Bloody 'orrible," said Dan1. "And then this shit 'appened at work...."

As the brothers' metro slid silently towards the 1st arrondissement Dan1 told Locky about the whole week, about El9 at the fight and taking her home in Slit's limo, about the N106 and how they all suspected him of tipping off Paris, and finally about the date in the Boons and the strange restaurant and the club and the whole crazy night. He was about to tell him about the pic of Slit and his suspicions when Locky angrily broke into his monologue.

"You've got to stay away from that organik." Locky leaned towards him and jabbed a finger into his side. "This shit at work. This politics. Take it from me, you've got to stay away from that. You're not going to get another bite at Slit's cherry. If you hang around this PETSO bitch you'll end up on the manufacturing floor the rest of your life. Simple as that."

"So what am I 'sposed t'do, watch people get torn to shit with Freya n' that? That shit's sick. I don't wan' no part a that."

Locky shook his head with his jaw set. "Stay away from the organik," he said.

The metro stopped and Locky slid into the mall. Ten minutes later the brothers were standing in sharkskin suits admiring themselves in the enormous monitor that covered the rear of the tailor. Dan1 shook his head.

"This ain't me."

The tailor's pseudopod slipped around his waist and found its way down his leg to the floor. "It's a perfect fit," hissed the diminutive assistant.

"You look neat," said Locky.

"Yeah," said Dan1. "It ain't me."

In the metro home Dan1 could feel Locky's disappointment. The day had been a failure. They had fought over El9, fought over Biota, even fought over what clothes Dan1 should wear. Suddenly a fault line that had always existed was shuddering open between them. Dan1 felt powerless to stop the shift.

The two of them were silent as the translucent membrane dropped towards their apartment.

"Been thinkin' o'gettin' me own place," said Dan1. " I c'n afford it now."

"Yeah," said Locky, "that's great. Real great news. Any idea where?"

Dan1 shook his head. Reaching into his pocket he could feel something soft and wet. He slowly extracted the fleshy mass with a hesitant hand—it was an apple core.

The top of the town

Professor Wilson trundled through the city's most exclusive shopping district in the sophisticated 1st arrondissement. The figures around him sashayed, promenaded and sauntered past, wearing the finest and most fashionable integuments money could buy. Wilson was wearing overalls.

He kept his head down, resolutely examining his heavy leather shoes. An ornate staircase swept upwards from the arcade and led to an expensive restaurant perched at the apex of the city's western wall. He gripped the banister and moved slowly up the broad, curving incline.

At the top, diners were seated around tables inspired by giant flowers, their meals resting on elegant petals. A maitre'd stopped him and asked haughtily whether he was looking for the service entrance.

"I need t'get up t'the roof," he said, affecting the weary attitude of a parasurgeon while broadening his Melbourne accent to such an extent that it was barely comprehensible.

The maitre'd looked surprised, but recognized Wilson when

the old man lifted his grinning face.

"Please come this way."

He led Wilson into a private room to the side of the main dining area. A giant chrysanthemum bloomed in the center of the room, surrounded by intricate coralline chairs supporting comfortable fungal cushions.

"Well this is new," commented the maitre'd. "Slumming it this time, are we?" His voice was high-pitched and quivering with the deliciousness of his own mirth.

"I thought this cover would be as good as any," replied the professor dryly. "It managed to fool you."

The maitre'd looked slightly pained and bowed instinctively as he pulled the doors closed, leaving Wilson alone in the room.

In a movement more sprightly than his old frame should have allowed, Wilson leaped onto a chair, skipped lightly over a petal and landed solidly in the center of the floral table. He firmly gripped the mid-section of the stamen. The petals of the flower lifted, gently enclosing him. The stem began to grow upward, pushing into the ceiling, the cuspidate tips eventually piercing through. The flower emerged into a dimly lit space and opened again, releasing Wilson from its protective envelope.

He stepped onto the gray floor and walked through to a circular chamber where seven silhouettes sat evenly spaced around the edge.

"It is getting dangerous," boomed a voice. "It is the right time to intervene." The Circle's alertness had caught him unawares, but he was used to their demanding methods. The professor shook his head and slowly began to outline his case.

A common sequence
Dex uploaded the scene-map to his perineurals, marking every detail of the crime scene, including the location from

which each sample was collected. Next he verified identities, starting with a collection of dots at the eastern side of the corpse where a group of shocked neighbors had gathered to survey the scene at first dawn. The sequences were mostly from hairs found in the dust, although one onlooker had stubbed her toe on a rock and left traces of blood. All the sequences matched control samples taken from the neighbors—nothing out of the ordinary.

He then identified the police present at the scene. Even though officers wore sealed masks and suits there was always some contamination. With so many people working simultaneously over the corpse, isolating their samples was an onerous task. The officers were trained to come in from one direction so that they only contaminated a single section, but it still took Dex until well after midnight to plot their presence on the scene-map.

The next day he woke early. After only four hours of sleep he was a little groggy, but he couldn't rest with so much work to do. He took a strong shot of analeptic and returned to his desk.

The identifiable groups at the scene had been plotted, leaving the killer, the victim and the inevitable randoms. The killer's DNA was so unstable it had to be kept in an isolated cryopac, but Dex instantly recognized it—human yet fundamentally unstable, constantly shifting in form—the same killer from the woodlands and the alleyway.

He turned his attention to the randoms—mostly they would be people present before the murder. Perhaps there would be people who passed by the scene without noticing it—although that seemed unlikely. Dex was unsure of what he was looking for: any pattern, any aberration, anything that could form the basis of a lead. He was worried that the number of samples collected from the crime scene in the alleyway was insufficient. Unfortunately, there was nothing he could do about that.

He spent the day with the blinds shut—his office dark except for the sallow light of his desk lamp. His scanner hummed all day, by nightfall it was hot and sweaty to touch. The bluish glow of the monitor made Dex's eyes water, his vision blur.

He raised an instant meal of protein pats and took a walk; Dogbat followed, yipping, yapping and running in tight circles around his feet.

"Are we going on an investigation?"

Dex shook his head and kept walking in silence. He had things to turn over in his head. After working at the monitor for so long he could no longer think clearly. Dogbat tried to run in a figure of eight between his legs. He stumbled over the hyperactive furball, kicking out with his leg, but deliberately missing.

"Should I be collecting evidence, master?"

"Go back home and guard the house," growled Dex.

"Yes sir!"

The little freak dashed off, leaving Dex to wander through the suburban streets. He stopped for a quick nip at The Hoary Blandishment before closing time.

"Ya know what Rhon," his voice was a little slurred from the drink and lack of sleep, "there ain't nothin in this place but you and me."

Rhonda Le Guin swept her hand over the bar, clearing the evening's tips into her pouch. "That's true Dex. It's gettin' pretty late."

"Nah, I mean there ain't nothin', nothin' else. There's just you and me. There's no ghosts or spirits or gods. There's just bars and benches and…" Dex waved his hand unsteadily, "bollocks. There's just a whole shitheap of bollocks."

Rhonda, who was fully expecting Dex to make a move on her, had now lost the thread of the conversation. "What're ya saying Dex?"

"My dad told me that God made us whole. That God determined exactly who we were and what we could do. That some of us was saved and some of us was damned and there wasn't nuttin we could do 'bout it."

"That don't sound right to me Dex," Rhon put in from across the bar, shaking her head as bartenders are trained to do.

Dex grunted. "He was a Calvinist bastard, believed in predestination and all that. But it ain't right, is it Rhon?"

"Nup." Another professional shake of her head. "But you ain't right either Dex. There's more in this bar than jus' you n' me. There's history in here. There's stories an' that. All over," she waved her hand around, "all through this place there's stuff that means something t'people. And there's you and me Dex. That means something t'me too."

Dex seemed to have drifted away from the conversation. He was slumped over the bar whispering to himself. He hiccupped and abruptly shouted, "They can kill 'em all if they like, e'ery last nun, but it don' mean shit. They ain't gonna kill me."

"Time for home darl. Here's something to sober you up a bit."

She passed a small shot down the bar and Dex slung it back in one hit. He returned to the shack and went back to work on the case. It was past three in the morning when the scanner found a possible match. The initial probability was low, as usual. Dex's heart raced as it narrowed past fifty percent. The whirring numbers slowed as the machine compared the two samples. It passed ninety percent, then finally declared a match.

Dex grinned. Someone other than the killer had been present at both murder scenes. Even better, the matching sequence was from the blood found in the lantana, a perfect sample. He could study the blood that coagulated around the broken branch and work out exactly when the onlooker had been at the scene. The original sample was stored at the police station—he only had the sequence.

He jumped onto his cat and sped away, slipping through the streets in a fluid black movement. West Boons was empty, the houses dark and battened down. He flowed like a liquid snake around the corner and roared up the arterial.

The officer on the night desk reluctantly checked Dex's credentials, accepting he was working as a special consultant, but still not giving him access to the samples. Dex hustled the young bull into contacting Captain Warren at home. The grumpy captain gave his authorization, still half asleep, and Dex returned to West Boons with the cryopacked sample tucked safely in his pouch.

The sun was rising as Dex parked his cat in front of his shack. He rushed inside to boot the scanner, the exhausted machine groggily stirring to life. He began a careful analysis of the bloodstained branch and quickly concluded that the onlooker had stumbled back into the lantana around the time of the killing, cutting his leg on the sharp undergrowth. The principal killer may have been a gen-mod, but this onlooker was pure human, explaining the mixture of savagery and curious humor displayed by leaving the victim's head on the dumpster.

Dex had heard of this in other cities. Someone had a pet they were using to kill for their own pleasure—not so unusual. What was unusual, what remained, was the enigmatic DNA left behind by the mutant killer.

Dex needed to rest. His blinds were glowing pinky red from the morning sun. He placed the accomplice's DNA on his sample board, rising from his chair to stretch. A movement caught his eye—a blood red line tracing across the board, seeking a matching sample.

Brotherly advice: ditch the bitch
"Lock, I ain't gonna quit," snapped Dan1 angrily. His brother

had been on him ever since the shopping trip—ever since he'd told him about the illegal fight and El9. Dan1 figured he was jealous. Locky had always wanted to be a part of a design team, hell everybody did, and now that Dan1 had what everybody wanted he was wondering whether he wanted it after all.

He got why his brother was pissed at him. Thing was, he couldn't ignore what he felt. The fight, the N106, the conversations with El9, they were all adding up to something. He wasn't sure anymore if Biota was the place for him. Even so, there was no point quitting just a few weeks out from the Grand Final.

"Of course not," said Locky. "I can't believe you even thought of it. Especially now this Miklos guy has taken the blame for tipping off the board."

It was true—Dan1 was in the clear. Miklos Pohl had confessed to reporting the N106 to the board. The man who had worked at Biota for more than twenty-five years had been unceremoniously sacked from the gladiorg labs on the day of his confession. Dan1 didn't share Locky's sense of relief. He didn't feel vindicated. Instead, he felt guilty for not blowing the whistle himself.

"You're off scot-free," insisted Locky. "And Freyja and those other idiots will calm down about the PETSO girl thing. Let's face it, you rescue some chick and take her home in a luxury car—who's going to blame you for that?" He raised his arms in a comical gesture of submission. "It's not like you're going to see this bloody organik again."

"I'm seein' her ag'in."

"Don't be mad—what's so fascinating about some musky skank from the bush?"

"She got me thinkin' Lock. Got me thinkin' 'bout all this."

He waived his arm grandly towards the world at large. "Got me thinkin' big picture."

Locky sneered. "Ooooh, big thoughts from the big boy now, eh?"

"I don't wanna spen' th'rest a me life watchin' illegal fights and trappin' brains in tanks," snapped Dan1. "I don' see that as right. I know you is pissed coz you'd do it, but you ain't there. You ain't there."

Locky swung around the table and sat next to his brother. "Look, Slit obviously doesn't know about the PETSO girl thing. He's put you on a new project, right?" Dan1 nodded sullenly. "The others will forget about it soon and everything will go back to how it was before."

Dan1 shrugged. "That ain't the point."

"Yeah it is. Stop wondering why this organik is the way she is or worrying about illegal fights. Don't go if you don't like them. Listen to me Dan1 and take my advice, you're gonna have to ditch this bitch."

Dan1 shook his head, but didn't have the energy to continue the fight.

Locky patted his brother on the knee. "Just hang in there, bro. You'll be fine."

Dan1 didn't think everything would be fine, but he was not planning on quitting his job. He had been placed on Project Menos, and although Freyja was working on the same project, he would be spending most of his time in a separate lab.

"Just ditch the bitch," repeated Locky glibly, stalking off towards his room.

Dan1 rolled his eyes behind his brother's back, kicked up his feet and splashed a link across the wall. Dozens of local apartments for lease washed across the site.

The hungriest headhunter

Everyone knew that Jimmy Bex was the best, and most notably, this was the opinion of Jimmy Bex. He strolled through the camps in lizard skin brocade and ivory epaulets, those keen eyes pressing in to every tent, looking for the telltale signs of former management: French cuffs, a deal trophy, a permanent tan, that perfect blend of competence and desperation. He was the best headhunter on the strip, one of the first with perineurals and a straight link to Biota HR, and in the two years since the final subjugation of Leviathan he had become healthier, wealthier and wiser.

Traumatic events like Leviathan tend to give society a shake and sometimes resourceful men like Jimmy Bex find themselves floating to the top while everyone else drowns around them. He was not interested in the hard sell, he had a simple philosophy, "Proteins don't bind to cells coz they is forced to," he would say, flicking over the job description, "they bind coz they got chemistry. You think there's chemistry here?" He was a facilitator, someone who could connect the right person to the right position, and he was very proud of the fact that every day families were pulled from the hell of halfway houses in the Boons to the quiet comfort of an apartment on the Northern slope—all thanks to his unique understanding of chemistry.

More than a million job contracts had come from the citadel and he had his fingerprints on a good number of them, but pickings were getting slimmer—the camps were emptying out while the contracts just kept coming. Biota had moved from hungrily absorbing the excess human resources created by a near total collapse of industry and the state, to greedily expanding as prices remained low and exports increased exponentially. Post-Leviathan Melbourne was booming and everyone was taking advantage, the rough streets outside the citadel were crawling with headhunters—anyone with DNA was offered a contract.

As the labor market tightened, the corporation went looking for prospects in the so-called Lost Generation, kids without parents or schooling. A fresh teenager had been tailing Jimmy for months, a cocky eighteen-year-old with no experience, trying to catch a corporate position. He wasn't qualified for squat and Jimmy sent him away, tail between his legs. Two months later HR sent out a pic of the kid and his foster brother, offering positions.

Jimmy tracked them down to *Mother Umami's Magic Show and Lucky Protein Carvery du Jour* and wafted the contracts under their noses. It was too easy. The corporation offered the older one something in accounting and put the younger brother on the manufacturing floor. Jimmy flicked over the job descriptions a few times but just couldn't feel the chemistry— he knew immediately it was his exit omen, time to move on. The art had gone from his job—it was just a desperate search to put bodies behind desks.

"So how come a kid workin' dis dive got friends in so high places, huh?"

"Maybe Mother Umami put in a good word." The eighteen-year-old was flushed with pride. "Pretty sure she's wanted us outta here for a while."

"Maybe kid, but there's easier ways to get ridda kids like youse. Maybe you shoulda been called Lucky, not Locky, eh? Coz someone up there likes you, someone's got your back. Course you gots'ta remember kid, there's no such thing as a free lunch, eh?" Jimmy Bex linked his sequence to the contract and sent it off. "Speaking a'such things, how 'bout lunch ona house, a celebration like?"

The younger kid ladled a thick slosh of soup and passed it over to Jimmy's greedy hands.

Project Menos; Slit's surprise entrance

Two small organisms sat on the benchtop, little more than brains with a sharp bone protuberance at the front and a purplish Menos gland bulging from the top. Dan1 injected one of the organisms with a virus and waited for it to spread. After a few minutes he directed a laser at the bulbous gland and the small organism leaped forward, instantly impaling the second organism on its sharp horn.

The Menos system was simple and deadly, designed to remotely control the neurotransmitters in a brain, directing their flow, their intensity, their intention. It was a sophisticated implementation of optogenetics, designed to ensure that higher functioning neural processors, like the N106, would not get lost in an existential funk on the battlefield. It worked by infecting the gladiorg with a virus that delivered light sensitive proteins to specific areas of the brain. When laser pulses stimulated the receptors, neurotransmitters were strategically released throughout the cortex, causing intense rage to focus on a specified target. The brain still made its own tactical decisions; its senses were not impaired in any way. In fact, it was not even aware of the subtle manipulations of the device.

Unfortunately, the virus they had incubated was only compatible with the N106, so after the board confiscated the N106 the team was scrambling to develop a generic alternative for whatever neural unit they would be using. On Friday afternoon Dan1 uploaded an edited sequence into the database for genomic compiling, hoping it would assist with the compatibility issues.

"'Scuse me." Dan1 poked his head into Slit's laboratory, looking to discuss his changes to Menos.

The room was empty so he checked Slit's office, a fastidiously clean room off the back of the lab. He wandered around the office, keeping in his peripheral vision a window dedicated to the hallway so he could see Slit approach. The only decoration in the room was a quote—*Till taught by pain, men know not water's worth*—words paraphrased from a poem by Lord Byron.

There was a sliding sound and the front door to the laboratory closed. A moment later there was another sound, followed by footsteps and Slit's voice suddenly emerging into the laboratory. Dan1 hurriedly replaced the frame on the wall and dived under the desk.

"Project Menos will ensure our boy attacks with utter ruthlessness," said Slit. "But it's useless without the N106."

"Yes sir," susurrated Freyja, who had also miraculously appeared in the lab.

"Keep working on the prototype," continued Slit. "We need a conscious mind to be coupled with Project Menos—that will make for a right bloodbath."

He extended his index finger. "Here's the code for the lower laboratory, it works the same as the others.'

Freyja pressed her index finger to Slit's. "Thank you."

"Excellent." Slit turned and left, the door snapping shut.

Freyja loaded something onto the wall, just out of Dan1's sight. As she paced across the room Dan1 watched her from beneath the desk, her slim legs switching back and forth across the doorway. She was focused intently on the wall, silently reading and memorizing. Her lips moved and her head bobbed from side-to-side, but she made no sound.

Five minutes later she closed her eyes and tilted her head at the ceiling, looking pleased with herself. She wiped the wall with the back of her hand and left the room.

Dan1 crawled from beneath the desk. He stood, stretched gingerly, and stared at the blank wall. Wiping information never deleted it permanently; cells on the surface had a memory. By tracing through the cellular permutations Dan1 recovered Slit's code and downloaded it to his perineurals.

Something like a DNA sequence passed across his vision, ending in an unusual sequence of 34 Ts: 34 consecutive Thymine bases in a chemical chain. He buried the unusual sequence deep in his architecture—safe from anyone finding it.

Dex's shack; two goons and gray matter

Dogbat skittered into the house with a small, gray cylinder clamped between his jaws.

"Package for you Sir."

It was unusual—Dex wasn't expecting anything—so he cautiously approached. The package was made from plastic; not a biopolymer, but a genuine non-bio wrap. It had a timing system at one end. The cap at the top slowly unpeeled and a grayish goop leaked out. Dex instinctively grabbed Dogbat and ran for the door. The gray matter spread rapidly across the room.

He reached his cat and swung a leg over, his shack already consumed by gray cells, which were quickly making their way along the dusty patch that served as Dex's front garden, flowing towards his bike in a river of quicksilver. The emerald eyes on the panther twinkled to life. Dex threw her round to face the gate. Clutching Dogbat awkwardly under his arm, they launched forward out of the dust. A line of gray cells attached to the left hind limb of the bike. She swerved wildly out of the gate and sprinted off down the road, Dex hugging close to her, digging his heels into her haunches. The gray matter was already eating up her back leg and she was limping badly.

Behind him he noticed two goons following on moto-leopards, the yellowy eyes of their machines bobbing in his rear vision. They were steadily catching up. With his panther injured there was little chance Dex would be able to escape. He considered getting off his bike and facing them hand-to-hand, but a quick observation of their size convinced him that would have been a mistake. They followed, sitting in his rear-vision, one on each side, keeping a respectful and funereal distance.

Dex maneuvered up the onramp, his bike limping onto 1st Arterial, barely able to keep to the minimum speed in the slow lane. The gray matter on her legs was a deadly enzyme, a fast acting lysin that destroyed organic material. He glanced down at the necrotic flesh trailing in ragged strands from below the cat's knee. He needed to stop and cauterize her hindquarters, otherwise the lysin would begin to act on his own body— explaining why the two goons on moto-leopards were not rushing to catch up with him.

He pulled into an exit lane and hobbled towards the service center wedged into the median strip of the arterial. The toxic mass had reached the top of the hindquarters, consuming the entire left limb. It began to spread down the right side and up onto the back. Dex squeezed the flanks of the cycle and heaved himself forward to keep away from the encroaching gray cells. His pursuers were enjoying the spectacle.

In a swift movement he turned and hurled Dogbat behind him. The solid brown ball yelped before collecting the larger rider square in the chest. The giant reeled from the blow, then recovered, accelerated swiftly and pulled a tail-whip from his jacket, leaping within range and lashing the whip down Dex's back; the teeth snatched his skin, dragging him onto the roadway.

When the whip tore away it left a deep channel of wet flesh. Dex turned onto his back, pressing bloodied marks onto the black surface of the road. The second moto-leopard was approaching, the rider's colossal arm swinging another savage whip. Dex stood unsteadily to face the man.

The whip was aimed at Dex's midsection: the intention to

cleave him clean in half. Moments before the leopard passed, Dex dropped quickly to the ground; a stray tooth cut a long gash from his cheek. The whip extended over him and wrapped around a solid lamppost. The rider's arm was unexpectedly yanked backward. The giant fell heavily to the ground and his moto-leopard skidded away.

Dex stumbled in a half run towards the fallen moto-leopard. Picking up the bike with his remaining strength, he kicked it into life. The other giant was fast approaching, swinging his whip through the air.

Dex took off. For a moment the giant was gaining ground, swinging the whip dangerously close to the hamstrings on Dex's vehicle, but Dex was a lighter and more skillful rider. He managed to get ahead.

He raced out the entrance to the service station and headed the wrong way up 1st Arterial, sending a Beetle scurrying out of his path. He jumped the median strip and swung the leopard around, leaving both giants far behind.

His old precinct station was close by—he could take shelter there. He left the moto-leopard slumped on the front steps and stumbled awkwardly to the station house door, his back shredded and his cheek flapping open.

The new girl at the front desk didn't believe he was a specially commissioned officer—she figured he was another splitter freak fired up on endo. He demanded to see Captain Warren, his labored breaths bubbling through the blood leaking from his cheek. She refused to help and called for assistance. Dex struck out, flying into a rage, furious and bloody—ending up paralyzed, twitching in a mess on the floor of the station house.

From high peaks to back lanes; snakeboards and ladders
"What the hell happened to me the other night?" E19, wearing

daisies on her shoes, was smiling brightly. She landed a soft kiss on his cheek.

"What the hell 'appened t'*me*?" countered Dan1. "I woke up with blood all o'er me shirt."

"What?" she cried.

"I musta slipped tryin' t'get back home. I broke me nose!"

"No way. Man, we were toasted."

"Yeah," he said, "I can't even remember leavin' the club. I can't remember sayin' goodbye. I can't remember nuttin'."

"Well you were a perfect gentleman, so don't worry," said El9 reassuringly. "A little too perfect for my liking." She flashed him a cheeky smile.

Dan1 felt a deep flutter in his chest. She slid an arm around his waist and they walked towards the Metroduct. Dan1 was happy to be with El9. Maybe it wasn't a permanent need, but he knew he wanted to be with her, to talk to her, to hear her thoughts. At work he'd reached a point where it was hard to be around the brains—he couldn't think of them as neuro units any more. After witnessing the illegal fight a gnawing discomfort had metastasized into something more serious. Locky wouldn't listen, Slit and the design team couldn't understand, but El9 was there with an ear and a smile.

She had insisted on going out in Central Melbourne to see where he normally spent his time—what she referred to as his "natural habitat". Dan1 was not really sure what to show her. He spent a lot of time hanging around the back of the snakeboard shop, but didn't figure El9 would be interested in that.

They caught the Metro to the shopping precinct in the 1st arrondissement and wandered along the broad malls, Dan1 keeping an eye out for the fanciest restaurant he could find, something to impress El9.

He wondered up to a place on the Western slope with enough

cutlery laid on the tables to be classy. As they approached, the maitre'd gave them an appraising glance.

"Do you have reservations?"

"About this place? Nah, not really—looks real swank."

El9 giggled. The maitre'd sighed. "I meant sir, did you book a table in advance?"

"Um," Dan1 flushed, "noooooo."

"Well perhaps sir, may I recommend another..." Dan1 conspicuously patted his distended account, swelling with weeks of unspent wages. "...table along the Western wall? The sunset is breathtaking tonight, don't you agree m'lady?"

"Quite," breathed El9, mocking the snobbish affectations of the maitre'd, "but I wonder if you could make the clouds more violet? All this orange is far too enervating, do you not agree?"

"I'm sure m'lady's wishes will be fulfilled in due time." The maitre'd ushered them towards a table with a beautiful view over the city's Western slope.

Dan1 spent most of the dinner trying to act ten years older than he actually was. At first he playfully tried to coax El9 into telling him more about the "research project" she was conducting in the city. She avoided his questioning with practiced diplomacy. After they had placed their orders she leaned over and gently wrapped both her hands around one of his.

"I will tell you more about me, when you show me the real you." She looked conspicuously around the fancy restaurant. "Don't look so stunned, Don Juan. I'm just saying I don't think this is the kind of place you normally hang out."

Dan1 gave a guilty smirk, fiddling with one of the forks elegantly laid in front of him. "What the hell is this fork for?" he asked. "Why do I need all these forks?" he said in mock exasperation. "No wonder this place is so pricey, they must spend a pile on forks."

El9 chewed her hand, trying to stifle her laughter. "So where is it," she asked between giggles, "that you normally hang out?"

"Behind the snakeboard shop," admitted Dan1.

"Sounds ginchy. Let's go there."

They ran from the restaurant and back into the mall. After catching a Metroduct, Dan1 led El9 into a narrow alleyway that had been converted into a snakepark. They sat on a stoop and watched the fluid arc of a snakeboarder flowing up the edge of the pipe and into the air. The rider spun and flicked and slipped the board under his feet moments before landing.

"Slik!" called El9. "I've never seen anything like this!"

She applauded enthusiastically. Dan1 gently took her hands and pushed them down into her heavy skirt.

"This ain't the place t'clap," he smirked. "I mean, y'can if ya like, but it ain't normal."

The snakeboarder was looking at El9 with a puzzled expression. He laid the board under his feet and snaked away.

The street had half pipes at both ends; a bank mounted on one wall faded into a long curving rail and up the center was a snake-run. A kid slid along the spine next to the snake-run, popped up, pulled a neat three-sixty and slipped back up the bank. El9 instinctively raised her hands, then stopped herself and smiled at Dan1.

"Can you do this stuff?"

Dan1 nodded enthusiastically. He borrowed a board and jumped off the top of the bank, slipping down to ollie the run, rail slide up the spine and pop off into a seven-twenty back onto the bank again. El9 whistled and clapped. Dan1 was sliding along a smooth section of the alley, taking a bow from his board. He pushed himself forward, building speed, then whipped up the half pipe.

After twenty minutes he returned to the stoop. She begged him for more while pulling him closer. He looked at her from beneath his hood, still breathing heavily from the ride. She kissed him quickly on the mouth.

It was past midnight when they left. They walked back towards the Metroduct and grabbed a chickpea roll on the way.

"This is more like it," said Dan1, taking a large bite of the roll.

"Hey! Leave some for me, ya guts!" protested El9.

"I didn' think ya ate GM food!"

"There's always a first time," she demurred. "Anyway, a girl could starve!"

They arrived at the Metro with sauce dribbled down their fronts. Dan1's shirt greedily absorbed the stain, El9's natural cottons held on to it, leaving a brown line snaking between her breasts.

"You know, I can't tell you where I live," whispered El9, "but I can tell you that my last Metro has already left."

"The Metroduct runs all night," objected Dan1 stupidly, before catching himself.

She took his hand and wrapped it around her waist.

"I can't resist a man who smells of chickpeas and garlic."

Later that night he woke next to El9. His coverall, just big enough for the two of them, wrapped around their hips and drew them together. He looked out through the bulging eye of his room. He was happy—for sure—but there was a dark swirl of concerns nagging at him.

He rolled from the coverall and reached his shelf where Slit's hair was still sitting in its vial. He held it against the light from the city, watching it drift in the liquid. He had been avoiding the question. He hadn't returned to the sequence since Slit's dinner party—leaving it in two states simultaneously, Schrodinger's hair.

He decided he would visit Mother Umami and ask some questions about his past, specifically whether she knew why Theodor Slit made a cameo in his mother's music box. He slipped back into the coverall and was enveloped by sleep.

Through the miasma of dreaming he gazed from his coverall. Just outside his room there was something moving, hovering— an eye bobbing gently in the sky, a single eye with short wings fluttering desperately to keep aloft. It bobbed a few more times and darted away.

The Captain loses faith; ends with a good question

Captain Warren sauntered down the stairs to find Dex bleeding and handcuffed to a bench. He immediately regretted hiring him. He had no idea why working on the woodland killing had this effect on Dex, but he felt responsible for dragging the man back in. He sat Dex on the couch in his office and offered a hot drink.

When Warren returned Dex was swaying unsteadily.

"So, you using again?"

Dex shook his head. The wounds on his back and cheek had not healed properly, leaving dark stains all over his clothes. He was hunched over and breathing in gasps. He sipped from the steaming mug.

"Can you remember what happened? How did you end up like this?"

Dex looked up from his mug and straight into Warren's eyes. The captain nervously chewed the strange growth on his lip.

"My house was destroyed. Totally flattened." Dex was still short of breath. He'd been beaten pretty good and the ready-aid hadn't fully kicked in. "Everything in the house is gone— the evidence, the files, everything." He took another shallow breath. "I was chased by the guys who did it."

Warren looked at him dubiously. Dex's story sounded like endo-fuelled paranoia. "Will you take a blood test?"

Dex offered his arm without hesitation. The captain took a bug from his desk drawer and plugged into a vein. After a few seconds the bug cheeped.

"Your system's clean. Assuming you're telling the truth, who would want to destroy your house and chase you down?"

"Theodor Slit," replied Dex.

Captain Warren shook his head. He walked back around his desk and sat down. "Why would Theodor Slit be interested in you?"

"I got a match on my sample board," panted Dex. "So here's a better question: why is Theodor Slit hanging out at murder scenes in this city?"

Warren sighed and pushed his neck around so Dex was entirely outside his field of view. It took some effort, but it was worth it. He suddenly wanted Dex out of his office, out of his precinct, off the case. He turned his head slowly back to reality.

"What do you mean?"

"Slit was at the first murder scene. He was at the second too and I can prove he was there around the time of the murder. He's involved in this somehow."

Warren sighed again. "Shit."

It had made sense to put Dex on the case when it was just some brutal killer stalking the streets. Warren was aware of the reputation Dex had built as a hunter and collector, it seemed like the perfect fit. But if Slit was somehow involved that would bring a shitstorm of politics. It would require a defter hand.

"Samples are a lock here? No chance of error?"

Dex nodded. "No mistake."

Warren looked across the table, squinting at the thrashed biopunk sitting opposite. Everything, from Dex's forehead spikes to his clobber boots, told him he was now the wrong man for the job. And yet he had managed to make progress far quicker than any of Warren's team would have.

"Theodor Slit," Warren half-whispered the name, shaking his head.

Visiting Mother Umami; reading the fatty folds

The thing about Mother Umami's milksteaks was that they usually lasted just one sip—depending on your lung capacity. After first intake of the gelatinous sweety meatness there were certain neurochemicals that instructed the motor cortex *more is required, urgently and immediately.* This visceral response led to painfully puckered cheeks and bulging eyes as the body raced to drain the last of Mother's goodness from the vial. Afterwards, satisfaction lasted one or two hours before the cravings resumed.

This intensity of desire was both the best and worst aspect of Mother Umami's unique brand of cuisine and had led to her being arrested for selling highly addictive foodstuffs to minors, a trumped up charge almost certainly instigated by her former lover at Biota. The incident occurred around the same time Locky and Dan1 left her employ and to everyone's surprise she hadn't disputed the calumny, instead, she had sold the franchises and moved to a remote property outside the city.

The Saturday morning train slid down the travelduct, heading for Mother Umami's. Dan1 stepped into the carriage—on his new wage he wasn't forced to ride the roof—and followed the conductor to his assigned seat.

The train moved swiftly on an express line, bypassing the suburban stations, then slowed as it approached a cluster of hills to the north of the city. At full speed the train had been a liquid mirror, but as it lost momentum the body compressed, the fluids in the rear caught up to those in the front, the skin slackened and the carriages suddenly looked like plastic bags full of water. To the passengers the loss of momentum was barely perceptible, but to a spectator the once slimline locomotive now looked like an obese worm struggling to heave itself over an apple.

The train inched its way up the slope. Dan1 tried to relax

and settle into his chair as they slithered towards the summit. The front of the train rounded the crest of the hill and slipped like a tear down the cheek of the hill. Suddenly the city was far behind and the train was a silver blur gliding across the level fields, low and flat in the travelduct.

When Dan1 woke that morning El9 was sitting up in bed holding the vial containing Slit's hair. She had laughed when Dan1 told her what it was. "Who collects their boss's hair?" A fair question, but he hadn't answered. He didn't like the idea of ancestry. He'd grown up believing that only the privileged had a past—people like Dan1 got a record, and they could even avoid that if they didn't get caught. His bloodline, always buried behind some unknown trouble years ago, was suddenly spilling back into his life, bringing with it an unwanted undercurrent of loss and fear.

He got off at the station and began the half-hour journey on his snakeboard, winding along the main roadway leading from town. Mother Umami's house was on a small parcel of land accessible via a dusty back road and he snaked swiftly under the shadows of the tall weeping trees, their branches diffusing the morning light, protecting him from the rising heat.

He reached the front gate and followed a smudged pathway winding through Mother's wild garden; untamed roses with fierce thorns twisted across a low shrubbery of earpod acacias and swordfish banksia; a few tall eucalypts rose from the undergrowth, their knotted trunks shedding long chunks of cracked bark.

The house, a two-story antediluvian home constructed entirely from traditional materials, had survived Leviathan untouched. Its large second-story balcony was hewn from ancient wildwoods, as were the boards on the outside walls, all covered in curious lime green paint that was chipped and splintered with age. The kitchen, filling the front of the second floor, was light and airy despite the hooded balcony.

As Dan1 skipped up the steps a maid approached, one of Mother's avatars, dressed in a short skirt and apron.

"Heard you got a promotion!"

Dan1 was disappointed that Mother Umami hadn't come out to see him personally. "It's not a promotion."

"According to Locky you're working with Theodor Slit, his right hand man." The maid avatar mangled Mother Umami's flat Melbourne brogue until it sounded faintly cockney.

"Yeah," said Dan1, noncommittal. *Where could he even begin?*

"Hmmmm, feels like there's somethin' goin' on there—had any breakfast?"

"Not really."

"Then sit down and I'll fetcha something."

The maid swooped around the kitchen collecting ingredients. As she tilted over the hotplate Dan1 could see the soft fold of her cheeks. She was frying farm-fresh baconeggs, straight from the hutch, and something green that she had plucked from the garden. For guests, Mother liked to maintain the aesthetic sensibilities of an organik, without the inconveniences. She handed him the meal and they both took seats at a worn wooden table.

"So tell me 'bout it," she said.

"Well it's kinda complicated." He paused for a long time, baconeggs dawdling in front of his mouth.

"Locky told me you were havin' trouble with office politics."

"Locky doesn't know shit. There's more'n jus' that." He reached into his pocket and took out the pic of his mum standing with Theodor Slit. "I found this'n that ol' music box."

"Ya mum's music box?"

Dan1 nodded.

She calmly studied the pic. "Who're these folks?"

"The guy is Theodor Slit. I figure the woman is me mum."

"Hmmm. I dunno if I should get into this." The maid's mouth suddenly twitched uncontrollably—crossfire emotions coming from the perineural interface. Mother was unsure about something. "You should come in'ta see me, inta me room. Be better t'have this face to face."

"Sure." Dan1 hoofed the rest of his breakfast and headed down the corridor to Mother's room. She was even larger than he remembered. Her massive folds now filled the circular bed, spilling over the edge in places, her arms barely distinct in the mountainous pile.

"Don't stare like that," she snapped.

"Sorry." Dan1 turned his eyes to the ground and found a place to sit near her bed.

"I always meant to tell 'bout this, Dan1, but I didn' wanna upset ya," she began. "Just before you left, a fella visited from the rent-a-runt scheme, where I gotcha from. They gave me the music box and some ... links."

She leaned slightly to stretch a bulge of her stomach, then threw up links across the taut skin. The first one read FAMILY ATTACKED IN MUTANT SLAUGHTER. Dan1 touched her damp fold, turned bluish from the text, opening the link. The story was horrific: a family went hiking in the woodlands behind Melbourne, the mother had been torn to shreds, father and daughter both went missing and were never found, and somehow the boy had survived. The folder contained a pic of his slain mother—the same woman he'd seen with Slit in the music box.

"That boy is me?" he asked.

Mother Umami nodded.

There was a pic of the missing man and metadata that read

MISSING: PETA SINGER, THEOLOTRICIAN. Dan1 studied the pic. The man had a broad, happy smile. His face was round, reminiscent of Dan1's, and his eyes were squinting into the sun. Dan1 finished reading, but his hand was left hovering over Mother Umami's stomach.

"Ya reckon he's me dad?" He tapped the pic of Peta Singer. Mother enveloped his hand into her fatty mitt.

"Back when I found out," she heaved a huge breath. "It's so bloody godawful. I figured you'd rather not know." She reached for something fresh to eat. "Must be a lot t'take in."

"I thought Slit was me dad." Dan1 was overwhelmed. "Fa' months now I thought it was Slit."

Mother Umami strained to raise the folds of fat above her eyebrow. "Ya gotta approach this calmly," she counselled, churning through the archive, the links on her stomach spinning past. "I was given these by the bloke from rent-a-runt. I always figured this Singer fella was ya dad. It makes sense from my vantage."

Dan1 looked back at the picture. If he was forced to know his father, he was glad it could be this genial image, rather than Slit. Singer's was a countenance he could take after.

"Did ya say ya thought it was 'im?"

"Say t'who?" asked Dan1.

"Theodor Slit."

"Nah way! I don't want 'im t'know shit. I don't want none of this. I just wanted to tell you coz… coz…" He let the sentiment drift away and she squeezed his hand.

"Stay for lunch. I'll make curd burgers," she offered.

"Sounds slik."

"Slik? Where'd ya pick that up?"

"Must've got it from a friend." Dan1 shrugged, smiling happily. "Ya know, I found a girl I like."

"Nay, ya never mentioned that!" She feigned a look of exaggerated shock. "You better stay for lunch," she said, waving a finger of meat at him, "and ya better tell me all 'bout this girl."

Saturday call

Locky knew that most people didn't think he deserved his job—and he didn't think it was because they were jealous, it was because they thought, quite rightly, that he was massively underqualified. He had little experience in the field, no formal training, and absolutely no interest in accounting as a profession or a practice. But as a manager of people Locky was unparalleled, and if his nameless critics had understood the full breadth of tasks required by his position then they would have been awed by the deftness with which he fulfilled his role.

Locky's department was the Accounts Integrity Group. The police of the police, they audited the numbers flowing in from the accounting subunits that managed expenses from within the departments of Biota. It was Locky's particular obligation to ensure that no one was allowed to scrutinize the accounts of the gladiorg department too closely.

Money always decides the outcome of conflicts; from Italian duchies in the Renaissance to cotton growers cut off in the port of New Orleans, the free flow of cash is the lifeblood of war. The previous evening Locky had watched Rex demolish a bear-like Moscovite named Ursus Borealis. He liked to consider that he had made a personal contribution to that victory, for in the epic battles of the arena Locky saw himself as a facilitator, or perhaps a vasodilator, someone who kept the blood flowing.

His collaborator in this deception was none other than Theodor Slit, who was given a free hand over the gladiorg department's accounts in return for giving Locky a much

needed hand up, helping him escape the Boons and take his
rightful place at the executive suite. In return Locky was never
allowed to contact his benefactor, nor speak of his benefaction,
and was always required to be available, even on weekends.

Locky was enjoying light Saturday morning chitchat with a
woman wrapped in light cotton sheets when he felt the dark
presence of Slit drift into his perineurals.

Time to get up.

"I better clean up," said Locky abruptly.

"But we were just about to get dirty," breathed the woman
through cotton sheets.

"I'll be back, just give me a sec." Locky hurried from the
room, blowing kisses at his paramour.

Pathetic Kallikak, hissed Slit, *Her body isn't even corporate.
Why did I bother raising you so high if you're going to stoop so low?*

"Sorry Mr. Slit," mumbled Locky on the way to the
bathroom, "what can I do for you?"

I need to move money out of Account K. Make it happen.

Slit was referring to a rather large pool of discretionary
funds that had been collecting under Locky's purview,
unnoticed by Biota.

"Of course, how much are you after?"

All of it. And I need it by tomorrow.

Locky's throat tightened.

So there will be no more playtime today, Mr. Kallikak.

"No sir, I'll get right on it."

*I am aware that your so-called brother is still keeping dangerous
company. Do you want me to deal with it?*

"No sir, I'm on it."

*I'm running out of patience. If you can't persuade him, I will be
forced to. Do you understand?*

"Yes sir."

And Locky, make sure you report to me if Dan1 *exhibits any ... aberrant behavior.*

"Yes sir."

The dark presence receded leaving Locky leaning on the bathroom door, his head aching from the night before.

A visit to the professor; the end of politics

The professor pulled his mail from Biota and collected it on his desk. He dumped the messages from his perineural into the pile then scrunched his hands across the display to permanently delete them. He grinned at the young student sitting on the other side of his desk.

"Too many invitations," he said. "It's as if they don't want us to do any research—just attend cocktail parties and conferences and summits and industry sponsored gabfests where we all listen to what an incredible contribution Biota makes to Melbourne. Sometimes I get so tired of hearing about Biota ... Oh well, I guess that's the downside of living here."

The young girl nodded eagerly and clutched a notebook to her chest. She was wearing a light floral dress and open-toed shoes. The professor could smell the faint bouquet of her daisy dress intermingled with the usual mustiness of his office. She had her hair tucked into a large net—a popular style on campus.

"I've been thinking of taking a sabbatical. Perhaps travelling to one of the maritimes, or an emerging city, something outside the WTO. Somewhere non-aligned. Did you take a year off before university?"

"No," she replied defensively. "I didn't have the time."

"Time is very much on your side, my girl."

He stepped over to the small hexagonal window, standing slightly to the side and behind her. When she had arrived she moved her seat so it faced away from the display of taxidermy he kept in a glass cabinet. She could not hide her disgust. It had been the only thing that gave her away.

"So," soughed the professor. "You wanted to ask me about Theodor Slit."

"Yes," replied El9 curtly. "I'm writing a biography on him as part of a series on great gladiorg designers."

"And I suppose you want to know why he was expelled from the university?"

He sensed her discomfort. She had not revealed her agenda, but he was prepared to be generous with this PETSO girl. Her resourcefulness had impressed him. She had managed to become extremely close to Dan1 in a very short time.

"Yes, I am interested in that," she said calmly. "And I know that you are familiar with the incident because you served on the Ethics Committee that expelled him."

"I like a student who does her homework. Although it makes me suspicious. You're far too organized to be a poli-sci student." The professor laughed tightly.

"We don't study politics anymore, professor; we study behavior and organization, as per the Biota curriculum. I thought a man in your position would refrain from even mentioning politics."

"In my position?"

"I've read your articles in support of the Circle of Seven. It's pretty impressive that you managed to keep your position. You must be an expert at...well, at politics."

"I do my best, with the resources I have. Politics is, as always, the art of the possible." The professor stopped abruptly and stepped back from the window. He stroked his salt-and-pepper goatee. "So you want to know the story of Theodor Slit? Well, I can accommodate you there.

"The man was a brilliant student and he worked on

extraordinary projects. But he was pushing the boundaries of science, he and his collaborator, Thomas Wotan. The two of them did not understand politics, they didn't understand the threat their work posed to the established order..."

"You mean the Circle of Seven," interrupted El9.

"I mean the Charter, dear girl. And community standards. Their work threatened to undermine basic morality, it threatened to redefine our understanding of humanity, of the nature of being, of the physical boundaries of the individual. The Ethics Committee really had no choice but to send them down from the university."

"Do you still belong to the Ethics Committee?" asked El9.

"Sadly that institution no longer exists. It was disbanded after the reformation of the university."

"You mean when Biota took over."

"Yes," sighed Wilson.

"So they won?"

"What do you mean by that?"

"Well Slit is working in a powerful position at Biota, while the Ethics Committee, the Circle, everything you supported, has been discredited and disbanded."

"We still have the Charter." Wilson's sharp nose had been put out of joint.

"But there are no courts, no commissions, nothing to enforce the Charter," pushed El9. "You're a toothless tiger."

The professor spread his arms, placing a hand at either end of the desk, apparently for no other reason than to demonstrate his impressive reach. "In my opinion, it is better to be a toothless tiger than a dead cat."

A tense silence stretched between them.

"PETSO," said the professor. He paused and looked at El9 to let her know her disguise had failed. "Protests, hacks, demonstrations. None of it will change a damn thing. PETSO wants war, but war is exactly how Biota wins."

"So what is your plan professor? To hide out in here with this junk," she looked disdainfully around his messy office, "waiting for the whole thing to stop? For everything to go back to what it was before Leviathan?"

"You will not win a direct confrontation with Biota," said the professor. "It might feel good to take them on, but my aim is not to die on a hill. I want to win."

"So do I." El9 surprised the professor with her forcefulness. She stood and walked from the room without saying goodbye.

He sat behind his desk and looked around at the memorabilia he had collected over the years.

"Youth," he sighed. "I can't believe I was once one of them."
He went back to his work.

Terminal goop; off the case

Dex's shack had been reduced to a pool of gray scum. Half a dozen officers in white HAZMAT suits with clear plastic visors were cleaning up the mess. A short woman was standing at the edge of the remains, peering across the wreckage with interest. Leaning down, she extracted a vial from the plastic pocket of her suit and carefully dipped it into the sludge, removing a small sample of gray goo, which she plugged into her perineural system.

On the street Dex and Captain Warren were sitting in a squad car. Dex had caught two hours sleep on the couch in Warren's office and his wounds were mostly healed.

"Let's go and speak with Hui," said Warren, squeezing his generous gut through the door of the squad car. Dex eased his way out and limped towards the woman in the white suit.

"You little idiot," sneered Dex to Dogbat, who had bounded

up to greet him, enthusiastically wagging his tail. "You brought it in, didn't you?"

"Yes I did Sir," responded Dogbat, tail still wagging sprightly.

"Morning Hui," called Warren happily.

The woman was staring at the complex chemical analysis flashing across her peripheral vision. She swayed a little as she refocused her attention on the fat captain.

"Good morning Warren," she said gaily. "I'd shake your hand but it would probably kill you."

"I understand," acceded Warren with a nervous smile, looking at the dangerous gray stains on Hui's white HAZMAT suit. "This is Declan, he owns the house, or he used to own the house, now I guess he just owns the land."

Dex smiled wanly.

"It was nasty stuff that did this," said Hui, getting straight to business. "It started over there." She pointed to a patch on the ground where Dex's living room had been. "Then it spread rapidly through the house. Took everything with it—every organism anyway. Nothing left but gray goop. We're damn lucky it didn't spread further."

"Dex was in the house at the time," said Warren.

Hui raised her eyebrows. "Well, you were incredibly lucky to escape. If this had touched you…"

"I saw what it did to my cat," interrupted Dex.

"You were lucky." She reiterated the phrase like a mother chastising her child. "I haven't seen a strain this destructive in a long time."

"Who could get their hands on something like this?"

"No one," replied Hui flatly. "It could be a force—maybe WTO—but then it would have to be a top secret project that I haven't heard of."

"Is that possible?" asked Warren, half-joking.

"It is possible." Hui's response was typically modest. "Usually HAZMAT gets access to all research, but it's possible someone was working on this at such a high level that they didn't share information."

"Could this have been made by someone else?" asked Dex.

"What do you mean? An amateur? No way," she said flatly. "I don't know exactly what this is, but it's extremely sophisticated."

"How about a rogue within the corporation?"

"Sure." Hui shrugged. "Don't know how they'd pull something like this off without getting caught, the board finds out about this stuff eventually. No one has enough control over their budget to hide the resources required for this kind of project. It's pretty unlikely."

"Unlikely?" Dex already had his own ideas about who was responsible.

"Unlikely," repeated Hui, "but not impossible."

Back in the squad car Warren looked directly at Dex. "I know what you're thinking, Declan."

"Nah." Dex shook his head emphatically. "You have no idea what I'm thinking."

"Coincidences happen all the time." The sentence was benign, but from Warren it sounded like a threat. Dex stared straight ahead.

"Don't do this, Declan. Don't go chasing after Theodor Slit just because of some crazy coincidence. The guy is a seriously well-respected designer; he's a Melbourne legend."

"That doesn't change anything."

"He could have been passing by, or the samples could have been contaminated. Anything could have happened," insisted Warren.

"I know what happened," growled Dex.

"No you don't. You just have a theory—one theory out of millions of possibilities. Don't treat this as conclusive evidence."

Dex looked over the remains of his shack. There was a reason why someone destroyed his home and had tried to kill him, same reason why those goons had been sent. Dex was getting very close to identifying the killer.

"Declan, I'm handing this case to homicide."

Dex shrugged. "Homicide can't help. They won't bring in the killer, not before I do anyway."

"You're off the case, Dex. I've had to decommission you. You're no longer a special consultant. You have no rights or privileges associated with the police force."

Dex glared at Warren. He tried to look unaffected but he was seething with rage.

"I'm sorry Declan but you forced my hand. The incident this morning," he shook his head, "you knocked the desk officer unconscious. You were out of control. I have to do this for the sake of the department. You can stay on my couch while you look for a new place, okay?" Warren booted the squad car.

"Can I bring Dogbat?" asked Dex, holding him in Warren's face.

"Yeah sure. All I ask is that you don't harass Slit, stay away from the guy. Just relax at my place, recuperate a bit, it will do you good. Andrea can cook you five square meals a day. You'll feel like a new man in no time." Warren laughed and patted his bulging belly.

The squad car pulled away from the curb and crept through the quiet streets of West Boons. They arrived at Warren's home in the northern suburbs. His wife, Andrea, had been forewarned and was waiting at the door.

"I have a book club meeting this afternoon," said Andrea brightly. "But I've set you up in the den. You'll be able to sleep there undisturbed. There's plenty of food in the parlor so just help yourself."

The mousy woman disappeared into the kitchen. Dex

stretched out on a comfortable cot in the den. He placed his hands behind his head, the wounds on his back still aching. He closed his eyes and slowly drifted towards sleep.

"I'll deliver him first," he muttered before slipping away.

The cat stalks; catches the rat unaware

"I nearly had to kill for it, but I got a pass for tonight's battle." Locky was triumphant.

"Noice, first round of finals. It'll be a good'n." Dan1 wasn't really in the room, his mind off probing an obscure patch in the hydra.

"So you want to meet up?"

Dan1 snapped back to reality and dumped the feed from his peripheral vision. "Nah man, I got plans t'night. I'm gonna drop by, say hi t'everyone in Slit's box, then head out."

Locky looked dubious. "This is the finals bro."

Dan1 stuck out his chin. "I know, but I work with gladiorgs all week, and I'm just not innerested in spending me weekends on'em too. I already got tickets t'a show in the Boons."

"With her?" Locky didn't disguise his hostility.

"Yeah, with El9."

"This is crazy—this is madness. You can't have this girl staying in my apartment."

Dan1 seethed. He'd been trying to find a new place for weeks but it was tough—there were options, but none of them good.

"What happens when the cops come looking for her here?"

"They won't."

"How can you be sure? All we know is that she's some organik nutter. Anything could happen. Have you thought about your job? Have you thought about mine?"

Dan1 had. It's all he'd been thinking about, but when he

raised it with Locky he just got a wall, no discussion, not interest, just a wall of anger. His head boiled.

"This one's a bark short of a bitch," snarled Locky.

"Back off! And stop tryin' to protect me from shit, it ain't your job no more."

Locky stared maliciously at his little brother. He unfolded his arms and walked up so close Dan1 could feel the breath tickle his ear. "What makes you think I'm trying to protect *you* from *her*?" he spat. "Maybe I'm protecting her from you, ratboy."

He stalked into his room.

Dan1 angrily threw the apartment listings onto the wall and quickly scanned through them: all bad choices, but better than staying put. He threw down bond on one, impetuously sealing the lease with his sequence. He wanted out, immediately.

He walked to his room, threw some things into his coverall and slung it over his shoulder. He left the music box on his shelf; he'd come back for that later.

Cooking it, old school; the missing hair

Dan1 woke in his own apartment on Sunday morning. The light just managed to penetrate the heavy lids of the outer wall. He had no view, no appliances, no furniture and very little space. He sorted through the small pile of belongings he had brought with him. Somehow the vial with Slit's hair had stowed along. He ran a full test on the hair and discovered it wasn't Slit's after all, it was his own.

He laughed bitterly. If DNA is destiny, as Slit believed, he'd spent the last few months trying to unshackle himself. When he believed Slit was his dad he saw himself in the great master—a comfort with sequencing he'd never come across before in someone else—but he was also deeply cut by the differences. Slit treated everyone as a meatbag of chemicals. Dan1 had realised he was cut from a different cloth—he had come to question everything, not just the illegal fight but everything Biota was founded to do. Suddenly, with his paternity resolved, he felt fully liberated to explore these questions with El9. He tossed the tube back onto the pile.

El9 had planned to visit so they could play some games. Without a perineural system she couldn't hook into the hydra and play a real game, so she brought around some ancient boards, which limited the gameplay to just three dimensions, sometimes four, but even within such a simple environment the permutations were complex and entertaining. They played intensely for hours, until it was so late El9 decided to sleep the night.

The next day he left work early and caught a train out to the Boons. El9 had promised to come around for dinner and Dan1 was going to cook a special meal. After some searching he found a store selling historical foods. He arrived home early and began preparing the meal: peppers stuffed with ratatouille.

It was not a simple task—made more difficult because the apartment didn't have a conventional stove. He cautiously followed the recipe, consulting a culinary dictionary for definitions of unfamiliar terms. After two hours of sustained effort he managed to cook something that was, strictly speaking, edible—in the same way that toenails, strictly speaking, are edible. He was tremendously pleased with himself.

El9 was due within the hour. Excited, he skipped up the steps into his room to get dressed, trying on a white cotton shirt he had bought in the Boons. He was augmenting his pheromones when he noticed the tube containing the hair was missing.

He searched through the small pile of his stuff. It had disappeared. He returned to the kitchen feeling a bit deflated. There was only one person who had had access to the tube: El9. Did she take it? Why? Perhaps she had thought it could be useful for one of her PETSO operations? Dan1 was disappointed she hadn't asked him directly—he would have let her have it.

El9 was nearly two hours late for dinner. By the time she arrived Dan1's stuffed peppers were sagging.

"Hungry?" he asked.

"I could bite the nuts off a low flying duck," she grinned. Dan1 did not respond.

She apologized for being late and smiled as they ate the soggy peppers.

"You pissed about something?" she asked after a few bites.

Dan1 shook his head. "Nah, just knackered. Real tired."

"What is it?" she pressed.

He grimaced and looked pained, squirming in his seat. "Did ya take Slit's hair?"

El9 was silent for a while. "Dan1, you know I work for PETSO?" Dan1 nodded. "It's a very important thing for me. It's not a *part* of my life, it *is* my life." Dan1 nodded again, looking miserable.

"At this point I should tell you that I cleaned the hair away... or accidentally threw it out, or... I should make up an excuse and not tell you the truth, because that's the way it is with PETSO. We never jeopardize the success of an operation." She shifted uncomfortably in her seat and wrinkled her forehead.

"I'm going to tell you the truth, Dan1. But you have to promise to keep it to yourself. Okay?"

"Yeah course," he said.

"Well, maybe it's easier for me to show you the truth." She got up from her chair and led him from the room. "We need to catch the Metro to get to my place. It's not far."

The brown shag; his beautiful eyes
A short while later Dan1 was standing in a small apartment

not dissimilar to Locky's. The floor was covered in a deep shaggy brown rug, the walls were an inoffensive beige, only the furniture was atypical of a residential apartment. Against the back wall was a long bench covered in scientific equipment from the twentieth century. Perched at the end was a giant data drive hooked up to an ancient-looking monitor. An incubator filled the opposite corner and a small desk covered in mess occupied the center of the room. El9 switched on a desk lamp.

"While I'm here in the city my research project is on Theodor Slit," she explained. "I've been trying to track him since I got here. I've also been doing some research on his past." She passed her hand over the data drive. "We're almost positive that Slit was thrown out of university for performing illegal experiments on humans. His crime was covered up by the faculty and now we think he's conducting the same experiments at Biota. I was sent to find proof. When I said I was working an operation, well, you're the one I'm operating. You're our way in."

She paused from her confessional, sitting in the shadow of the lamp, her dreds swinging like thick rope from her temples.

"I'm sorry I wasn't honest with you, Dan1. I'm sorry I didn't tell you that I've been researching your boss. And I'm sorry I took the hair without asking. I just saw the opportunity and took it."

Dan1 stepped through the cluttered room and sat down on the carpet.

"What were ya gonna do with it?"

El9 got up, opened a cabinet and removed two pouches.

"I incubated a set of Slit's hand prints," she said. "And a set of irises as well. I thought I could use them to get past biometrix at Biota."

"Aaah," sighed Dan1. "Well then I've something of me own

to say. Ya see, that's my hair."

El9 looked puzzled. "I don't understand."

"I thought Slit was me dad, so I took a sample from 'im." He grimaced. "Then I realized I'd just foun' one of me own hairs on 'is shoulder."

El9 stifled a giggle.

"So these are your hands?" she asked, reaching into the pouch. "And these are your beautiful eyes?"

He nodded and laughed. She clambered over him and gently pressed his shoulders to the floor. They kissed deeply.

"I wish ya'd told me all this before," he said.

"I should have."

They rolled onto a narrow stretch of carpet between the bench and the desk, the only empty space in the room. El9 deftly removed Dan1's white shirt while he struggled with the still unfamiliar buttons and hooks that kept her body pinned behind light cotton. With a little help from her they were finally both naked. She rolled onto her back, allowing the thick tendrils of carpet to massage her back and buttocks while Dan1 stroked and kissed her neck. There was nothing separating them: no aides, no auxiliorgs.

Later, panting and exhausted, they sank back into the plush carpet on the floor of the cramped apartment. El9 looked across at him; even in the dim light Dan1 could see she was smiling.

"Thank you for forgiving me," she said.

"Thanks for being straight up." He rolled over to face her and placed his hands between her naked thighs. "Here's th'thing. I wanna know what they're doin' too. I ain't comfortable there no more. I ain't comfortable with what 'appened t'Miklos Pohl. I think they is doin' somethin' sketchy—all'a 'em—Slit, Freya, Wing—all'a 'em. Maybe like that illegal fight. Maybe much much worse.

"I can get into Slit's lab," he said as she nodded at him enthusiastically. He pressed his hand onto her chest to stop her from interrupting. "I know there is somethin' goin' on with that lot—somethin' I ain't 'sposed to know. They is planning somethin' for the Gran' Final, I heard Slit talkin' with Freyja. I reckon they is hidin' it in another lab, one the board don't know 'bout—one they is tryin' t'keep secret from Paris."

"Why do you think that?" she asked, sitting up in surprise. She wrapped an arm around her knee and gazed down at him.

"I heard 'em talkin' 'bout a lower lab, he e'en give her a code."

El9 stared wide-eyed at Dan1. "Tell me you…"

"I gotta copy," he grinned.

El9 bounced on her bum and clapped her hands, throwing her arms around him and kissing the top of his head.

"I can't believe I found you," she said. "You really are the answer to everything."

Dan1 shrugged. "I's pretty darn good."

She pushed him down and pressed her mouth against his stomach. "So when can we break in?"

"I gotta plan for how, it'll take a bit ta get it all together, but we gotta do it before the Gran' Final."

She kissed him deeply.

Father knows

The radio crackled and through the static came her father's voice. "What the hell are you doing, El9?"

El9 raced over to turn down the volume. "He's in the apartment—what the hell are *you* doing?"

"I'm trying to make sure that one of my agents hasn't been compromised—and from what I've heard she has been very compromised indeed."

"I'm undercover Dad; this was my mission, get close to the

kid. What else was I supposed to do, learn how to snakeboard in a week?"

"You're in a relationship," snarled her father.

"This was the mission you gave me, dad. The other night I ate junk food, it's all within the rules, it's part of the project. It's what I'm supposed to be doing, don't freak out."

"You ate GM? El9, darling, how could you compromise yourself like this? I've obviously made a huge mistake."

"It's just junk food, dad, and this is just junk sex, you know? Just junk sex, roll it up and throw it away. Nothing to worry about."

"El9 you're not in the compound anymore, the city is dangerous. They can make junk food so addictive people get hooked. I've seen people kill for the stuff. Junk food is no joke, it's dangerous. And junk sex even more so."

"I'm doing this for the cause, Dad. I know what I'm doing and you'll just have to trust me."

"You're playing with fire, El9."

The toilet door retracted and Dan1 stepped into the living room.

"That a radio?" he asked.

"Yep." She hurriedly turned the dial. "Everything is old school in an organik's world."

"Yeah," Dan1 laughed and shook his head. "You guys sure is crazy."

Dex in suburbia; cornered beasts

Andrea, Captain Warren's wife, was a nagging busybody with far too much time on her hands. She filled some of her day with work for various charities, but on the whole her marriage to Warren was one of those curious arrangements where the husband brought home a wage and the wife slowly killed him with undying selflessness. Dex spent much of his day hiding in the den to avoid her.

When Warren came home the two men stood on the back porch slugging beer. Warren enjoyed having Dex around. He was quietly proud of his neat suburban life. As the sun sank behind the back fence he fired up his Ye-Olde Grillmate™ and they chatted while barbecuing a perfectly quadrilateral steak.

Their conversation centered around the difference between police work and collecting samples. Dex's years in the private sector had given him the freedom to explore alternate methods that the police force could not have accommodated. Meanwhile police forensics had improved their technologies and data collation. A mutual respect developed between them, not the rekindling of an old friendship, because they had never been more than distant colleagues, but admiration for each other's professional accomplishments.

Dex spent the next few days recuperating. He tried to keep his mind off the case. Luckily there hadn't been another killing. He trailed around the house looking for something useful to do. There were many rooms to explore while Andrea was out shopping or volunteering. He found a fitness room in the basement and spent a few hours working out and listening to Warren's collection of new soul music.

While poking through Warren's study he found a top-of-the-line scanner and a sample board. He suddenly felt a pang for the case. He desperately wanted to get back to it. He'd been yanked away right when the killer was within reach.

Tracking beasts in the pits outside Melbourne was tough work. It was dark in there and impossible to know the terrain. He usually had limited visuals on his target, making it hard to know when they were vulnerable, when to strike. But one thing he knew: when a beast was cornered it panicked. Suddenly they got jumpy. Suddenly they lashed out, rushed the trees, stumbled into crevasses. They made mistakes.

It's also what people did when the investigation closed in. When they feel their options narrowing, they panic. That's what Slit had done. Sending his goons around to destroy Dex's house was a huge mistake. Warren was right, it *could* have been a coincidence that Slit was passing by two of the murder scenes close to the time of the attack. But sending his goons wasn't a random act. It was an admission of guilt.

The grey goop, his house and all the evidence destroyed, that should have been a temporary setback. But Warren had also panicked. Pulling Dex from the case, denying him access to the police's own store of samples, that had blocked Dex from progressing his case. Dex trusted that Warren was acting to save the department's reputation, not trying to slow walk Dex's investigation for any other reason. But he wondered.

Either way, there was nothing he could do without the samples. He looked hopefully at Warren's impressive sample board, but it was empty. He shut the door and tramped back upstairs.

A rabbit's foot; some luck

By the time Warren came home Dex was already feeling claustrophobic. He wanted to leave the house and find somewhere with a room for rent.

"Come on, the steaks are juicy, the wine is flowing, where else would you want to be?"

Dex smiled. He'd warmed to the Captain since seeing him in his natural environment. This wasn't the kind of place that Dex could survive in, but Warren obviously thrived here.

"Righto," nodded Dex. "I'll take your free food one more night."

They laid out another huge meal consisting of enormous amounts of protein and drank a bottle of red wine before the meal head even begun. The lights were warm and Dex was relaxed.

"Whenever I get tired at work or stressed or whatever,"

Warren waived a fork around his living room, "I remember I'm coming back here. Every day ends here. That's not so bad."

Warren grinned broadly, then checked himself. Dex could feel his embarrassment at being boastful. Warren probably thought Dex wanted all this, probably thought he'd humiliated him, but he knew Warren meant well, the wine had just led him somewhere unexpected, somewhere awkward. These things happen.

"Ya know, Warren, I don't mind where I'm at either."

Warren looked pained. "I…"

"The thing is," Dex interrupted, "I never come home from my work. I carry it around with me. Always have. I get that now, is who I am."

Andrea emerged with a huge white pudding shaped like a rabbit's foot.

"Wow," Dex grinned. "This is amazing." His tone, his eyes, the relaxed slope of his shoulders, it lanced the moment that had built between them and Warren smiled appreciatively.

"Let's dig in."

Warren hoed into the rabbit's foot and uncorked a sticky wine before ladling out seconds.

Andrea retired to bed and the two of them sat, nursing the remaining wine in their glasses.

"I'm lucky," said Warren. "But I admire you Dex. You really get it done. For me," he waived around the room again, "this is my buffer from the world." He pointed at Dex a little drunkenly, "You don't have one do you? You just get out there and bring them in. No process, no bureaucracy, no one to answer to. You just bring them in. That's lucky."

Dex nodded. "I'm lucky."

They finished their wine. Warren stumbled a little unevenly up the stairs. He looked grateful for the bannister. Dex stretched out on the cot in the den, his back fully recovered, well-rested and well-fed. Tomorrow would be a good time for him to leave.

The next morning he woke with a start as the door to the den snapped open. Warren stood in the doorway, curling his lip and gnawing at it for a moment, then slipping a pouch onto the desk. He quickly closed the door and trotted off down the hall.

Dex jumped from the cot and picked up the pouch. Inside the first fold were rows of tiny vials, all the samples from the crime scenes: the woodland, the alleyway, West Boons. Each was neatly labeled. The labels corresponded to the scene-maps still stored in Dex's perineural system. He raced from the room and ran downstairs to the sample board.

The head of the body; the spine spy

"You're going to need clearance for that."

Dan1 hated dealing with the city bureaucracy. It was made up of talentless drones from head office in Paris, begrudgingly sent away to serve their time in the antipodes. They tended to be haughty people with mustaches, strangely antiquated uniforms (livery was a better word) and an attitude that suggested the third millennium had generally been a mistake and it would be better to revert to the old ways.

"There are adequate plans available publicly in the hydra," suggested the bureaucrat.

"We need something with more detail, for the refurbishment." Dan1 had concocted an elaborate story to justify his request, but so far it had come up against the might of an even more elaborate bureaucracy.

"Yes, this refurbishment. There isn't any note of it in our database."

"It's a minor matter, nothing worth troubling the honorable corps d'ingenieur."

The man's mustache preened at this compliment, seemingly adopting an independent personality, even as its owner maintained a grim mien.

"So you don't actually need the source codes, just the modeling?"

"That's right," said Dan1 quickly, sensing a way around the impasse.

"We can't provide that."

"I see."

"Unless you request it for an artistic program. Then we can release the information without board approval."

"Do I need to register as an artist?" asked Dan1 hopefully.

The man guffawed loudly. "Of course you don't need to *register* as an artist. No one registers as an artist, they either are, or are not, artistic."

"Righto. Well then I'll take the model for an arts thingy," said Dan1, perking up.

"Of course, sir. Just let me test to make sure you have the requisite levels of creativity and you can be on your way."

Dan1 sighed and unfolded his arm. The man plugged a bug into his soft flesh and waited. The bug withdrew and sang happily.

"Well done, sir, arty as an old master. Press here for the plans." The man and his mustache gestured at a pad in front of them.

Dan1 was thrilled—both at having been considered an artist and having been given access to the city models. He touched his forefinger to the pad and the model uploaded to his perineurals.

On the way home he spun the model and zoomed to Slit's lab. It was immediately obvious where he and Freyja had appeared from. The lab was pushed against the spinal column of the city, so there was plenty of room to house a secret facility inside. There must be a concealed entrance from Slit's lab and Dan1 guessed that the code Slit had given Freyja would open it for him.

Back at it; a trapezoid forms

Dex threw open the door to Warren's study and placed the pouch of samples on the desk. He happily booted Warren's scanner. He was eager to get back to it. The greenish glow of the scanner swept up his face. This was way better than his old equipment. He thrilled at the responsive touch.

He unrolled the pouch and found the killer's sample stored in a clearly marked vial. Previously Dex had been forced to keep the killer's DNA in a cryopac, but the officers at forensics had somehow managed to stabilize it. He held the vial in the green light, turning it over in his fingers.

He had gone from a decimated shack, broken body and destroyed files to back in the hunt. He was ready to roar into the morning. Having the killer's DNA stabilized meant he could finally mount it on the sample board with the others. He had emerged from Slit's sabotage ahead of the game—he may have lost his official status with the force, but he'd gained better equipment and superior samples.

He knew these killings centred on Slit, he just wasn't exactly sure how. Maybe the great gladiorg designer had bred some transgenic humanoid pet he was using for murderous thrills? Perhaps it was Slit himself, dynamically transforming his DNA through some process Dex had never encountered? Either way, he finally had the equipment to pursue his theories.

He decided to start from the beginning, tracing what he knew from the woodland killing forward. He started by placing Dan1's DNA next to a sample taken from the survivor of the woodland killing, knowing that these two samples would match. After placing the vials a short distance apart on the board, a thin red line extended horizontally from each of them, meeting in the middle.

He took the killer's now stabilized DNA from each of the three crime scenes and pushed them into the board in a neat row. He grinned as the thin red lines extended outwards, connecting the three samples.

Now for the big moment. He took Slit's sample in his hand and held it to the light. Out of the corner of his eye he saw a movement. Lines began extending up from the killer's samples. The lines traced their way up the board, slowly converging. They connected at each of Dan1's samples. Suddenly the neatness of two red lines had given way to a cross-crossed trapezoid that connected Dan1, the boy at the woodland murder scene, and the humanoid killer present at all the crime scenes.

Dex leaned back and sighed, pinching his nose in frustration. He placed Slit's sample back in the pouch.

"How is this possible?" he almost choked on the words. It was suddenly too much and he rocked violently forward on his chair, nearly ramming face first into the board. Suddenly, before he'd even begun, the momentum of the morning came crashing into this red trapezoid.

He checked the samples again, making sure the labels matched. He checked the equipment, plugging in a few more matching samples to make sure there weren't false positives.

That Dan1 was the boy at the woodland murder—well that was no surprise. That it was the same killer at all three scenes—he'd established that. But how could Dan1 have been the killer? He was just a young boy at the time of the woodland murder—his own mother was the victim. It didn't make sense.

He removed all five samples from the board and tested them independently. They all matched.

Normally this would have required a walk to Rhonda's, maybe a drink or two. Instead he wandered along the sloping footpaths of Warren's suburban dream, circling the nubby ends of cul-de-sacs.

The boy was the killer.

He turned this insane idea over in his head, trying to find some other possibility. His pace slowed. The idea had sat long enough now that it lacked its original shock. It was just a fact, something to synthesize into the story.

"Sir! Sir!"

Dex was snapped from his thoughts.

"This is a private lot sir." The pathetic security was a lot more bark than bite. "You'll have to leave."

"I'm a guest of Captain Warren," said Dex.

"There is no resident here by that name."

Dex looked across the suburban expanse and wondered where the hell he was, where the hell he had started, how the hell he had arrived here.

He shrugged. "I'll leave."

He wandered back through the rounded streets, not tracing his exact path, but always heading in the general direction of Warren's house. The security followed him at a cautious distance, dropping off as he crossed into Warren's section of suburb.

He sat down in front of the red trapezoid. The walk had resolved nothing really. Sure, the boy was the killer. He got that now. But the question that had been buzzing into his brain, the thing that really bore into him, was how had he not noticed that the woodland victim and killer shared the same DNA until now?

The semifinals; cracking the code

The man was wearing khaki overalls with the Novagen

213

trademark clearly emblazoned on the back. He looked around, his hollow, panicked eyes watery with fear. The woman next to him grabbed his hand and dragged him across the sandy surface, away from the howling crowd.

Rex pounded up behind them and plucked the man from the sand with his mouth like he was bobbing for apples. He ground the man's body between his teeth, letting the head and feet fall from both sides of his mouth.

Dan1 watched as the rest of the humunculi were cleaned up in the bloody half-time spectacle. He had seen the same thing every year of his life—it was an expected feature of the finals' season—but this time it shocked him, or embarrassed him, like he was seeing it with new eyes—with El9's eyes. The humunculi weren't really human, just auxiliorgs dressed to look that way, but he still found it disturbing. He turned away from the arena and disappeared into the hydra.

Sometime later there was a loud whooshing, whirring sound as a gigantic beetle from Buenos Aires floated a lap around the arena, just above the reach of Rex Australis. It paused for a moment, lightly hanging from the transparent chitin covering the balconies opposite Slit's box.

"She's pretty impressive," said Fuego Wing, who had caught Dan1 deeply lost in the hydra. "Nice speed work, but no strength. Rex will smash her."

Wing was leaning on a chair at the front of the luxury skybox nonchalantly munching on shrimp.

"She's bloody tough." Dan1 pulled some battle stats into his peripheral and read off the beetle's vital signs.

"The flesh is strong but the spirit is weak," said Wing. "She's all amygdala, barely any cortex work."

"No tactics," agreed Dan1.

Wing sniffed loudly and wandered off.

Dan1 flicked the battle stats away with his pupil and pulled El9 back into his peripheral. They hadn't made any progress deciphering Slit's code. He had run it through the proteomics database without any luck; there was no organism in the library with a sequence ending in 34 Ts. A search string through the hydra didn't turn up anything. So he was helping El9 incubate it, instructing her on how to compile the sequence into a comprehensible genome and prepare the cell. Much to their disappointment, what emerged from the incubator was nothing more than inert gray goop. El9 carefully removed a sample and slipped it into a vial.

"You seem distracted tonight, Kallikak. You're not worried about Rex, are you?" Freyja's slinky presence appeared at Dan1's shoulder.

"Course I'm worried." Dan1 quickly pulled himself from the hydra. "It's the semifinals."

"I'll sleep easier after Rex destroys this beetle."

"Me too."

"I'm looking forward to it." Freyja smiled gently and slipped off to the other end of the box.

A short while later the beetle found itself in a difficult position. The large hard wings that covered its back had been forced apart and pinned open by Rex's massive haunches. Rex swiped at the beetle's head, ripping the antennae off, but the beetle snapped its mandible across Rex's right claw. The giant lizard roared in pain, tore the beetle's back open and literally ripped its insides out.

The arena exploded with cheers—their Rex was through to the finals.

Dan1 slipped from the box to avoid the champagne celebration. He wanted to get back to El9's apartment, where the two of them had been planning their mission to find Slit's secret lab.

"This here's all eaten by cancer," said Dan1, pointing to the plans for the Biota building. "We can easy get to the foyer from there, then use me pass to get t'the labs."

"And what about the code?" asked El9.

"Don't reckon we can rely on that, so I got a crack as back up."

"Any good?"

Dan1 nodded knowingly. He had tracked down a 16-year-old biohacker from Shanghai and traded a copy of his genome for a powerful decryption virus. If the virus failed he could always use brute force—they would be packing a laser-edge too.

"We gotta be certain that Slit's outta his office, so I asked Lock to help out, lure Slit away."

"Can we trust Locky?"

"El9, he's me brother. Course we can trust 'im."

"Well, he's not really your brother, not from what you've said."

"He ain't blood but he's brother enough. It ain't physical, not a material thing, it's mind-like."

"Okay," said El9. "Guess you know what you're talking about."

Shifting sands; time to hunt

Handling the killer's DNA had always been a challenge. It was the central challenge of the woodland investigation the first time around. It was chronically unstable. Nothing their scanners or boards could manage at the time. Everything had to be done manually, and even that was tough—it seemed to shift and swirl away whenever they tried to pin it down. Everything it came into contact with caused fundamental mutations.

He'd compared the killer's sequence to dozens of suspects. He'd analyzed it extensively, desperate for anything that might push the case forward. But he'd never compared it with the boy found in the woodland. That had simply never crossed his mind.

It wasn't until forensics had managed to stabilize it and get it into a vial, keeping it biovital but contained, that Dex had an opportunity to manage it on the board.

He felt ashamed. He had missed it all along. A central mystery of the woodland killing—how had the young boy survived?—had been answered by the enigmatic DNA. Dan1 had survived the woodland because he was the killer. He slipped through their fingers and survived for all these years. Who knew how many victims there had been since? And who knew what happened to Peta Singer and his daughter—torn to shreds? Spread about the woodlands? Devoured?

Dan1's DNA was a stable version of the killer's mutant DNA. The boy was some kind of sophisticated gen-mod. Perhaps something could trigger his DNA to become unstable? Dex couldn't be sure. But other aspects of the story were coming into focus.

Dex now understood the significance of Dan1 and Slit being reunited: Slit was planning on using Dex to keep an eye on Dan1, but in the end the boy walked straight into his workplace. Theodor Slit—the master designer—had made himself a humanoid gladiorg and taught it to hunt and kill.

Dex was a licensed bounty hunter. If there was a mutant loose in the city and Dex thought that it could kill again, he had an obligation to take its head. He studied the blood red trapezoid marked across on the sample board. He'd missed it all these years. He could be responsible for god knows how many subsequent deaths. More than just the most recent two, he assumed.

He wasn't going to miss his target now—it was time for the final hunt.

Before the Circle; a firm response
A circle of seven silhouettes emitted a low humming noise,

a sign they were in deep communal meditation. Their heart rates were slowed to effect their hibernation. Their bodies burned no fuel except to sustain their brains in a deep trance. They had been in this state for nearly a week.

The deep resonance of their steady chant flowed into the room, riding on broad soundwaves running at low frequency. Indeed, the frequency of their chant was perfectly matched to the low running delta waves that dominated the rhythms of their combined consciousness. Even the light was dim, permeating evenly throughout the dull chamber.

Professor Wilson felt the tendons in his neck unwind as he stepped silently through the door.

The chant began to modulate, at first imperceptibly, but with increasingly dramatic swings in amplitude. Their brains were slowly shifting from the deep sleep of the delta rhythms to the relaxed wakefulness of alpha waves. Even the light in the room brightened gently as if powered by their conscious energy.

Wilson waited silently on the edge of the circle.

"Are we ready?" asked one of the wakened silhouettes.

There was a low hum of consent.

"I assume you are aware of the developments," began Wilson.

"We are," stated Cadden.

"I was visited by a young member of PETSO recently. She has insinuated herself into the situation."

"We are aware," intoned Brabazon. "The boy is becoming a liability."

Wilson stepped forward. "With respect, I agree that the situation is precarious, but I do not believe it necessitates direct action. Our previous methods have proven effective."

"We are inclined to intervene," said Hiroake. "We cannot afford another Leviathan."

The Circle hummed with consent.

"I appreciate that and assure you there will not be a repeat of the Disaster."

"Your assurances only go so far," said Cadden. "We offer you grace, but expect results."

"Of course, Your Honor."

"Should the situation deteriorate, expect a firm response." Professor Wilson bowed his head and withdrew from the chamber.

Locky's favor

On Friday morning Dan1 went to see his brother. It was almost a week since Dan1 had moved out, long enough for Locky's grudge to be in remission.

Locky had his own office at the head of the open plan area where his team worked. He was sitting in a comfortable chair staring wall-eyed at his monitor.

"Hello my brother," he greeted Dan1 with an extended hand. Dan1 had not seen the office since his brother's big promotion two years previously, when he had been forced to come and observe the evidence of his brother's success.

"So, what can I do ya for?" Locky was being genial—surely some kind of trap.

"I need a favor." Dan1 was already feeling unsure about how this was going to work. "I need you to call in a service 36."

"Whose account has been hacked?"

"No one's. But I need to make it look like that."

Locky rocked forward in his chair. "Why do you want me to do that?"

"I can't say, but I need it tonight."

"What time?"

"Nine-thirty."

"Nine-thirty? PM?" Locky looked at Dan1 like the idea of staying past five on a Friday night was a criminal offence. "No way!"

"You could go out for dinner and then come back," added Dan1 hurriedly.

Locky looked dubious.

"Plus you can claim overtime right up to the end of the service." Dan1 had come with a swag of pre-planned sweeteners. He knew that on the night before the Grand Final, Slit was guaranteed to stay in the office until late. He needed to use his brother's authority in the accounting department as a decoy. If Slit thought his personal account was being hacked he wouldn't ignore it. It was guaranteed to get him out of his laboratory.

"Well," said Locky with a resigned sigh, "I guess I can do with the overtime."

"Thanks bro," Dan1 put in quickly. He didn't want to give Locky a chance to change his mind.

"So, who do you want me to issue it on?"

Dan1 paused for too long; enough time for Locky to know there was something suspicious going on.

"Theodor Slit."

"What? No way!" Locky slammed a fist on the table. "This is for that bloody girl, isn't it? You better not be helping her sabotage the Grand Final."

"I'm not," insisted Dan1, "this has nothing to do with her."

"Then what the hell is this?"

"I can't tell you," admitted Dan1. "But it's important. Real important." Locky contracted the door to his office and jammed an accusing finger at his brother.

"If you're lying to me Dan1, I swear to Alu I'll go bat shit crazy!"

Bat shit crazy was an old Locky threat, his highest level of anger. Dan1 shifted nervously on his feet. He had never asked his brother for a greater favor, nor betrayed his trust so blatantly, but he needed to find out what Slit was up to. Dan1 looked his brother square in the face.

"Trust me Locky," he began unconvincingly, "this ain't nuttin' to do with El9. Just a favor to me. I'm doing research on me dad—me real dad. Ask Mother if ya like."

Locky sagged back into his comfortable chair. He tapped at his monitor distractedly.

"Okay Dan1," he sighed, "I'll do it. I'll notify a service 36 on Theodor Slit. I'll do it at 9.30pm. But if this blows up in my face," he waved a threatening hand at Dan1, "I'll never forgive you."

"Thanks Lock. You've always been a good bro."

"Yeah, whatever." Locky waved him away with a circle of his hand.

Preparing to hunt; the sweet Jaguar

Dex was not preparing for an arrest; he was preparing to kill. Dan1 may have appeared human, but there was an animal under his skin—a savage gen-mod programmed to kill. As far as Dex was concerned, he was caught on the wrong side of a one-way equation: he had displayed the savagery of an animal, so Dex would hunt him as one.

He loaded his rifle, slipping a round of hair-thin ballistics into the chamber and setting the gauge to maximum toxicity. When he hit Dan1 he did not want him to fight back: one shot, one drop.

Dex was in the empty living room at Captain Warren's house working by lamplight. Pulling a vial of Dan1's DNA from the pouch, he took an ovum containing a tiny bug and pressed the two together. A hollow spine instinctively extended from the bug to take a taste of Dan1's DNA, just enough so that when the time came it would recognize his sequence. Dex repeated the process with several other bugs, then stashed the ova safely in his pouch.

He slung the rifle onto his shoulder, walked through the kitchen and opened a door leading to Warren's garage. In the corner the sleek outline of a sports car was covered in a protective membrane. Dex pulled back the cover, revealing the powerful haunches of Warren's Jaguar XV6.

Dex slid into the driver's seat, low in the body of the beast, and called for the garage door to open. As the door retracted, the afternoon light poured onto the car's fine black coat, giving it a reddish tint. She hummed quietly in the cold garage, the warmth of the sun bleeding into her muscles, the beast slowly rising as he wrapped his hands around her motor-cortex. Just as he was slipping his thumbs gently up the cortex Dogbat scampered into the garage and looked imploringly.

"You stay here," he commanded.

The Jaguar padded softly out of the garage and swung into the street.

Dogbat bounded up the street behind.

"Wait for me sir. Sir! Sir! Wait!"

He headed for the city, hoping to catch Dan1 on his way home from work. He wouldn't mind killing him in public, but would rather corner him in a quiet alleyway. He was always patient when stalking prey.

He stroked the motor-cortex and they took off down the street, pouring around a corner, the Jaguar's long tail swishing behind, keeping balance and tethering momentum. He dug his thumbs harder into the motor-cortex and was thrust back into the seat, his neck straining as she pounced up the arterial onramp.

She thrust herself into the traffic. A Golgi prime-mover swerved suddenly to avoid a collision, the heavy vehicle straining and howling as the Jaguar leaped on, sliding between two terrified Beetles scuttling in tandem. She was so much faster than the rest of the traffic that Dex was having a hard time keeping her under control. He rushed past a galloping Mustang, swung around a bend and came up rapidly behind a Ford Taurus clip-clopping in the fast lane. The Jaguar howled and the Taurus moved aside. Dex and the beast sprinted past.

He almost missed the exit ramp and struggled to restrain her as they slipped back into the slow-moving city traffic. A swarm of teenagers on Vespas surrounded him at a red light, nodding at his sleek Jaguar.

"Nice legs!" called a girl at the front of the pack.

Dex ignored her.

The light turned green and the waspish Vespas buzzed off down the street, humming just above the ground. Dex waited a few moments before taking off, wanting to avoid the swarm.

He took the next left and proceeded at an even pace towards the Biota buildings. He was beginning to think he should not have taken Captain Warren's car—not for any moral reason, but simply because she was too conspicuous. He parked a short distance from the main entrance and waited for Dan1.

He didn't have to wait long.

The splitter; and the snakeboard chase

Dan1 met El9 behind the snakeboard shop, as planned. She was wearing slim dark clothes with her hair tied up behind her head and was sitting on the stoop at the dead end of the alley with a duffle bag slumped over her lap. Dan1 snaked towards her, pulling a few subtle tricks off the bank. She smiled as he glided up and kissed her across the lips.

"Heya handsome thief," she teased. "Wanna break into my house?"

"Nah," he replied, "I only do corporate jobs."

He fell next to her onto the stoop and they quietly went over their plan. She showed him the laser-edge and the vial containing the decryption virus, then pulled one of the recording devices from the bag and placed it onto her eye.

"Wow," laughed Dan1, "that be ol' school equipment ya got there."

"Well, we don't have perineural systems," complained El9, "organiks have our own way of doing things."

"I got that," replied Dan1 dryly.

She was calibrating the zoom when a dark shadow hiding behind the half-pipe at the other end of the alleyway came into focus.

"Dan1," she said quietly. "Don't be obvious about it, but I think you should take a look. There's someone over there."

Dan1 turned and focused the eagle-eye of his perineural onto the half-pipe, resting his head in his hands to avoid being conspicuous. He located the silhouette, adjusting for brightness and contrast, and recognized the man immediately.

"Oh shit," he whispered under his breath. "We gotta lose this guy."

"No kidding. Who the hell is he?"

"The splitter punk from the arena."

"When we first met?"

Dan1 nodded.

"Wow. He just won't quit."

"Here," he took her hand.

They climbed onto the platform above the half-pipe at the dead-end of the alley. Dan1 showed El9 how to stand on the snakeboard and then stepped onto it himself, wrapping his arms securely around her stomach.

"Okay," he said, edging the board towards the ramp, "ya ready for this?"

El9 bit her lip and shook her head. "No," she whimpered.

Dan1 glanced towards the shadowy figure at the end of the alley. The silhouetted point of a barrel peered back. He took a sharp breath and leaned forward on the snakeboard. They raced down the curve of the half-pipe.

Before El9 could scream they were launching through the air on the other side. Dan1 twisted his hips, desperately trying to push El9's frozen body around. They managed to spin just in time to catch the lip of the ramp and go speeding up the other side. Dan1 was ploughing all his weight into the curve of the ramp, urging the board higher, trying to gain more speed. They took off from the edge at an angle, flying up the wall and riding along it, heading towards the open end of the alley.

They landed with a crash on the platform at the other end and with newly acquired momentum slipped down the face of the ramp and onto the street. Dan1 looked behind and saw the splitter emerge from the shadows with a rifle slung over his shoulder, running towards a car parked on the opposite side of the street.

They swerved across the hectic flow of traffic. The splitter had jumped into a Jaguar—an unlikely car for a punk—and was pursuing them down the busy street. Dan1 dodged skillfully between cars with the Jaguar wildly pulling between lanes to keep up.

As they approached an intersection the light turned red. Dan1 and El9 slipped between the lines of cars slowing for the light and flew into the intersection moments before the opposing flow of traffic had begun. Behind them the intersection flooded with vehicles.

Dan1 was elated. They had escaped.

Suddenly they heard a cacophony of howls as the intersection erupted into dispute. From above the howling came a roar. Dan1 looked back and saw the elongated body of the Jaguar leaping across the flow of the intersection.

He quickly swung into an alley, heading for a shortcut to the

Biota buildings, a long pedestrian walkway snaking from the end of the shopping precinct. The Jaguar roared up behind them.

They slipped across the road and hopped a low barrier, crashing onto a pedestrian walkway. The Jaguar exploded onto the street behind them.

They quickly weaved through the pedestrians, bumping into arms and elbows, apologizing as they went. El9 looked over at an arterial curving in parallel with the walkway. There was a sleek black form bounding alongside them, traveling much faster than they were. It would have enough time to cut them off.

The Jaguar stopped near the bottom of the walkway and the splitter emerged, swinging the rifle from his back and lowering onto one knee. Dan1 and El9 were traveling too fast to stop, flying towards the open road. Dan1 pointed the board towards the entrance of Biota and leaned into the incline, trying to build as much speed as possible.

He closed his eyes and prayed as El9 screamed at the top of her lungs. Moments before they hit the bottom of the ramp a bulky shadow loomed from behind the Jaguar, raised an enormous hand, and rammed it hard into the shooter's back. The splitter dropped the rifle and fell heavily onto the pavement. Dan1 and El9 raced across the road, narrowly missing a speeding Stingray, slipping into the embrace of the Biota courtyard.

Keeping his promise
"What is it?" snapped Slit as Locky insinuated into his perineural. "I thought I told you never to contact me."

Sir, you said I should keep an eye on Dan1.

"Yes," hissed Slit, still sounding venomous.

You wanted me to report any aberrant behavior.

"Yes Kallikak! I remember the conversation. What is it?"

I need to tell you something. In fact, it would be better if you came over and saw this for yourself.

"Very well. I will be there shortly."

Locky withdrew.

Cancerous columns; The Ride of the Valkyrie

It was nine-thirty and the courtyard was almost deserted. Dan1 and El9 snaked through the grounds towards the gladiorg labs. Neither of them understood what had happened to the splitter, nor why he had suddenly pursued them, but it was clear he was no longer a danger.

They could feel the security eyes following them and when they reached the western side of the complex they gladly slipped into a little used thoroughfare running alongside the cancerous wing of the building. The cancer was well developed and had killed off a large part of the outer wall; necrotic chunks of the building's fascia had peeled off, smashing into the ground around the site. Dan1 brought the snakeboard to a stop at a gap in the fence.

He checked his watch. His brother's diversion should have worked by now. Slit would be panicking about his hacked account—hurrying to meet with Locky.

El9 and Dan1 squeezed through the loose gap in the fence and began working on a column supporting the eastern edge of the main foyer. The column was a mixture of cartilage and bone, but its base was a tumescent bulge, largely eaten away by malignancy. As they worked at the cancerous flesh with a laser-edge a pungent smell wafted over them, the tumor slowly opening like a spring bud, the flesh inside wet and liverish. It cauterized as Dan1 continued to open the wound.

Eventually he had cut through to the other side. The column shifted unsteadily, supported by only two spindly sections of cartilage. The slimy surface of the tumor brushed his shoulders as Dan1 stepped out into the foyer. El9 followed, stepping into the tiny gap, pushing her hands against the walls for support. Midway through, the column groaned and slumped. She leaped forward as the tumor closed around her. Dan1 yanked at her arms, but her legs had been clamped as the two walls of the tumor sealed closed like giant lips.

Dan1 struggled to pull her free. She squirmed and writhed as the walls pushed tighter around her hips. Dan1 pushed his feet against the base and with a heave El9 slipped out onto the floor of the foyer. The massive support collapsed closed behind her.

"We gotta get outta here," whispered Dan1. They fled through the foyer towards the entrance to the gladiorg laboratories. "At least the collapsed column hid our way in," he said, still panting from the run.

"It also just cut off my exit," countered El9. Inside the building she could move with impunity, as long as she stayed under Dan1's biometrix, but getting into or out of the building required clearance from main security. "We'll worry about it later."

They hurried along the darkened corridors, passing the gladiorg laboratories, empty the night before the Grand Final. They rounded the corner and headed for Slit's personal laboratory. Inside the light was on but Slit was not there. Locky's diversion had worked.

Dan1 felt along the wall until his hands pressed a subtle indentation. He pushed gently and a strange keypad unfolded. He grinned at El9, who passed him the vial containing the decryption virus. Hunching over the panel, he carefully injected the vial. They waited for a few moments.

Nothing happened.

"Damn," said Dan1 under his breath. "It shoulda worked by now."

"Maybe you need more," suggested El9.

"It's a virus, if it's gonna work it'll spread itself. One cell shoulda done it." He slapped the keypad in frustration. El9 looked over Dan1's shoulder at the black and white keys on the pad. They were arranged in a curious pattern, with long white keys interspersed by shorter black keys, but nothing printed on them—no symbols or alphanumeric annotations at all.

"That's a piano," said El9 in surprise.

"Wadda ya mean?"

El9 leaned down on one knee, placed her hands along the keys, and pressed them delicately.

"It should make a sound—maybe it's broken."

"Ya seen somethin like this before?" asked Dan1.

"It's a piano; an old analog musical instrument. We have one at the compound. Dad taught me how to play."

"If I hummed somethin, could ya play it?"

"Sure," said El9.

Dan1 hummed Slit's favorite tune, the one he had heard Slit humming a thousand times in the hallways: Richard Wagner's *Ride of the Valkyries* from *The Ring Cycle*. El9 took a while to get the chords, stumbling over parts, sounding out the notes in her head. Dan1's re-creation of the tune was not perfect, but eventually El9's fingers made out the familiar Wagnerian refrain.

A small section of wall retracted revealing a mottled bone platform. Dan1 took El9's hand and they walked across the uneven surface to the edge. Just behind them the wall contracted, sealing off the light and leaving them in gloomy darkness. As their eyes adjusted they realized they were standing on a vast vertebrae. Above them in the darkness they could just make out the collocation of bones stretching to the top of the city. They were standing in the city's spinal canal. El9 squeezed Dan1's hand tighter.

Facing the music, again

Dex was stunned by the blow. Looming over him was a giant man with a club-like arm, face contorted, a blood-red nose twisted and gnarled and eyes full of emotion.

"Yu hert Reggin," the giant said—the shadow came crashing down.

When Dex woke he was being pulled along the roadway. The giant was dragging him along on his back. His nose was bloodied and mashed; his vision blurred. He reached down and felt at his side; he still had his pouch but his rifle was missing.

The giant stopped and twisted Dex's ankle, a sharp pain shot up his leg. Dex groaned. The behemoth twisted again. Dex's body spasmed and he kicked uselessly with his free leg.

"Yu awayke, punck? Can yu here mee, punck?" He twisted Dex's leg still further out of position.

"Yes," howled Dex, nodding his head furiously. "I can hear you." His body relaxed as the vise-like grip loosened.

"Yu nerely kiled Reggin." The giant shook his head. Dex finally recognized him from the cycle chase after his shack was destroyed.

"Why did Slit send you?" growled Dex, preparing to flick a venomous barb into the giant's chest.

"Nobotty send us." He lifted Dex by the ankle and held him over the edge of the roadway. Dex tucked the barb back into his sleeve. He couldn't poison the giant now that he was the only thing stopping him from plummeting two stories. He swung sickeningly above the drop.

"You can't kill me." Dex could feel the giant's grip loosening. "I've come here with a message for Slit."

"Slitt has nuttin to do wid dis."

"It's about the boy."

The giant waited, his grip tightening again. After a considered pause he asked, "Wot do yu knoe?"

"I was hired by Wilson, but the bastard won't pay me. I'll tell you guys whatever you need to know. I don't care. I don't have allegiances. I just want to teach Wilson a lesson for trying to rip me off."

Dex was hauled back over the railing and thrown onto the roadway. He pushed himself away from the giant, squirming along the ground, then lifted himself up against the embankment.

The giant snatched his wrist. "Don't tri anyting." He clasped the venomous barb to Dex's wrist so it was almost piercing his skin. Dex was trapped, threatened by his own weapon. The thick hand tightened.

Dex heard the frantic scurry of feet coming up the road. Dogbat leaped, landing with a solid *thwump* on the giant's chest, before rebounding over the edge and down onto the roadway below. The colossal man stumbled back in surprise and released his grip. Dex quickly flicked a barb into the giant's neck. The man collapsed, unconscious.

Dex stepped over the body and looked down at the vivid red splat on the pavement, marked with tufts of brown hair. He paid his respects to Dogbat—loyal and stupid to the end—then limped back to the Jaguar.

He removed a small ovum from his pouch and loaded the bloodhound tracker. He knew his prey would still be nearby. The tiny bug zipped off, instantly lost in the cool evening air. The medikit in the back of Warren's car made a temporary fix for his nose; anesthetic flooded his face, icy and relieving. He lay back to rest while his nose healed.

It was not long before Dex was woken by his perineural system; the tracker had found a match. His sat-map told him the tracker was still close by, just inside the Biota building.

Dex leaned forward and searched under his seat for the

stout pistol strapped beneath. He would get a shot at his target tonight after all.

Spine of the city; the essence of a Scottish waltz

Dan1 and El9 were standing in the spinal canal, a cavernous hollow running down through the city's spine, the heavy bones shifting and grinding around them, filling the well with an eerie resonance, like wind over wire. A soft glow from the spinal cord threw long shadows across the bone walls, into which was carved a long spiraling staircase, falling beneath them like a ribbon to the floor.

"Let's go," said El9, taking the first cautious step.

There was just enough light for the two of them to follow the shifting stairs. They walked in silence, their footfalls barely audible over the creaking of the spine.

It was a long trek down. Slowly the steps lost definition, becoming smoother, rounder and harder to grip. As the light faded the stairs turned into a rough, uneven ramp. Dan1 adjusted his perineurals to the dark, but El9 was having trouble. She stumbled and lurched towards the black drop in the center. Dan1 only just managing to grab at her shoulder to steady her. They stayed crouching for a few moments in the darkness.

"I reckon I should go first," said Dan1, heart thumping.

El9 agreed and the two of them continued into the darkness. After some time they could see a dusty gray light coming from below. They had reached a point where the spine fused with the solid bone plates of the foundation, but the light was coming from a large well bored into the bone. As they sank deeper into the foundations they passed buildings from the old city, yawning through the bone, their doors and windows choked by the organic mass as it had grown around them. Finally they reached the bottom of the well.

"End of the line," murmured El9.

The circular room was filled with more than fifty steel containers, some pushed up against the wall, others scattered around the spine. The containers were overflowing with various animal parts; a lion's hindquarters placed clumsily next to a rhinoceros head; piles of limbs stacked next to a box of wings. The air was dry and dusty.

"What's that smell?" asked El9.

"It's argon. Keeps the flesh from rotting."

"What is this place?" El9 began to record footage of the butchered menagerie. "Why would anyone do this?"

"Guess they're 'speriments," replied Dan1. "Ya can't build the greatest gladiorgs on the battlefield without experimentin' a bit."

El9 steadily documented the sickening details.

Meanwhile, Dan1 approached a large concrete structure that loomed from the bone foundation. No wonder Slit had gone undetected: there was no DNA trace, the stairs were carved into bone and the concrete structure was hermetically sealed—no DNA could get in or out. There was a door at the far end and he pushed his hand into the cold wall, feeling around until a panel popped open.

"El9," he called, "get over 'ere—there's another piana."

El9 knelt down in front of the piano-style keyboard and played the same chords as before, but there was no response.

"What now?"

"Try this." Dan1 hummed another tune from Wagner's *Ring Cycle* and El9 played it—again no effect. "Hm. What else can ya play?"

El9 shrugged.

"Dammit!"

"I know a nice sonata," she suggested.

Suddenly it hit him and he threw the code across his palm.

"Can you play this?"

"No, that's a DNA sequence."

"What if it isn't? What if it's music? Ya know, A—G—C."

"Chords."

"Exactly."

"I guess it could be annotation from the pentatonic scale, but there's no T chord. Unless…."

"Unless what?"

"Well, if the letters are an arrangement of chords A, G and C, then the 34 Ts might represent the timing that the other chords are meant to be played in. You know, as in ¾ time."

She picked up the code from the ground and carefully played the notes, sounding a familiar Scottish waltz.

"This is pretty clever," said El9. "Music is a simple way to remember long and complex codes, without actually needing to store anything permanently." She kissed him gently on the cheek. "Lucky you caught them in the act."

"Lucky that my girlfriend knows all this ol' instrument stuff, I reckon." He grinned as the door slowly retracted. They were engulfed in blinding light.

Bottom of the city; the number of the beast
As they stepped through the doorway the air was torn with screams. A long white room stretched for nearly a hundred meters. On both sides solidly built cages were stacked to the ceiling with howling animals rattling at the bars. Dan1 and El9 walked slowly into the room, thousands of eyes focusing on them as they crossed the threshold. The further they walked into the room the louder the screams became. El9 carefully documented it all with her cam.

She approached a cage containing a strange looking primate covered in fine red hair. She moved toward it warily, preoccupied by its humanness. Peering down the line of cages she realized they all contained animals with humanoid features. Whether grafted onto horse-like heads, or reptilian bodies, or even birds, there was a distinctly human aspect to every living beast in the laboratory. She stepped back from the cage and panned the cam up and down the room.

Dan1 made his way toward a small recess in the far wall. Inside was a large bench scattered with various surgical tools. A cube covered in cloth sat in the middle of the table. He pinched the cloth, slowly removing it from the cube. Immersed in greenish cerebrospinal fluid was a human brain.

On the other side of the room El9 examined the small keypads mounted on the cages, each keypad marked with a series of numbers from 0—9. She dialed in 009 and pressed the hash key. The cage sprang open and the small primate with fine red hair climbed down the bars onto the floor. With a grateful look, he scampered off towards the door. El9 dialed in another number.

Soon the room was swarming with humanoid creatures. Some were able to read the numbers on the cages and help their friends escape, embracing with cries and howls of freedom, running chaotically about the laboratory, dancing and hooting. The room was suddenly like singles night on Noah's ark.

Dan1 called to El9 as he struggled across a current of freed creatures. He dragged her back to the small recess where a number of humanoids had gathered around the table. While he was away they had hungrily helped themselves to the grayish flesh. Cerebrospinal fluid covered the table and there was nothing left but a few chunks of the human brain. Dan1 stepped back in shock. One of the tiny humanoids reached out to take another bite.

"Hey!" shouted Dan1. "Get outta that!"

"Come on." El9 tugged his jacket. "Forget about this. Help

me open the rest of the cages."

Dan1 paused, looking back at the scattered remains of the brain, then joined El9 on the other side of the room.

They released the rest of the humanoids and herded them towards the door, where a long procession of beasts climbed, flew and stomped their way up the city's spinal column.

One cage was left unopened at the end of the room, a large transparent door, four meters wide and over five meters tall. It had a number—like the cages on the wall—and a keypad, but the interior was arranged like a comfortable hotel room—albeit for an oversized guest. Inside, a large animal covered in coarse brown hair groaned, as if in distress.

"I don't know if it's safe to release that one," cautioned El9.

It looked like a grotesquely swollen human, the architecture of its body transformed and disfigured. Its calves and thighs were taut with powerful muscles that had contracted, crooking its legs. Its back was hunched, its shoulders burdened with a hulking musculature, pushing the head and neck forward, resulting in an upper body posture reminiscent of a bison. It stared out at them with a distinctly human expression.

"We gotta let it go." As Dan1 reached for the keypad, the beast heaved forward in the cage and examined him closely.

"I'm really not sure about this," said El9 nervously.

Dan1 dialed in 9—9—9 and then #. The door slid open. El9 and Dan1 both stood back.

The enormous beast lumbered out, sat on its powerful rear haunches and stretched its back. With two arms it reached outwards, the massive chest heaved, releasing a terrifying roar. It turned to face El9.

In a quick movement it tore the cam from her face and smashed it against the wall. El9 and Dan1 both turned and ran. El9 barely made it four steps before the beast grabbed her around the throat, dragged her towards the line of cages against the wall and threw her in, locking the door.

Dan1 was halfway down the room before it caught up with him. The beast seized him around the neck and threw him into a cage. It snarled viciously through the bars then heaved away down the laboratory. For a few moments the long white room was silent.

"Dan1." El9's voice echoed off the blank walls.

"Yes," he replied.

"Are you in a cage too?"

"Yes."

"Shit." She stamped her foot in frustration.

"What are we going to do?"

"Dunno," he called back.

"Can you read the number on your cage?"

"Nup."

"Shit."

They heard someone walking towards them and both fell silent. They were finished now, trapped in cages at the very heart of Slit's secret sanctuary.

The shot; big jump

The bug was buzzing uselessly around the front entrance of Biota looking for a way in when suddenly it darted into a maintenance duct beneath the building, heading determinedly towards a point near the city's spine.

Dex checked his sat-map and moved closer to the exit point of the duct. He slipped out of the Jaguar, crouched behind the car, and checked the ammo in his pistol, setting the gun at maximum toxicity.

The bloodhound tracker was within fifteen meters. He could hear footsteps echoing in the duct. He nestled in closer to the

Jaguar and took aim. The enormous cover of the duct groaned as it was forced open.

Dex could see light reflecting from a single eye and heard the steady breathing of a giant set of lungs. He stepped back from the Jaguar, his gun still pointing into the duct. An enormous beast covered in a thick mat of coarse brown hair emerged into the streetlight.

Dex's tongue suddenly tried to hide down his throat. "Holy Alu father of chaos," he whispered.

The animal snarled and crouched as if ready to pounce.

Dex squeezed off the rounds, emptying the pistol into its head. The hairline ballistics pierced straight through the skull, leaving thirty highly toxic darts wedged in its brain, but they had no effect.

"Ah, shit."

The beast stalked forward, a line of spittle running from its salivating jaws, razor sharp claws extending and retracting as it approached, one eye trained on Dex, still crouching in the shadows behind the Jaguar.

He rolled twice, leaped in through the passenger door and jammed his hands on the motor-cortex—she roared to life. He heard the heavy thump of the brown beast landing on the roof of the car. From the passenger side he dug his thumbs into the Jaguar's cortex and she surged forward.

A single talon sliced through the roof, the car instantly a convertible. Dex slid onto the driver's side and headed for the pedestrian walkway. Looking up, he saw the enormous brown beast towering above him, about to swipe. He turned the Jaguar sharply. The car lost its footing. Its tail swung desperately to maintain balance, but Dex had pushed it too far. The body of the vehicle twisted as its powerful limbs collapsed hopelessly underneath. The extra weight of the beast on the roof flipped the car with enough momentum to spin through several rotations.

The tangled mess of man, beast and car finally came to a stop. The beast was dazed. It rolled away from the wreckage. Dex hauled himself through the bloodied doorframe and staggered towards the edge of the walkway. The beast looked up at him and seethed. It pushed from the ground and glared through its one savage eye. Dex hopped onto the railing.

Standing at the edge, he looked down at the precipitous drop below. He would surely die in the fall. He looked behind him. The beast was poised to pounce. Dex turned back to the edge, sucked in a deep breath, and jumped.

Ranga Rescue

There was a quick scampering of claws on the hard floor. The small primate with fine red hair hurried past Dan1's cage and headed straight for E19, stopping in front of her cage.

"Can you read the numbers?" she asked in a high clear voice, as if talking to a child. The primate smiled back at her. It hopped over to the keypad and punched in a code. The cage door swung open.

"Oh thank you so much!" cried E19, hugging the little monkey. She ran down to Dan1's cage and punched in the number.

"Now we have to get out of here," she said.

"Quickly."

E19 took the little red-haired monkey in her arms and they ran towards the spinal column. As she started up the staircase Dan1 grabbed her wrist, putting a finger to his lips. There was a distant pounding, getting closer. Someone—or something—was coming down.

They had to hide. Surveying their options, Dan1 headed for

a container of severed wings; their broad expanse would easily cover them. He lifted the top layer and gestured for El9 and the primate to clamber in. He followed after them, crouching down in the morbid darkness.

The huge beast they had released from cage 999 paused and shook its shaggy brown coat. From deep in its throat came a low growl. El9 and Dan1 could hear it sniffing at the air, searching them out. They both froze. It would not take long for the beast to discover them. The huge creature was moving about the room with its nose stuck out, inhaling deep breaths of air.

Dan1 was seized by panic. He could feel his heart pounding in his chest. His throat was tight and his breath shallow. He tensed tighter into a ball and felt the muscles straining on his back. Then suddenly, hiding in the darkness with the smell of flesh and panic about him, he felt something squirm on his back.

He relaxed his muscles and bristled uncomfortably. Reaching out for El9, he tightly wrapped his arms around her waist. Heaving her up, he boldly brushed away their cover. He was clutching her to his stomach; she in turn was holding the red-haired primate.

The huge beast turned towards them, cocking its head and examining them with interest. With a series of broad lumbering strides it rapidly approached, extending one arm and flashing its savage claws. Moments before it was within reach Dan1 unfurled an enormous set of wings and launched powerfully into the air. The beast leaped and swiped at them.

They watched as the beast disappeared into indistinct darkness, Dan1's arms wrapped tightly around El9's waist while wings flapped powerfully from his shoulder blades. She struggled against him, trying to find a more comfortable position, then turned her head to look at him. His face was set. He was staring straight ahead, seemingly in deep concentration.

The three of them continued their precipitous climb all the way up the spinal canal, weaving their way around the opalescent cord between the dark bones moaning in the hollow tunnel. They flew upwards towards a small cleft opening into the moonlit night.

They were suspended above the city, all the Boons, all the lights, stretched out below them. The little primate chirped cheerfully and kicked his feet into the air. El9 laughed. Dan1 laughed too, and for a brief moment, faltered on his newly acquired wings.

Musica delenit bestiam feram
"What the hell happened?" snapped Slit.

The beast was sitting in the middle of Slit's laboratory, coarse brown hair covered in blood, chewing at a ragged chunk of meat caught in his claws. He looked up at Slit and grunted, returning to his meal.

"Who let you out of your cage, Tom?" Slit walked over and placed a bloodied parcel wrapped in cloth onto the bench. The beast ignored Slit's question.

"I scared away your private detective," he growled.

Slit seemed placated. "Did you kill him?"

"I don't know. It's not my business. You can clean up your own mess, Theodor."

Thomas Wotan heaved himself from the table and walked towards the curve in the wall. He pointed at the panel hiding the black and white keyboard.

"You'll have to let me back in," he snorted. "I can't play that bloody thing."

"That's the whole point," Slit retorted. "Who let you out, Tom?"

"I think you better come down and see the lower lab."

241

"I've already seen it," said Slit, "over my perineurals."

The brown-haired beast flashed his long claws and winced, as if every movement was painful. Slit picked up the bloodied parcel from the bench and walked over towards the keyboard. He played a short tune with one hand and the wall retracted. The tiny man and the disfigured beast began their trek down the stairwell.

"Where were you while all this was going on?" Tom's voice was deep and gruff, gurgling from his throat and echoing around the hollow chamber.

"I got a call from our young accountant friend." Slit's voice was sharp with indignation. "I don't know what his game was, but I dealt with it."

"Dealt with it?" growled Tom.

Slit raised the bloodied parcel wrapped in cloth and opened it just enough to reveal Locky's vacant eyes staring from his severed head.

Tom grunted his approval. "Good work. We'll need that now."

Destroy this abomination

"We have reports the boy found Thomas Wotan alive," intoned one of the silhouettes.

"Yes." Wilson hung his head and looked uncomfortably at his shoes.

"Does he know what he is doing?"

"It was inevitable."

"We must intervene. It is time to take these matters in hand."

"He has made more progress on his own than we have as a group. He has earned the right to proceed unimpeded," interrupted Wilson. The professor had prepared the argument in advance, anticipating this line of thought, having learned long before to be prepared when appearing before the Circle.

"Your insistence on this point concerns us," said Cadden. "We understand that you want the boy to control his own destiny. We have already given you significant leeway because you found the boy and have offered a guiding hand throughout his development. In this you have helped us, but there is now too much at stake to be taking these risks."

"It is true that when he found the beast, he freed it. But only because he felt sorry for it." Wilson spoke in an even voice, but his words were forceful. "He did not know who or what it was. He is young and proud, but compassionate. He will choose his own allegiances. Any attempt to force his hand is a mistake."

There was a murmur of disapproval among the Seven.

"Remember Professor, you too are young and proud in our eyes. Between us we have seen many centuries. Do not underestimate our collective wisdom."

"That was not my intention, Cadden." Wilson addressed the most senior member of the counsel with his head inclined as a mark of respect.

Cadden harrumphed from his shadowy chair. "Do not attempt to persuade us with your rhetoric," he continued. "We will make the ultimate decision on the boy's well-being."

"Of course," acceded the professor. "I merely place my opinion before the Circle. In this particular circumstance there is much to be gained from an alliance with the boy. He will be a very powerful ally, something the Circle needs in these challenging times."

"The whole reason we agreed to risk involving ourselves with Leviathan was to kill the likes of this boy," noted Hiroake. "That course of action was approved by you at the time, Professor Wilson."

"And by the time Leviathan turned on us it was too late," growled Brabazon. "We let it become too strong."

"We hesitated when we should have ruthlessly terminated," agreed Li.

"The boy is an abomination and must be destroyed," said Cadden in a powerful baritone. "Terminate the project."

Flight to the compound; looking peaked
"What the hell just happened?" Dan1 had the terrified and exhilarated look typical of earthbound mammals that have very recently discovered they can fly.

"I have no idea," shouted El9 over the wind, trying to collect herself. "I lost the cam, so we won't have any footage of the lab. But we've got something better." She passed the small primate onto his back. It wrapped its arms around his neck and nestled into his hair. "We got living proof!"

She kissed him, running her hands over the unusual protuberances that had miraculously grown from his shoulder blades. The monkey chirped and kicked its legs into the air. El9 laughed and turned back to face the city.

"I've never been up in the clouds!" shouted El9.

"Neither have I," replied Dan1. "Let's go check 'em out!"

He turned and soared upwards. He didn't even think about how he was doing it, as if he had flown his whole life. He headed up into the clouds with El9 clamped to his stomach and the monkey clinging onto his back. As they pushed through the wet fog she turned to face him again, shivering as they increased altitude.

They burst through the wispy top of cloud cover and into a nightscape painted in tones and shadow; white tufts of cumulus stretched like a blanket for miles to the horizon, the moon was a polished stone set amongst the diamond stars. This world was perfectly monochrome, aglow with soft light reflected from the heavens.

In that moment, in the thin crisp air above the clouds, shivering, she kissed him deeply—their icy lips shrouded with condensed breath glimmering silver off the full moon.

"It's beautiful up here," she shouted, withdrawing from his lips, her teeth chattering and her voice unsteady from the cold. "But we need to find a place to hide. We should go to the PETSO compound."

Dan1 nodded and descended rapidly through the crystalline clouds. El9 directed him northwards towards the compound. She twisted around to face the ground, looping her legs over the back of his and cuddling her head into his neck.

Dan1 had no idea where his newfound abilities had come from, but he held El9 to his chest with ease. He arched his wings and glided effortlessly towards the farm.

It was well past midnight when they arrived at the edge of the sawgrass forest. The long blades swayed in the gentle evening breeze.

"Don't go near them," warned El9, pointing at the razor-sharp points. "They're deadly."

"That's pretty impressive home security," said Dan1 into her ear.

"There's no way in except through an underground passageway," she called back as they soared over the forest. "Unless you've got a flying boyfriend." He pulled her tighter to his chest—she had never admitted that, never named their relationship. She pointed excitedly at a group of dark shadows far beneath them. "They protect us too. We think they're part kangaroo and part Saurolophus."

"That's a curious mix," replied Dan1 into her ear.

"We found them here when we bought the place. We call them Kangasaurs," she laughed.

The huge creatures bounded through the giant sawgrass, their strange bodies wrapped in coarse reptilian skin, their huge hindquarters pushing them high into the air.

"Set down over there." El9 pointed towards the center of a large clearing where a dozen or so buildings were gathered. Flying in low over the orchard Dan1 circled once and gently landed outside. A man hurried to greet them.

"Get inside," he ordered.

"Dad, what's the matter?" asked El9.

"Please El9, just get inside."

Dan1 was last through the door and turned from closing it to find El9 with a frozen expression.

"It just appeared as breaking news," said El9's father while he fixed drinks for the three of them.

A monitor displayed pics of El9, Dan1 and Locky, the headline read:

Brother Murders For Lover.

"Locky is dead," said El9.

If there is a certain amount of shock doled out by the universe then Dan1 was receiving his in a lump sum. El9's father handed Dan1 a drink. The drink passed straight through Dan1's hand and fell to the floor. Before him stood the clandestine leader of PETSO. Dan1 instantly recognized the man from the pictures in the old news article Mother Umami had shown him. It was only his hair that had changed—no longer a neat cut—it was coarse, shaggy and brown, blown about like tumbleweed.

Dan1 stared stone-faced in utter disbelief. He was standing in front of Peta Singer—the man last seen with his mother before she had been savagely killed in the woodlands.

"You look a little peaked," said Singer. "I'll fix you another drink."

PART THREE

THE GRAND FINAL

Hath not the potter power over the clay, to make one vessel unto honor, and another unto dishonor?
—*The Holy Bible, Romans 9:21*

A brand new day, a brand new car
The paramedics were scraping Dex from the pavement. As he jumped from the pedestrian walkway his perineurals had sent Captain Warren an emergency signal. He had fallen fifteen meters and landed on the roof of an Uyghur day surgery, rolled from the roof and fell another two stories to the pavement below. The paramedics had arrived soon after.

"Dex!" barked Captain Warren, crouched next to him in the rear of the ambulance. "Dex, can you hear me?"

He had fallen in such a way as to protect his brain, but the rest of his body was badly broken. Warren slapped what was left of Dex's cheek. The paramedic rebuked him for being too rough, but he persisted, determined to bring Dex back to consciousness.

Slowly, Dex opened his eyes and blearily focused on Warren's face. Warren grabbed him by his crumpled shoulders.

"Dex you bastard!" Warren shook him violently. "That was a brand new Jaguar!" The paramedic pushed Warren away, struggling with him to the back of the ambulance. "A brand new Jaguuuuaaaaaaaarrrrr…"

A poisoned mind
"How dare you bring a god damned gen-mod to the compound? What were you thinking?"

"That gen-mod just saved my life and got us hard evidence that Slit is splicing humans in his lab—don't you think we can trust him?"

"Never."

"Then just try trusting my judgment, Dad." El9 was standing in the back room of her father's cabin, arms tightly crossed under her breasts.

Singer's countenance quickly shifted from anger to a

condescending pity. "It's no choice between what you believe, what you were raised to do, and your false affection for this gen-mod."

"This isn't about that."

"It clearly is about that, otherwise your judgment would not be clouded. I just hope that his, his *talents* don't extend to his liver."

"What does that mean?" asked El9 urgently.

"I have dealt with the situation. That's what it means."

A brand new body

It was the early hours of Saturday morning when he woke in a brand new body. Warren was sitting by the bed reading a fashion magazine from the late 20th Century.

"They had to use your spare," he said casually.

Dex groaned and sat up further on the pillows.

"I'd forgotten I even had a spare." His voice was tight and a little irregular.

He stretched his jaw around and peered down at his new body.

"Every ex-cop has a spare, Dex. It's part of the health plan. What do you think?"

"What's still mine?"

"It's all yours Dex—new and improved."

"So only my brain survived?"

"Everything was destroyed, right up to the brain stem. You really did a number on yourself."

For the first time Warren looked up from the magazine. His eyes narrowed, pushing them further into his chubby face. He folded the magazine and rested it on his gut.

"So what happened Dex? I'm imagining that you were so overcome with guilt for wrecking my brand new Jaguar that you decided to throw yourself from the walkway and end it all.

That what happened?"

"Something like it."

"Of course," sighed Warren, folding his arms and crossing his legs, "that doesn't explain why the roof of my brand new Jaguar was completely removed. Nor does it explain why you were driving my brand new Jaguar up a pedestrian walkway. And according to Biota all their surveillance equipment was temporarily shut down by the genius who broke in, killed one of their accountants, and stole the designs for a new neural unit. So we have no footage of whatever the hell happened there."

Warren leaned in close and flared his nostrils like a wild hog. "Perhaps you can shed some light on all this?"

Dex slowly shook his head, his gaze fixed on the dull beige wall. He suddenly leaped from the bed and ran for the door. Two guards stationed on the other side quickly brought him down. They had him pinned to the floor with his bare arse sticking up through the gap in the back of his hospital gown.

Warren walked around him. "You're not going anywhere until I get some answers. That was a *brand new Jaguar*, you know."

Dex tried to nod but a guard's elbow was driving his neck into the ground, smooshing his lips against the smooth green hospital floor. He made a slight gurgling sound.

"Are you trying to say something?" Warren waved at the guard to loosen his grip.

"I found the killer," he gasped.

On the way back to the house Dex told Warren about Dan1's DNA being a match for the killer's and expanded on his theory about Theodor Slit being an accomplice. Warren sat in silence, treating Dex with the detached incredulousness he had developed over years of listening to liars and criminals.

When they reached the house Dex headed straight for Warren's office. The first thing he saw was the sample board crisscrossed by a tight web of red lines. The neat trapezoid was gone. The strange mutating DNA found at the murder scenes had matched itself with every piece of DNA on the board. Dex stared at the complex pattern of blood red lines tracing across the board.

"I noticed it before I came to the hospital," said Warren from the doorway. "I've never seen anything like it. Somehow the killer's cells reorganize themselves to mirror the cells around them."

"So Dan1 wasn't the killer," sighed Dex. "The killer's DNA mutated to match Dan1's DNA on the sample board."

Warren stood with his arms crossed, his head jutting forward as if his deep concern was pooling in his generous chin.

"Lucky I didn't…" Dex trailed off.

Warren allowed the silence to linger before interrupting Dex's thoughts. "Is that the only connection you'd made between Dan1 and the killer?"

Dex nodded slowly. "I don't get it," he snapped suddenly. "If Dan1 isn't the killer, what the hell was that thing outside Biota?"

Warren shrugged.

"You know, I've spent a lot of time working out *who* the killer is, when I should have been focused on *what* the killer is. I need access to a police lab," he said abruptly.

"Not tonight, Dex. You need some rest."

"Are you kidding me? This is a brand new body. I've never felt so rested." Dex placed his hands on Warren's shoulders and looked into the captain's piggy little eyes. "I'm sorry about the car, but I nearly had this bastard. Just give me some time with his DNA and I'll bring him in. I promise."

Warren looked at his watch: 1am. "You can have a lab until eight, but after that full shifts clock on."

Dex grinned. "That's enough time to make a start."

The morning after; she speaks

Dan1 knew there was something wrong with the drink Peta Singer had prepared for him—he could smell the poison. But what had disturbed him more was the angry conversation he heard coming from the back room. He took off, fleeing like a wounded animal across the PETSO compound and through the orchard into the sawgrass forest, stopping to drink at a waterhole, where he could sense beasts observing him from the cover. He drank enormous gulps of water and kept running, out of the sawgrass and across the arid salt plains.

He ran through the old growth forest and up into the hills, emerging from the other side overcome by hunger, a furious ache in his stomach stretching to his head. He instinctively followed his nose to an old shed on a nearby farm where he found a two-kilo block of protein—and ate it all. He ran for another thirty kilometers, heading for Mother Umami's, or at least that general direction, his mind was not ordered—he was not in control of himself.

He ran up the old lane leading to Mother's house and jumped the fence into the garden. He didn't follow the path, instead bounding over the thick tangle of undergrowth, launching himself from the trunk of a tree and swinging onto the verandah. He opened the door to the kitchen and rushed inside. Again he drank, sucking the water from the faucet with inhuman strength.

Mother's avatar heard the ruckus and emerged to find Dan1 rummaging through the kitchen gorging himself.

"Get in my room," ordered Mother, taken aback by his deranged appearance. "Now!"

Mother's voice somehow brought him back, abating the animal urges. He slipped into the room and slumped on her chaise lounge. "Locky's dead," he said. "And they reckon I killed 'im."

253

"What?"

"I wanted to break in t'Biota, so I got Locky t'help, an' they killed 'im."

"You're gonna have to give me a bit more detail there, sonny."

Over the next couple of hours Dan1 explained everything. He told Mother about El9 and PETSO, about the break-in and their miraculous escape, and finally he told her about meeting Peta Singer.

"I reckon this whole thing with El9 is God punishing me for killin' Lock," he said.

"You didna kill Locky," replied Mother curtly. "Someone at Biota killed Locky for their own reasons. I'm surprised 'bout Peta Singer but. Musta been a right shock. You still got ya mother's music box?"

"Sure."

"I reckon we should go get it. I wanna track down that fella from rent-a-runt. He might have some answers here."

As Mother lurched forward on the bed a gaggle of avatars rushed to support her from behind. She heaved again and with the avatar's assistance rolled from the bed. "Get the Deux Chevaux ready. We're going in t'town."

Dan1 watched her procession down the hall with amusement; it brought to mind a Thanksgiving Parade balloon being pushed through a narrow alley. A few times the avatars found themselves rolled between the wall and their mistress, caught in the folds like a fly in dough. She placed a foot on the running board of the Deux Chevaux and with a final heave mounted the beast. Dan1 mounted the other side, which was at least a foot higher due to Mother's sagging weight.

"Let's hope the ol' DCV starts then." She was tugging at the knotted stocking of second skin pulled inelegantly over her legs. "Open the garage!"

Mother's old Deux Chevaux whinnied loudly and shuddered, sending a tingle through the saddle that in turn quivered up Dan1's spine. It staggered to its feet and began a labored and lurching clip-clopping along the dusty track leading from Mother's place to the arterial.

Mother sat happily at the reins, her first fresh air in nearly a decade. "The man from rent-a-runt told me if you had questions about the box you could find his contact details inside it," shouted Mother over the noise of her dual-driven car.

"Who was he?" Dan1 was perched next to Mother at the front of the cab.

"No idea," she replied. "He was an odd bloke, though. I never really reckoned the box was ya mum's. And I definitely didn' want ya trying to find the fella who dropped it off. Struck me as a loony." Mother smiled warmly at Dan1. "Guess we don't have any choice now but."

They came to a halt outside Locky's apartment. As Dan1 rushed through the door he was hit by an overwhelming wave of remorse that stopped him, physically, in the middle of the room. He couldn't imagine living without Locky: no strange women in towels, no smart suits, no hair product. He forced himself up the stairs to his old room and collected the music box, leaving as quickly as possible to escape the ghosts.

Back in the car he carefully opened the lid and checked for the man's contact details in the underlay, the same place he had found the pic. He gently peeled back the carpet, revealing nothing but blank board. He pushed his hand backstage, feeling for anything that might come loose. His rummaging disturbed Adeona, who walked out onto the stage wearing her petite ballerina costume.

"Maybe he was a loony after all?" suggested Mother.

Dan1 sighed and began to close the lid. Their journey into

the city had distracted him from his other worries. Now he could feel them creeping back in nauseating waves that seemed to emanate from his stomach.

"Are you looking for Professor Wilson?" asked Adeona in a high-pitched voice.

Dan1 was so startled he nearly threw the box off his lap. He turned to Mother, who was staring back in disbelief. Neither of them had the presence of mind to respond to the tiny toy.

"I can send for a guide," offered the diminutive ballerina politely.

Singer hears them first

The black hawk-copters approached in a traditional v-shaped squadron, coming in low over the sawgrass, their whooping cry scattering the kangasaurs.

"You did this E19," shouted Singer. "You never should have brought him here."

Tin rattles went off and the security marshals began ushering people towards the bunkers, but it was too late. The hawks quickly swooped, releasing dragnet webs that trapped the frantic organiks, wrapping their struggling limbs and pulling them together into groups of twenty or more. Behind the front line a sweeping hawk clutched the waiting sacks in its craw and dumped them into the waterhole. Within minutes hundreds had drowned.

They landed in the center of the compound and an unmarked official stepped from the copter, surveying the subdued settlement. Another agent approached carrying a chitin sack; the red-haired primate E19 had rescued was suffocated inside. The unmarked official took the sack and tossed it back into the copter.

"Find them," he ordered over his perineurals. "We need

them back at the citadel before the Grand Final begins. Slit is impatient."

Wilson's place; dynamic totipotency
Professor Wilson's lodgings were nestled into a quiet corner of the university campus. Mother and Dan1 had been following a flying eyeball that Adeona summoned to guide them. Their ancient Deux Chevaux staggered up the drive and collapsed onto an overgrown clump of lawn grass.

"I'll wait here for a moment," said Mother, as Dan1 dismounted. "Let me know if you need me to stay."

Dan1 walked towards the small sandstone cottage covered in thick creeping rose. Professor Wilson emerged from between the roses, offering his shoulder to the flying eyeball, which settled there, tucking its wings behind its spherical body.

"Excuse my appearance," he said, "but I like to keep things casual on the weekends. I'm Professor Wilson and I believe you have had quite a stressful 24 hours."

"Yeah," agreed Dan1.

"Would you like to come in?"

Dan1 turned to Mother, who was eyeballing the Professor suspiciously from her saddle. Dan1 waved her away and stepped into a small room at the front of the professor's house. The walls were covered in shelves holding rows and rows of ancient leather texts. At one end was a large wooden desk, also covered in books and papers, and at the other end a couch and sofa were arranged around a low coffee table.

"There is no need to tell me what has happened," said the professor. "I have always kept a close eye on you."

Dan1 stared at the flying eyeball perched on Wilson's shoulder. "Mate, I didn' come here t'talk. I come t'listen."

"Good. There is a lot that I can tell you."

"I wanna know 'bout Peta Singer and I wanna know what happened in the woodlands on the day me mum got killed," said Dan1 impatiently.

"Well you've come to the right person." The Professor sat up and stretched his back. "I was there that day."

"You were in the woodlands?"

"I was the one who found you. And I've taken a close interest in you ever since. But before we talk about that day, we need to talk about something else."

Dan1 nodded.

The professor leaned forward. "Dan1, when we are first conceived we are just a single cell. And that cell divides and divides again into a tiny cluster of cells. Those cells have the potential to develop into every other cell in the human body. Do you understand?"

Dan1 scrunched up his face. He understood perfectly well. It was basic biology. "Course," said Dan1. "Ya talkin' 'bout totipotent cells."

"Yes," agreed the professor. "Every other cell comes from that single cell. It's amazing, isn't it?"

"Yeah," agreed Dan1.

"The thing about totipotent cells is that they can turn into other cells. For instance, many mature plant cells remain totipotent, so if you take a branch cutting from one plant it can grow into an entirely new plant. The cells that used to be cells in the branch reorganize themselves to become cells in a root system. Isn't nature simply extraordinary?"

"Yeah…" Dan1 was beginning to suspect the professor was a loony after all. "Of course, in most mammals their totipotent cells become increasingly specialized, turning into multipotent and pluripotent cells, and once they have become specialized it is impossible for them to return to their original form. You

258

see, for mammalian cells, totipotency is a starting point, one to which they cannot return."

Dan1 nodded, unsure of the professor's trajectory.

"Now Dan1," the professor leaned even closer towards him, "have you ever heard of dynamic totipotency?"

The dynamic cell; the modus operandi
Dex had all the samples from the crime scenes spread out before him, but he was only interested in the killer's. He slipped it into the scanner and isolated a single cell. He'd never been able to get a handle on the confusing and contradictory properties of the killer's DNA. Now, with a stabilized sample and new equipment, he had a fresh chance.

He took some skin from his hand and isolated a single cell, placing it in the scanner. The killer's cell immediately mimicked the structure of the skin cell. In direct contact it took less than a second. Dex recorded the result and uploaded it to his perineurals. Next he took a sample of his hair and fed it into the scanner. The killer's cell quickly reorganized to form a simulant of the newly introduced hair cell.

Dex had a new idea. He ran outside, picking over the dark parking lot for feathers, animal hairs, the remnants of roadkill. He was thrilled to find a fleshy, squashed rat. He gathered his horrible finds together and brought them back into the station.

He isolated cells and placed them near the killer's sample. Each time the killer's cells would mimic the newly introduced material. It was extraordinary to watch.

Dex had assumed the killer was some kind of humanoid gen-mod. He had thought its highly unstable genetic makeup was a flaw in it design, the mark of an impressive hacker but not an experienced designer. He realised it was not a flaw, it was *the* feature. It was this trait that set this killer apart from any other he had hunted.

The killer's modus operandi was suddenly apparent: it could replicate the characteristics of other animals during its frenzy. A mutant with those abilities accounted for the extraordinary destruction of the corpses. He didn't let his mind wander too far into the implications; he wanted to remain focused on his study of the cells.

He now understood that the cell could dynamically mutate into another cell, the next question to tackle was how it returned to its original condition.

Dex took a number of cells from the killer's sample and laid them out in row on the scanner, each isolated. He then took a series of samples from the parking lot and placed them next to the killer's, watching them mutate to replicate the others. He compared the DNA inside the mutated cells with the DNA from the killer's original sample. Incredibly the DNA itself had changed. It wasn't just the cell structure changing, it was the DNA.

He then removed the foreign cells and waited for the killer's DNA to return to its original form—but it was not quite the same. Each time the killer's cells mutated, the DNA mutated slightly as well, retaining seemingly random properties from the foreign cell.

Dex tried to stay focused on the forensics, but there was a story that kept pressing into his thoughts. No matter how hard he tried to keep to the hard science, somewhere in the back of his head a narrative was weaving together. He knew if he let these narratives take over they could lead to impulsive actions, like hunting Dan1. But sometimes they led straight to the killer.

A rather satisfying concatenation of ideas slowly dropped into his mind. This thing, this beast, this killer, was not designed and bred from scratch. This thing had been a human. That human had altered their DNA with the help of Slit. Maybe it was Slit himself. Those modifications allowed the killer to emulate animals and return to human form, but not exactly. They always mutated slightly.

This was the key. What if he could trace back through the permutations and find the killer's original DNA sequence? Was that possible? There was no way of knowing how many times the killer's DNA had mutated. It could be billions. If the mutations were truly random, there would be no way of finding the relationship between the DNA in the pre-mutation cell and the DNA post-mutation.

He sat back and pinched his nose so hard his head began to vibrate in anger. Anger at what? Maybe it was just frustration. Frustration at being so close, yet again. Frustration at being so close, but seeing between now and any kind of resolution an ocean of work, an almost impossibly large ocean of facts to collate: the billions of possible mutations that had happened to the killer's DNA from billions of possible sources. How could he possibly trace back through it all? How could he unwind all that history?

It was approaching 6am. There was a chance that Rhonda would still be serving at The Hoary Blandishment. He found his way into the Boons just as Rhonda was pulling the shutters.

"One last?" he asked.

"Sure," she said. Dex was grateful that she pulled the rest of the shutters anyway, he wouldn't want the morning light to infect her establishment. "Dark and stormy?"

Dex shook his head. "Nah, just a water."

Rhonda cocked her head, but kept her expression indistinct. She quickly pulled a water and placed it in front of him at the bar.

"I gotta thing," he began. "I gotta thing that's almost impossible to do."

"Almost?" interjected Rhonda.

And in that moment, that quickly, Dex knew that he had to try. That no matter how incredibly difficult, no matter how much work, how many hours at the scanner it was going to take, he had to do it. Because while it was almost impossible, it wasn't actually impossible. And while it may all come to nothing, maybe it would be the final piece to solve the woodland killing.

Rhonda passed him a shot of caffeine and refilled his water. He shot them both, swung his leg off the stool and walked out into the cool morning.

The impossible; an algorithm

He took an isolated cell from the killer's sample and noted the DNA sequence. He placed the cell next to a foreign cell, watching it mutate. He then removed the foreign cell so the killer's sample returned to its original form but with the newly introduced mutations. He noted the new mutations in the killer's DNA sequence and filed them.

He repeated this test dozens of times in the now full police lab. Warren had let him stay past eight, but the others in the lab were uncomfortable with his presence. He knew he didn't have much more time before they would start to complain and Warren would have to succumb to the pressure.

By testing a large number of samples and mutating the cells multiple times Dex began to understand that the mutations weren't random. If he exposed the killer's cell to the same foreign cell twice, there would only be one set of mutations. Likewise if he exposed it to two different cells from the same source. There was a relationship between the DNA in the pre-mutation cell and the DNA post-mutation. That relationship was determined by the nature of the foreign cell. If he could document enough of the mutations, perhaps he could express that change as an algorithm.

He continued documenting the changes manually. He worked without rest, the bench in the laboratory filling with his scrawling and the detritus left behind from many experiments. Dex was hunched over the scanner when the captain appeared.

"Come on Dex," said Warren wearily. "I gave you until eight o'clock. It's nearly noon. Sorry mate. Time to pack it up."

"Ten more minutes," said Dex without looking up.

"No, Dex. Time is up now," demanded Warren.

"It's ten more minutes to noon," insisted Dex.

Warren sighed and shrugged at the officers in the lab. Ten minutes later he returned to the laboratory to find Dex cleaning away the last of the mess, a computer tucked under his arm.

"Can I take this with me?" Dex half-whispered to Warren.

Warren nodded and gestured for Dex to pass him the unit.

Out the front of the police station Warren placed the computer into a pannier on the haunches of a powerful looking Cheetah. "I got this for you, it's police issue. They use it for undercover jobs against the cycle-cat gangs. Don't wreck it."

"Thank you," said Dex with a smirk. "Do you mind if I set up in your den? I still have some work to do."

Dex threw his leg over the Cheetah and slipped his thumbs across the motor-cortex, the beast shivered and purred.

"No worries," said Warren. "But Andrea will be using the living room; she has a book club meeting today."

"Okay," shouted Dex over his shoulder. The purr of the Cheetah turned into a screech as the agile cycle leaped into the street. He was distracted by his work, hardly concentrating on the road in front.

He now had the pre- and post-mutation DNA gathered from hundreds of different samples. Sorting through the raw data he needed to find some kind of relationship, something that would allow him to formulate an algorithm that he could apply more broadly. With an algorithm to work back through the permutations of the killer's DNA, unscrambling the sequence to arrive at the killer's original identity was just a step away.

Dex screamed through the streets, clinging to his new vehicle.

Wotan's story

It was midday but only a lamp illuminated the professor's features, making his angular face all the more distinctive. He sipped from a cup of tea, drawing his breath across the steaming surface in an effort to cool it down, then continued his history of the early research into totipotent cells.

"When I was beginning my career at the university, scientists were looking at the idea of cellular totipotency surviving the initial stages of mammalian development. I was invited onto the university's Board of Ethics, which was investigating two students in the honors program who had taken their research into an entirely new field, using the human genome as the subject for experimentation, clearly in breach of even the loosest interpretation of the Charter.

"Although it was never conclusively proven, Theodor Slit and a student called Thomas Wotan were suspected of conducting experiments on humans. They were sent down from the university and their case was referred to the Committee for Public Safety, probably known to you as the Circle of Seven.

"Slit found a job at Biota, as you know, while his lab partner set up a private laboratory in the suburbs, funded mainly from Slit's family money. In the beginning they continued their experiments on vagrants, but as The Committee for Public Safety cracked down they became increasingly desperate. I happen to know for a fact that Thomas Wotan conducted experiments on himself. I saw the results."

The professor paused from his story, took another deep breath and exhaled across the lip of his teacup. He studied the chaotic swirls of steam dancing over the dark brown surface of the tea.

"The thing is, Dan1, he very nearly got it right. He was able to inject a plasmid into himself that successfully gave his cells totipotent characteristics; he could turn his hands into claws or his arms into wings; he could absorb the properties of any animal he came into contact with. He had discovered a form of dynamic totipotency that was unheard of then, even in lesser species, and he had managed to successfully sequence it into the human genome.

"The problem was, he couldn't control it. His body was highly unstable. Every contact with organic material resulted in some cellular mutation—he couldn't even feed himself without risking mutation. Worse than that, his cells would always retain traces of their mutations, they never returned to their exact original form. By the time I saw him his body was horribly disfigured."

He took another deep breath through his nose and sipped at his tea.

"But you see Dan1, a man like that does not simply give up. He continued with his research and completed it. He found a way to stabilize the process, so that mutations could be brought about at will and then the organism could return to its original state without complications."

"So he fixed himself?" interrupted Dan1.

"No." The professor's eyes were downcast; his breath was heavy and the cup in his hand trembled slightly. "His condition was beyond repair so he started with an entirely new genome. He bred a new version of himself with sequences that would control the mutations. From the lab reports we knew he'd uploaded the sequence into a zygote and injected it into clay, but we lost track of it after that. Until you came along."

"That's me?"

The professor nodded. "Except for a few stretches of DNA, you share the exact same genome as Thomas Wotan."

"I'm made from clay?"

Mary in the Woodlands

"But if their lab equipment was confiscated, how did they incubate me?"

"The old-fashioned way." The professor looked evenly at Dan1. "Mary was with a religious order, a nun who offered spiritual guidance to Slit. They were friends, I suppose."

"So they used her," said Dan1, eyes downcast.

"Yes. They knew she wouldn't terminate any pregnancy because it was against her beliefs."

"And what happened to her in the woodlands?"

A tightened look of discomfort pinched the professor's face. "I will never forget seeing him come through the trees. It took me a long time before I could admit that it was Thomas Wotan—the very same man who had come before the Board of Ethics. He had come to claim you.

"Mary tried to protect you—she didn't know who or what you were, she loved you deeply and thought of you as a blessing. She didn't know that you were a bomb set to go off. She tried to protect you, but Wotan tore her to shreds and ... well, the bomb went off. I've never seen anything like it."

A strange and distant smile came over the professor's face, replacing the slight look of anguish that had drawn his sharp features into a tightened bunch. "You were barely half a meter tall, could only just walk, but when he attacked you, you fought back. Singer and the girl managed to escape while you and Wotan fought. I still remember the shocked look on Wotan's face.

"You managed to wound him badly; he was forced to flee. Then you returned to the rock in the middle of the clearing, lay on your back, and started bawling. After a while your body returned to its normal form and I decided it was safe to get you, so I picked you up, carried you away, and called the police. But I never told them what I saw.

"After that, you escaped from police custody, this was during the Leviathan panic and everything was chaos. I lost track of you for a few years, but when I saw the ratboy story come through the hydra I knew it was you. Slit was watching out for you too, no doubt. I planted Adeona in the music box to administer a plasmid, a temporary inhibitor for your condition. It dampened the fuse, Dan1, but I knew I could never stop you completely. When you moved to El9's apartment Adeona couldn't reach you anymore—hence your condition."

The professor looked at the clock on his wall. "I think it's time to have a snack. Let's have sandwiches and discuss the woodlands afterwards. Okay?"

Dan1 had been looking at the floor for some time. He slowly shook his head. "If I'm made from clay, how come I'm different from a machine?"

The professor shifted uncomfortably.

"You are not a machine because you are somebody's friend and, if I am not mistaken, you are now somebody's lover."

"Yeah, me sister's. That's normal…"

"El9 is not your sister and Peta Singer is not your father. Mary was a nun, married to God. No man had a relationship with Mary: not Singer, not Slit, not Wotan—only God."

"But I'm the same as Wotan—I'm the exact same person…"

"No Dan1, you are not the same as Wotan. You are a completely different person. Don't believe those who say we are simply an expression of our chemistry. We are like a tapestry, our DNA is the warp, it sets the foundation, but our differences come from experience, these things are knitted through us, they form the weft, and we all choose our narratives. We tell our own stories.

"You are now faced with the same question you have always been faced with: *who are you?* You are the only one who can answer that question. Every decision you make is a part of the answer to that question. So think hard about the decisions you make—do so consciously and deliberately."

The professor shuffled off to the kitchen to fetch some food.

The possible; and source code

Dex spent the day running the sequence, the hum of the police computer tickling his fingertips. The powerful machine had unscrambled trillions of lines of code. The killer's DNA was like a palimpsest, with each newly mutated sequence written over the previous one. By feeding common sources of mutation into one end of the model, Dex was building an algorithm that could be applied across all potential sources.

Dex had a single purpose: to determine the killer's DNA before it was altered by contact with the foreign organisms. There were tens of thousands of mutations to sort through and many millions of lines to reorder. But Dex was an experienced biohacker, he was used to unscrambling an egg. And he had Rhonda in his head: *this was not impossible.*

He also had the help of an extremely powerful police computer capable of trillions of calculations per second. The bulbous left hemisphere stored and computed the staggeringly long sequences while the right hemisphere pushed them through the model. Ironically the computer had been manufactured by Biota and was derived from one of Theodor Slit's early contributions to neural computation theory.

He trudged on, working with the neuro unit, combining his intuition with its awesome computing power. He was not waiting for a satisfying breakthrough, he was not expecting a moment of clarity or a single inspiration that brought the case to a close. He knew what was before him: hard drudgery. First the model, then the algorithm and then the killer's pre-mutation DNA.

He was running the algorithm against the model and they were slowly converging. He was exhausted, but his work was now becoming more urgent. He had to link out to the Hydra, testing the killer's DNA in its current form with genomic databases.

After his shack was destroyed he had lost some of his old hacking tricks, so he was limited to public access databases only. A few quickly blocked his access. He was drawing massive amounts of data and users were suspicious. He could feel the attention.

Eventually he'd be shut down. He knew it. He had to run the algorithm against as many possible source mutations as possible as quickly as possible. If he was cut off from the databases it would all be for nothing.

The police neuro unit was humming hot, sweating as an ungodly amount of data was pushed through it. Meanwhile, Dex was pushing back into the history of the killer's DNA sequence, paring it down, drawing closer to its primary composition, searching for the source code.

Finally the process started to lighten. He was drawing less data and less attention. The computer was working its way through the final permutations, the cause of the mutations becoming more obscure. Rather than simple foods, the killer had obviously been experimenting with other organisms. An ursine sequence had been inserted into a gene controlling the growth of limbs; feline DNA wove into sequences determining dental development.

The computer trawled through its proteomics database matching mutations after running them through the algorithm.

The humming stopped and the monitor cleared. The streaming lines of code were replaced by the complete image of a single chromosome, which was in turn replaced by another, until each of the twenty-four matched chromosomes had been thoroughly checked and processed. Finally a complete genomic model was displayed across the monitor.

It was late afternoon and Dex had not slept since waking up in hospital. His body was fresh but his brain had been through massive trauma. He could almost feel the line of stress across the base of his brain stem where it fused with the spinal column.

He sat back in his chair. He had crossed the ocean. Somehow he had done it. Now he just had to see if it was all worth it.

The Circle speaks; who made the hydra We can't risk him returning to Wotan.

The professor staggered slightly as the Circle forced its way into his perineurals.

It's time to deal with him. Get on with it.

"Haven't you been listening? He won't go back to Wotan, his beliefs are allied with ours. He will join us if we give him the opportunity."

Dan1 called from the living room, "You right in there, professor?"

"I'm fine Dan1, thank you." He turned away from the door. "We've all been watching him for so long because no one is strong enough to destroy him, everyone wants him as an ally. Now we have the chance and you are asking me to kill him."

We all remember Black Saturday; we cannot allow another. This boy has the potential to be worse; he is Leviathan in human form, with a human mind.

"Yes, that's exactly it. He has a human mind, he can

make his own decisions. That is the mistake that was made with Leviathan—it lacked humanity. It had god-like powers without an understanding of human frailty; it lacked mercy. Dan1 is different."

This is not your decision, Professor Wilson.

"I won't be a part of this."

Remember Professor Wilson, we created the hydra, we control your perineural link, and we retain the key to the interface. Kill the boy voluntarily or we will force your hand.

"Don't threaten me—none of you could hack my medulla."

It won't be just one of us, Professor. It will be all of us.

Demonstration

The professor returned from the kitchen without food and headed straight for a cabinet in the corner. He opened the glass doors and removed the largest piece of taxidermy—an impressive Andean Condor with its wings spread and its feet thrust forward.

"I want you to close your eyes." The professor took Dan1's hand and placed it across the roughened spicules of the condor's feet so Dan1 could feel the top of the bird's scythe-like talons pressed into his palm. "I want you to concentrate on the condor's foot. Try to picture it in your mind."

Dan1 pictured the bird's spiny bones wrapped in a thorny epidermis. He imagined the hooked talons reaching from his own hand.

"Think of it as an extension of yourself."

The bones in Dan1's hand started to shift. Not in a painful way, but in a subtle reorganization that became more rapid as he sought control of it.

He opened his eyes and saw that his four fingers had elongated into curved talons and the skin on the back of his hand had the same gray, horny cover as the condor's foot. He removed his hand and it returned to its original form.

"You have an ability, Dan1. It is certainly not the curse that Wotan gave to himself. You can replicate the features of any organism you come into contact with. Now that the condor is a part of your cellular memory it will always be there and most importantly, so will your humanness.

"But you also have a responsibility, Dan1. What happened in the clearing that day affected everyone; it convinced Peta Singer that the Charter must be strictly enforced, that's why he founded PETSO; even the poor police lieutenant assigned to the case eventually had a breakdown and left the force.

"You were changing the world even before you were born." The professor got up and returned the condor to the cabinet behind Dan1. "We knew you were coming and we wanted to stop you, that's why the Circle released Leviathan in such a hurry."

"I'm the reason for Leviathan?"

The professor gently removed a laser-edge from his pocket. "Not the only reason. When you live in a society where any misguided individual from the suburbs can splice up a virus that could kill millions there needs to be a technology that can be constantly vigilant, ruthless, omnipotent, omniscient and omnipresent; that was Leviathan. You always had too much power for an individual, Dan1, that's why the Circle needed to stop you, that's why they released Leviathan. But it failed."

Professor Wilson hinged on his hips, bringing his arm around slowly, methodically, almost robotically, drawing the laser-edge across Dan1's neck.

The killer's DNA; and a motive

He took the killer's DNA and uploaded it to his perineural

system, linking simultaneously with several databases, feeding the sequence out across the hydra.

He still only had access to the public databases but luckily the university returned a match for a former student, Thomas Wotan, listed as dismissed.

Dex hooked into the hydra and fed Thomas Wotan into a general search. Dozens of results were returned. As he sifted through the postings and publications it didn't take long for Wotan's name to be connected to Slit and the research they had been conducting at the university. Whatever Slit's interest in Dan1, he also had a close connection to Wotan.

The motive for the killings was clear: unlike Dan1, Wotan's mutations had permanent effects. Perhaps he needed to feed on human DNA to maintain his human form? If so, he would likely kill again.

Dex connected to Slit's network. "I have something to tell you about Wilson and the boy," he growled.

"Then you may make an appointment with Ms.. Sundew, my…"

"You need to hear these things today, in person."

"Very well," said Slit coolly. "Meet me at the arena."

Send in the Giants

Slit killed the line and considered the call for a moment. He did not trust the strange hunter and collector and was growing tired of his persistence. He turned to the giants standing near the buffet table.

"Regin! Fafner!" he snapped. The two giants lurched towards him, Regin still carrying a slight limp from his last encounter with Dex.

"Declan is on his way here," said Slit in low tones. "I want you to kill him." Regin and Fafner gulped down their food and walked towards the door. "And do it before he gets here!" shouted Slit.

The two giants carefully sealed the door behind them.

"You're losing control Theodor," sneered Thomas Wotan, crouched at the far end of the room.

Slit turned towards the window and watched the ground staff hurriedly preparing the arena for the Grand Final.

Dex and the cheetah; an inconvenient bullbar

The Cheetah was even sweeter than Dex imagined, custom made in a Monbiot laboratory, unlike the mass-produced Biota cycles. It was leaner and lighter than a normal cycle, built for speed, with more fast twitch muscle and an agile body that could change direction in an instant. Dex was lying forward along the spine of the graceful feline, his chin resting low on the beast's back, right behind the ocular units, so he could only just see the road ahead. The Cheetah wove lithely between the traffic along 3rdArterial, its blonde body pocked with black spots.

Behind it a large Golgi prime-mover was recklessly making its way up the middle of the lanes. Its deep horn let out a loud moan, forcing the cars in front to pull over. The bulky front cab had a broad windscreen, turned reflective in the westering sun. Its ocular units flashed aggressively to warn drivers they had to either get out of the way or risk being rammed by its enormous bullbar. The machine dragged a large trailer that swayed wildly back and forth as the driver forced his way through the late-afternoon traffic.

Return to PETSO

Dan1 removed the cover from an ancient panther-cycle in Wilson's garage. Its sinewy limbs appeared to have atrophied from years of disuse, the spine stiff and arched awkwardly, pushed up in a knobby ridge along its back.

He placed his hands on the grayish bulge at the front of the vehicle and pictured the nervous system of the cat: the sliverous skeins of silvery thread spreading and webbing throughout the machine; the gentle pulsing rhythm of the neurotransmitters, the tiny electric impulses coruscating into life. The cold, gelatinous touch of the motor-cortex slowly transformed into a lively and responsive interface. The ancient machine purred to life. He looked down at his hands, which had fused to the motor-cortex, and grinned.

He spurred the cat along the drive and connected to the nearest arterial heading out of the city to the northwest. He was determined to expose Slit, Wotan and everything they had done. He wanted to see El9 and present her with an even more damning piece of evidence than Slit's red-haired primate: himself.

He pushed through the sawgrass forest for as long as the cat could manage, the blades slicing his neck where Wilson had cut him, but the wounds quickly healed. Before long the forest was impassable by machine and he stashed the cat under a cover of vegetation.

After running for half an hour, leaping over the sharp sticks and between the thick clumps of sawgrass roots, he was confronted by the flat face of a giant creature. Without pausing to consider, he jumped up onto a broad blade of grass and sprang onto the beast's back. The enormous animal let out a piercing whine and stood on its hind limbs.

Dan1 clung to the hide as the beast threw itself around, deliberately rubbing itself along the serrated edges of the sawgrass. He closed his eyes and felt the rough hide melt into his hands; strings of protein reached out and threaded deep into the beast's fatty tissues, connecting Dan1 to the creature's neural network.

The animal quietened.

Dan1 was overwhelmed by a heightened sense of perception. He was suddenly confronted by a form of supra-consciousness: looking at himself through the eyes of the beast while viewing the beast through his own eyes. Two brains—both conscious, but only one imbued with consciousness—observed each other through a fluid link. It created an artificial sense of infinity, like holding two mirrors to face each other. He waited a moment to allow his senses to settle.

Feeling more comfortable, he and the beast turned around and began a slow bounding journey through the sawgrass. As his confidence built the power of his strides increased dramatically. Soon he was leaping above the sawgrass, hanging gently in the air for a moment, then crashing back towards the ground. He was not riding the beast, he had become part of it—like a benign parasite that had spread its way through the organism.

He found the best way to control himself while connected to the giant beast was to play a subtle game, slipping between his own mind and the animal's. All knowledge of how to control its body was locked inside its simple mind. In order to get this new extension of his body to do his willing he simply allowed the beast's brain some autonomy. There was a gentle tugging between the two minds, not unlike the physical reins connecting a rider's hands to the horse's bit.

He bounded out of the forest and into the clearing, heading for PETSO's compound at the center.

Sam recovers

The compound felt abandoned. He walked slowly between the buildings, frightened that if he ran into someone he would likely kill them with his enormous new body. There was a movement inside the main building and he hopped gently over to the window.

Inside, Brother Sampson, the enormous boy who had rescued him from the riot, was slumped in a chair. His long green hair had been replaced by fat white tendrils connected to a small box on the other side of the room.

"Ya wanna hear the voice of God, ya sunoffabitch? Or ya wanna let us know what happened to the DB?"

Sampson squeezed his eyes tight, ready for the blast. The man interrogating Sampson nodded to an associate by the box. The white tendrils stiffened and pulsed as Sampson's body threw itself into a series of painful positions.

"That wasn't even the voice yet, boy. That was just a taste." Blood trickled from Sampson's scalp.

The man by the box turned away and glanced towards the window, noticing Dan1. "Alu and chaos!" he shouted, scrambling to the back of the room.

His wiry companion stopped haranguing Sampson and turned to see the problem. Dan1 sniffed a thick spray of mucus onto the window.

Dan1 tore the roof from the building and picked up one of the interrogators in his mouth, flinging him across the PETSO yard. The man's body crumpled as it hit the ground and skidded into a ditch. The other man attempted to flee, but Dan1 pursued him, using the flat bone on his head to crush him against the rear wall.

Dan1 shuffled back from the building and with some effort drew his hands from the beast's back. The beast sat up onto its haunches and looked around, dazed. It looked down at Dan1 with its featureless face, then it bounded off towards the sawgrass forest, leaving Dan1 standing outside the wrecked PETSO meeting hall.

Inside Dan1 quickly removed the tendrils from Sampson's

head, untied his hands and fetched some water. Sampson tried to speak but Dan1 motioned for him to drink. The boy took a few deep breaths and drank from the cup. After some time he had recovered enough to speak.

"Thank you." He drank again.

Dan1 shook his head as if to say, *what else was I supposed to do?*

"We were invaded by men," gasped Sampson between gulps of water. "I think Slit must have sent them. Some managed to get away, but they captured me."

"And where is El9?"

"They got her, and Peta too."

Sampson's breathing was still heavy from the torture. His words came out in quick gasps. "They took them. But I don't know where."

The Grand Final was starting in less than two hours. Dan1 knew exactly where Slit would be. Many years ago Theodor Slit and Thomas Wotan had decided to play God with his life—it was time for him to show them all hell's fury.

Wilson's loyalty; the severed link Why did you let him go, Wilson?

"It was the right thing to do."

Why did you bother? You know there is no way he can hide from us.

"I am the Circle's hands, without me you have no way of reaching him."

We do not need hands, Professor. We are everywhere, we are the hydra.

A little lick of smile curled at the edges of the professor's thin lips. "Surely you know by now?" He let the Circle throw thoughts across the hydra before continuing. "I cut the boy, severed his perineural. You can't reach him now, you are stranded."

The professor felt a sickening pressure build at the back of his throat. His mind was opaque—not his vision blurring—his thoughts became soupy as the voices of the Circle crowded into his consciousness. His body slumped to the floor.

Earthly intervention

Fafner was in the passenger seat watching Regin wrestle the prime-mover through traffic. From their high perch the two giants could see Dex weaving his way up the arterial.

"Gett me a liddle clozer," said Fafner, "udderwise I'll neffer catch him on dat Cheetah."

Regin nodded solemnly. Fafner knew Regin would prefer to take care of Dex, but his back had been broken in the last confrontation and he still hadn't fully recovered.

"Don't let him see you," counseled Regin. "Just come up fast behind him and slice his neck. Then take the next exit and I'll meet you there."

Fafner grunted and raised himself from the seat, preparing to swing back through the cab and into the trailer. Regin grabbed his arm when he was halfway through the awkward action.

"Have you remembered to treat the whip?"

Fafner groaned. "Off corse I haff. Heel be brane ded. Dere's no comin bak dis time."

A dark look came over the giant's huge face as he stepped through the back of the cab. Fafner had used a special toxin to ensure that Dex would die, the same gray material they had used to destroy Dex's house.

Fafner looped the whip over his shoulder and mounted the cycle; the panther's narrow back sagged beneath the giant's enormous body—a scaled up scene of a dwarf trying to ride a tabby cat.

"Ar yu redy?" he called.

"Ready," replied Regin through their perineural link.

A small hatch opened and Fafner pointed the panther-cycle towards the traffic. He picked a gap and launched onto the road.

Dex's Cheetah was just ahead, moving quickly, but not pushing her limits. Fafner slipped between cars, approaching Dex's lane, making sure not to attract any attention.

He removed the tail-whip from his shoulder and with a deft snap of his wrist began a broad circular movement. At the same time he spurred the cycle faster, so she leaped a full car length in an instant, bringing him directly behind Dex, poised to remove the splitter's head with a quick flick from the tail-whip.

Out of the fire, into hell

Dex spun and fired a single shot into the breast of the leaping cat. The hair-thin ballistic pierced the beast's chest; the ataxins took immediate effect and the cycle crumpled, its front limbs falling lifelessly under its body. Forward momentum threw its rear into the air and Fafner was hurled upwards, his out-of-control whip slicing the top corner from the prime-mover's cabin.

Regin slammed the brakes, but there was not enough time. The panther-cycle and Fafner disappeared under the heavy tread. Dex slowed to watch Fafner's broken body being tossed about in the surging traffic.

Suddenly the prime-mover lunged forward—a fierce wind whistling into the cabin through the hole opened by the whip.

Dex threw his lithe beast around, avoiding the full force of the crash, but it was too late, the Cheetah's tail caught in the prime-mover's paw. Dex and the Cheetah were flung into the air, helplessly snagged on the massive forelimb. The prime-mover pounded the arterial, smashing them along the unforgiving surface, hauling them up and belting down again.

The tail was stuck fast. There was nothing for Dex to do but cling on as he was repeatedly slammed onto the roadway.

Each time he rose he saw Regin laughing mercilessly from the driver's seat, but the hole in the cabin was becoming larger, the windshield and much of the passenger side had been eaten away, rapidly replaced by a grayish goop.

As Dex rose, he caught Regin looking across the open cabin. Their eyes met and Dex grinned, before being rushed to the roadway again.

Regin slammed his hands on the motor-cortex. The prime-mover lurched towards the edge as Regin tried crushing Dex and the Cheetah against the barrier. The cabin was almost entirely eaten away now, the wind whipping into Regin's eyes, forcing him to squint. He pushed the prime-mover to its maximum speed and with a shove on the motor-cortex drove the massive machine into the embankment. The barrier gave way and the prime-mover reared over the lip, falling towards the suburbs below, the trailer twisting behind like the tail of a kite.

It crashed into a three-story residential high-rise and Regin was jettisoned across the building's flat roof. The trailer swung down, smacking into the apartments, the flat end wedging into the ground.

The forelimb of the prime-mover spasmed impulsively, waving uselessly through the air, tossing Dex playfully about like a mouse caught in a cat's claw. He clung to the body of the swinging Cheetah three floors above the ground.

There is no power on earth to be compared to him—Job 41:33
Dan1 had the wind at his back as he flew down 3rd Arterial towards the arena. In his rear-vision he saw a terrible accident. A panther-cycle stumbled and crumpled in the middle of rush hour traffic. The confusion led to a cascade of accidents as cars and cycles and trucks all forced themselves to a halt.

The first exit to the arena was filled with a long snaking jam from the car park to the arterial. Dan1 stopped at the end of the line. The vehicles were so densely packed there was not enough room for a cat to make its way in between. He pulled back into the stream of traffic and headed for the second exit.

As he rounded the bend he could see that all the off-ramps were clogged. The gladiorg Grand Final drew a capacity crowd, not to mention the thousands that gathered in the car park to celebrate and watch the event on live-fed monitors.

He turned his cat towards the edge of the arterial. With a roar and a leap he and the machine had cleared the embankment and were falling towards the suburbs below.

His cycle crashed onto the roof of a quiet suburban bungalow. The irate occupant emerged through the back door, shaking his fist and screaming something about needing to fix his roof for the second time in one year. Dan1 waved and apologized before skipping off the roof and into a quiet laneway. He fixed on the arena and quickly scampered off down a broad suburban street.

Follow my lead

Slit was standing near the front of the skybox, nervously surveying the battlefield. His body was rigid and his hands, clasped firmly behind his back, twitched occasionally as if flicking away some invisible insect.

Crouched at the far end of the room was the monstrous form of Thomas Wotan, a menagerie of transgenic characteristics; swollen hands punctured with horny knuckles of spiked bone, a fierce set of retractable claws slicing through the gnarled skin on his fingers. His hair dipped low on his forehead, framing the features on his face, which were arranged like a human, but with one eye clouded gray and a circle of skin around the socket roughened red, like a farmyard chicken. He yawned and revealed a set of savage teeth, somewhere between a mandrill's fangs and a feline's shearing carnassials. The skin covering his top lip was cracked and blackened like burnt rubber.

"I need to feed," he growled.

"Have you already finished the remains of that young accountant? You should save something for later," advised Slit.

"You can be rational about it, Theodor, because it's not your hunger." Wotan leaned forward and scraped a claw down the one-way screen. "Maybe it's not hunger," he mused, "maybe it's anticipation."

"You want to see Menos?" suggested Slit.

"Exactly."

"Well, Freyja is supervising the service engineers and ground staff. You don't need to worry, it has been expertly designed and tested."

"Wasn't the boy involved in that project?" snarled Wotan.

"I double-checked all the sequencing myself… but yes, it was a pity about that," admitted Slit.

"You have no idea what his disloyalty means to us," snapped Wotan.

"Well perhaps if you would tell me…"

"There is no need. Just do as I say, Theodor."

Slit was quiet for a moment. He knew better than to test Wotan's rage. "Despite all those complications, we managed to finish Project Menos," he continued, after an appropriate silence. "It's a huge innovation, all the tactics of the conscious mind with all the focus of the lower orders. Quite a feat to master the conscious mind, we have managed complete control of—"

"We'll see," growled Wotan. "Let's see it work on the battlefield first."

"Yes," agreed Slit. "We'll be unbeatable on the battlefield."

Wotan laughed loudly and Slit caught the condescension in his tone.

"You never quite get it, do you Theodor? Right from our university days you never understood the power of your own achievements. This is not just about gladiorg competitions. This is about dominating much more than sport." Wotan slurped at a stray line of spittle falling from his mouth. He looked down at Slit through his clouded eye. "Just follow my lead, Theodor, as always, just follow my lead."

Slit nodded curtly and looked out over the battlefield. A thin smile curled on his lips. Thomas Wotan had a knack for reconciling the conflicts that raged deep in Slit's soul. Slit had served Wotan for many years, managing to keep him alive and stabilize his mutations using a specialized diet derived from human bone marrow. Most importantly he had kept him a secret from the authorities.

Controlling the animal rage that had occasionally boiled up inside Wotan was always the biggest difficulty. He had only recently begun insisting on satiating his animal urges, hunting humans in the suburbs. Slit had carefully orchestrated the killings to avoid being caught, choosing deserted alleyways and inconspicuous back roads. After Wotan was satisfied, he ensured his safe return to the lower laboratory.

For many years Slit had used his position at Biota to continue Wotan's great projects. Now their work was nearly completed, and he was feeling so content that he was not the slightest bit perturbed when Dan1 Kallikak burst through the door and threatened to kill them both.

A rude interruption

Dan1 felt like he had been running for days. As soon as he pushed through the door he felt his resolve being undermined by exhaustion. There, before him, was the twisted wreckage of his clone and creator, Thomas Wotan, with a body so painfully mutated that Dan1's first reaction was one of pity. He paused as Slit turned to face him.

"The both of you is dead," he shouted hysterically, his voice cracking like a pubescent choirboy.

"Why?" asked Slit, evenly.

"Cos ya killed me brother," snarled Dan1.

"Locky?" Slit laughed mockingly. "That's no brother. More like your keeper. He's been working for me. How do you think I've been keeping track of you all this time?" He eyed Dan1 coolly, obviously enjoying his discomfort. "You have no brother. You have no mother, no father. You are a machine. A bag of chemicals. How have you not worked that out by now?"

"He had a mother," grunted Wotan, "she was delicious."

Slit laughed.

"Aaaah Mary," said Wotan in a mock nostalgic tone, a wistful look on his face. "She was my first decent meal in weeks."

"I'm gonna kill ya," said Dan1, rediscovering his resolve.

"Is Rex ready for his pre-match warm up?" inquired Slit to the room at large.

"Yes," came the reply into the room. Dan1 recognized Freyja's voice. "Menos is implanted and configured. Just use the panel to select the targets. We are ready when you are."

Slit pulled a monitor from his armrest and laid it across his lap. Dan1 noticed two tiny figures scurrying across the display. He looked out at the arena and recognized them immediately. The crowd roared as Peta Singer and El9 were released onto the battlefield.

"Someone's gonna stop this," said Dan1. "They ain't gonna watch humans killed for sport."

"I doubt the crowd will think they're human," jibed Slit. "They will assume they're homunculi. But *we'll* have the privilege and enjoyment of knowing who they are."

At the edge of the arena Rex Australis was slowly led from the preparation pit. There was a roar as he reached the battlefield. Slit gently tapped the screen, selecting El9 and Peta Singer as targets. Rex's brain immediately reacted with a surge of chemicals focusing on the two tiny humans.

"This is the technology you helped perfect," said Slit cheerfully.

Dan1 fixed at Slit and pointed viciously, a small spine of sharpened bone extending from his finger. "Later," he said, drawing the spine of bone back into his finger. He disappeared out of the room with inhuman speed.

"I'm looking forward to watching that boy die," said Slit, turning back to the battlefield. "Brother versus brother—it's so wonderfully biblical."

On the battlefield
Dan1's feet shifted uneasily on the sandy surface. It was not just the enormous crowd that had made him falter at the edge of the field, it was also the ten meter lizard standing in the center.

He could see El9 and Singer pressed up against the fence trying to climb out, but the crowd on the other side wouldn't let them.

"We're human," screamed El9. "Please believe us, we're human!"

"She looks like that organik from the protest!" screamed a splitter.

"They've bred humunculi that look like PETSO bitches!" called another.

"Maybe she really is the protestor?"

"Who cares?"

The crowd roared and laughed. Another volley of drinks was hurled over the fence. Singer and El9 ducked as the projectiles crashed into the sand around them.

"Please!" screamed El9.

Rex was approaching, an intimidating sight even for the crowd standing safely behind the mesh. El9 grabbed her father's hand and the two of them ran along the fence line towards the sealed exit leading to the preparation pit.

As Rex closed in, Dan1 was sprinting across the sand. He leaped up the gladiorg's back, using the bony plates on the spine like rungs on a ladder. When he reached the head, he dug his hands under the massive scales. Rex twisted around, trying to throw the unexpected rider onto the ground.

Dan1's hands seamlessly blended into the beast's skull, tiny tendrils of silvery material burrowed deep into the animal's cortex. Rex began to howl, throwing his enormous body around the battlefield. Dan1 felt the now familiar link as he delved into Rex's brain. The connection grew more intense. He was suddenly overwhelmed.

The mind he encountered in the beast at the PETSO compound had nothing more than the faintest echo of understanding. As he connected to Rex's mind he felt a deafening roar; a piercing and painful white noise filled his being, rattling through his teeth. His heart burst into sickening arrhythmic palpitations. The sound in his head, the feeling in his body, was like screeching audio feedback.

Through the blare came memories. Memories of the other mind's life. He saw some of his own memories in the beast, but they were strangely disassociated, as if he were looking at himself as a child.

Teaching him to train surf.

The Amazing Ratboy.

Magic tricks.

The images and sensations blurred and mixed, cleaving the core of Dan1's identity. Locky's voice...

I've got him under control.

The organik is on the way out.
I have something to show you.

The two minds were drawn together and he felt the ineluctable vortex of complete madness. He struggled to remove himself.

The beast was also in pain as the two of them wrestled for control of the one mind. Rex's body writhed. The massive beast flung himself about the battlefield as if seized by the most intense fit. He slammed himself against the fencing. The crowd was shocked by the suddenness of this inexplicable display.

All Dan1's higher neural capabilities were dedicated to a Pyrrhic struggle with Rex. From somewhere deep in the recesses of his brain a surge of chemicals, driven by self-preservation, began the process of withdrawing the tendrils. The two minds were drawn apart.

Dan1's exhausted body fell from Rex's back onto the sandy surface. The giant gladiorg staggered towards the center of the battlefield. After stopping briefly to recuperate the beast turned and fixed its gaze back on Dan1.

Taking the rooftop; where will it end?
The Cheetah's tail was still stuck fast in the tread of the prime-mover. The limb spasmed, briefly moving Dex closer to the roof and then suddenly throwing him further away.

Dex used his weight to gently rock the Cheetah back and forth, the pendulum motion bringing him closer to the edge of the roof, but not close enough to jump. He threw his weight more aggressively and the arc of the pendulum increased. He was almost over the roof, but he could feel the tail shifting in the tread. He had to jump on the next pass.

As he reached the bottom of the arc the tail slipped suddenly and Dex almost lost his footing. The machine began to fall away beneath him. He pushed off with both feet.

He missed the roof but managed to claw his hands onto the very edge of the building. He was still hanging three stories above the ground, only now he didn't have a firm grip. The Cheetah hit the hard surface below, splitting open like a sack of mud. Dex looked down and saw the horrible wreckage spread over several square meters of ground.

He heaved himself up the side of the building, his fingernails splitting as he worked his way onto the ledge. With his upper body and forearms resting on the top of the building, he swung one leg up the side and caught a foot on the corner.

An ominous scraping of shoes moved across the roof—Regin limping towards him. The man had a badly dislocated shoulder, but his good arm was holding a pistol. Regin unsteadily aimed the gun as Dex threw out an arm and cocked his wrist. A barb hit Regin in the neck. The giant staggered slightly. Dex rolled onto the roof, expecting to see the giant collapse, but instead he was bent over laughing.

"Biota makes the venom in those barbs, you idiot." Regin was standing above him now, the skin on one side of his face grazed off and only able to see through one eye. "We make the toxin and we make an antidote, which I made sure to dose myself with."

Regin laughed again and swayed, struggling to keep himself stable. Suddenly Dex kicked the pistol from his hand, sending it clattering away. The giant steadied himself, squinting through his one remaining eye. His depth perception was badly affected. He grunted at Dex and took off after the gun.

Dex heaved himself from the ground and made chase. Regin turned and swung wildly with his good arm—a lucky punch, catching Dex right under the chin. His teeth crashed together and the jarring sensation clapped his mind shut.

For a brief moment he was tumbling backwards into darkness. He caught himself from falling and leaned forward into a punch, striking Regin across an exposed cheekbone. Clotted blood and skin stuck to Dex's knuckles. Regin responded with a driving blow deep into Dex's gut, knocking the wind out of him. Dex coughed red, slaggy spittle down his front. Kneeling on the ground, with his arm clutched across his stomach, he tried to catch his breath.

Regin quickly delivered a powerful kick from the side, collecting Dex under the chin with the toe of his boot. Again, Dex's teeth smashed together, leaving broken shards of enamel in his mouth. His tongue was bloodied and swollen. He felt the darkness rolling over him.

When he regained consciousness Regin was standing above him pointing the pistol at his face. Dex immediately kicked Regin's knee out and rolled on top of him. He pushed his thumb into the giant's dislocated shoulder. Regin howled in pain as the joint moved further from its place.

Regin managed to spin Dex over and jammed his good arm over his neck. Dex was pinned heavily to the ground. He could not breathe. He reached up and cleaved at the giant's open shoulder socket. Impulsively the massive man's upper body spasmed, just enough for Dex to slip out from under the arm that had him pinned. Regin was still writhing in pain. Dex quickly grabbed him behind the neck. The two men made eye contact. A split second later Dex drove his head forward, cracking into Regin's forehead.

Regin's body slumped. Dex took two hands and pushed the dead man away, slowly extracting his long silver forehead spikes, now smeared with Regin's brain fluid. He heaved the heavy body off him. Regin's face was already turning blue. He left the body lying face down on the roof.

290

Getting up, he staggered towards the edge of the building. Much of the prime-mover had been eaten away by the grayish goo. The same process had spread into the lower levels of the apartment block. Dex immediately recognized the substance from his destroyed house. He looked up at the sky and shook his weary head.

"When will this end?"

Suddenly the foundation gave way and the whole building slumped sideways. He managed to grab hold of some loose cartilage on the fascia as the roof pitched violently towards the ground. The gray matter had consumed much of the lower portion of the building. It was only a matter of time before it reached Dex.

Rising ominously on the horizon were the reflective eyes of a black hawk-copter.

Facing up; ready for the deathblow

Rex Australis leaped forward, driving Singer against the wire mesh fence. The old man's body crumpled onto the sand, blood spilling from the deep gashes on his legs. E19 desperately assuaged the flow while Dan1 tried to distract Rex. Unfortunately, Menos was a very effective weapon and the giant gladiorg was obsessively focused on killing E19 and Singer.

Dan1 concentrated on reorganizing his hand into a sharpened, hooked talon. He threw himself at Rex, tearing into the beast's side and pulling open a line of fresh reptilian flesh. He fled to the other side of the battlefield, drawing the gladiorg with him.

A swinging blow from Rex's tail caught him through the shin, flicking him into the air. He bounced off the fence and hit the ground shoulder first. Rolling over, he ran his hand along the open wound. It was healing remarkably quickly, but he was still too maimed to keep running. The back end of a claw crushed him into the sand.

Rex towered above him and roared. The massive head came down and jaws closed around him, pinning him in the giant's maw. Dan1 felt the teeth sliding through his flesh. He felt his body being ground between two enormous incisors. He reached out and stabbed at the animal's eye with his sharpened talon, but it had no effect. The crowd was cheering at the brutal fight.

Just behind the eye, towards the back of the beast's head, Dan1 could see the purple Menos gland. He couldn't save himself, but he could still help Singer and El9. As the beast opened its jaws to take a final bite, Dan1 reached forward and severed the gland.

Exhausted, he slumped back, ready for the deathblow.

Rex paused. His jaw slackened and his gullet began to work like a child rejecting broccoli. Dan1 fell from the beast's mouth and landed on the battlefield. The giant lizard studied him with a puzzled expression, then looked at the raucous crowd.

Dan1 lay back on the sandy surface and started laughing— deep gurgling spasms that wracked him with pain. The self-organizing systems of his cells were rapidly repairing his broken body. He could feel the puncture wounds in his torso healing. He looked up at the now familiar features of Rex Australis: the cock of the head, the curious squint of his eyes, and a supercilious smile at the edge of his lips—Dan1 knew where Slit got his brain from.

Head office in Paris had stopped Slit from using N106 and the brain Freyja prepared in the lower laboratory had been destroyed when El9 and Dan1 freed the humanoids. They must have used Locky's.

Dan1 felt his body coming back into some kind of

manageable form, but his mind was still scattered. He'd seen himself in Locky's mind. He'd seen the years of betrayal. Locky was never his brother, never his ally, only out for himself. He looked up at the heaving beast.

The giant reptile stepped back. With Menos destroyed, the gladiorg was no longer obsessively focused on killing Singer and El9. The crowd was flummoxed—some started to jeer. The gladiorg slumped back on its hindquarters, thrust its head at the sky and roared in pain.

Wotan intervenes; a confused paramedic
"This isn't my fault," stammered Slit.

"You promised me a killing machine," slurred Wotan.

"The boy must have destroyed the Menos gland."

"Of course he has," roared Wotan. He tore open the wall and leaped from the skybox, bounding through the crowd, swinging down from balcony to balcony until he reached the ground.

The arena cheered at his arrival. Wotan paused, aware that he had revealed himself to the entire world. The crowd still hadn't decided whether this was the greatest pre-match spectacle ever devised or a shocking travesty of the sport. The arrival of this new beast tipped the balance towards the former.

Wotan headed straight for El9 and Singer, who were cowering at the edge of the battlefield. Dan1 had recovered enough to start a slow run in the same direction. Before Wotan reached them, Dan1 cut him off and lashed out with a hooked talon, catching Wotan in the gullet. He punched repeatedly into Wotan's breast, smashing at the rough hide until his knuckles bled.

Wotan threw Dan1 across the sand, but the younger man leapt back, swinging wildly with his talon. This time Wotan ducked the blow and responded, slicing at Dan1's shoulder, almost removing it. Dan1's arm hung by the shredded remains of a single tendon. His body closed the wound and stanched the blood flow, but he was suddenly defeated.

A terrifying smile breached Wotan's disfigured face, his yellowy teeth protruding from blackened lips. He reached out and shoved Dan1 back onto the sand.

"You put up a better fight when you were a baby. But I suppose you had the element of surprise back then," snarled Wotan. "Or is it possible that you have gotten weaker with age?" Wotan reached out with an extensible claw and brushed it against Dan1's cheek. "I thought you'd be my greatest creation." He grinned and raised his arm. "Goodbye."

A powerful tail knocked Wotan across the battlefield. The giant man rolled twenty meters before coming to a stop. Long bloodied wounds were ripped across his arm, torso and legs. He pulled himself to his feet and faced Rex.

The gladiorg lurched towards Wotan. Menos was no longer in control of Rex, but Dan1 couldn't recognise this as Locky either. This was something else, some wild, beastly mode determined to prove itself the apex predator on the battlefield.

At the last moment, Wotan leaped forward and drove a claw deep into Rex's neck. The reptile roared in pain and shook him free, once again sending the man skittering along the sandy battlefield.

Dan1 seized the opportunity, pulling El9 and her wounded father towards the pit.

"Open the gate," demanded Dan1.

A guard on the other side looked at them suspiciously. "I don't take orders from auxiliorgs."

"We're human, just like you," pleaded El9. "He's going to bleed to death." The guard shook his head.

Dan1 extended a long tentacle through the mesh, wrapping

it tightly around the guard's neck. "Open the gate," he demanded again.

This time the guard could see their point of view and pushed his palm against a monitor—the mesh retracted.

A confused paramedic arrived on the scene, also unsure whether they were auxiliorgs or humans. He took a look at Singer's injuries, decided it was not worth taking the risk, and immediately began the process of regeneration.

El9 was pushed away from her wounded father and Dan1 took her firmly in his arms. He leaned in to kiss her, but she raised a finger to her lips and unconsciously tilted her head towards her father. As he withdrew he slipped a small package into her hand. She quickly shoved it into her pocket, without her father noticing.

"Come on," said El9, "let's find Slit."

Looking over his shoulder Dan1 saw Wotan and Rex engaged in a savage battle. Dan1's wounds had healed quickly and if he joined the battle he could help Locky.

"Come on," called El9 again.

Dan1 hesitated, looking back, then followed El9 down the corridor leading to the skyboxes.

Finding Slit

They thoroughly searched the skybox. El9 returned from the ensuite to find Dan1 staring out over the battlefield.

"Slit's not here."

Dan1 didn't answer. Down on the battlefield, Rex Australis was locked in a fierce battle with Wotan. The noise of the crowd was intense. Just then, a hawk-copter appeared on the horizon, flying low towards them.

El9 and Dan1 both had the same idea at once, "The helipad."

The two of them rushed for the door and out into the corridor.

The hawk-copter was close to landing and the rhythmic beat of wings could be heard above the thunderous crowd.

As Dan1 rounded the final flight of stairs he saw Slit standing at the top, silhouetted against a transparent door. Slit turned and looked down his sharp nose. Dan1 was shockingly injured and his body had regenerated unevenly. Slit smiled wanly at his disfigurement.

"You look a little worse for wear," he said. "But you reap what you sow."

Slit stepped through the transparent door, firmly sealing it behind him. Dan1 and El9 rushed up the steps and watched as the hawk-copter glided towards the roof, stalling just above the helipad, before gently touching down. A door slid open on the side of the sleek machine. Slit turned to wave before climbing inside.

Case closed

Dex grabbed Slit's waving hand and twisted it behind his back. He snapped on the cuffs, tightly securing Slit's wrists. After nearly two decades on the case, he was making his first arrest—albeit a citizen's arrest.

Warren stepped from the cockpit of the hawk-copter and followed Dex across the pad. When they reached the transparent door Warren slapped a monitor and the door retracted, allowing Dan1 and El9 onto the helipad.

"You're still wanted for the murder at Biota last night," said Warren, matter-of-factly. "I'll get this guy booked, then make sure the warrant is rescinded." The captain looked at Dex. "You want to hand that guy over?"

"I never want to see him again." Dex grinned and threw Slit onto the pad. "But I still want the bounty."

Warren nodded, picking up Slit and cuffing him to the door.

"Slit ain't the only one ya should catch," interrupted Dan1.

"We know," said Dex. "We got him as a co-conspirator. If we could find Thomas Wotan, we'd bring him in too. Any help?"

"Try down there." Dan1 pointed towards the battlefield.

Dex ran to the edge and looked out over the arena. He immediately recognized Wotan from the Biota buildings.

"Holy Alu," he whistled. "That's him."

He grasped the silver cross in his pocket. The hard points pushed into his skin, a reminder to himself that after so many years, he was back on familiar territory. It may have all been quicksand and fog, but it was something he knew, and something he had missed.

Rex v Wotan

Wotan was winning on the field. Rex was bleeding profusely from one side, his responses sluggish and his movements slow. His height and weight, which should have been his two biggest advantages, were being used against him.

"We can't let this guy escape..." barked Dex.

Wotan scuttled between Rex's legs and drew a sharp blade across the reptilian undercarriage. The wound was deep and had seemingly opened the abdomen. The giant gladiorg stumbled, wavered, then collapsed to the ground—there was a heave and final sigh before the sand beneath turned deep maroon.

Wotan scuttled off the field. With the agility of a monkey he leaped up the balconies, reached the top, and paused, looking down at the broken body of Rex, then across at the figures standing on the helipad. He jumped from the edge of the building and disappeared.

"Get round there," screamed Warren.

What they came for

Singer dragged himself up the stairwell towards the helipad, his bleeding staunched but his body still hopelessly wrecked.

297

"El9," his weak voice echoed up the stairwell. She turned and raced down the steps towards him. "Here," he said, slipping a laser-edge into her hand, "take it. Finish Slit. Don't let him escape."

El9 walked slowly back up the stairs towards Slit, who was helplessly strapped to the open door. She raised the laser-edge, then dropped it back by her side.

"Kill him," pleaded Singer. "Kill him."

She pressed the laser edge through Slit's throat and pulled forward, leaving a heavy gurgling gash that spilled blood down the stairs.

"Now the boy," gasped her father. "You must kill him too."

"No," she said in a shaky voice. "Never."

El9 tucked the laser edge away and swept down the stairs, hauling her father up onto his feet. "We've got to get out of here."

"Kill the boy," repeated Singer between stertorous breaths. "While you can."

"I won't."

"He is not human, you know. How can you feel for something that is not human?"

"That's how I was raised, Dad." She pulled the old man down the steps followed by a slow tide of blood.

His purpose

"Alu motherfucker!" Dex ran back across the helipad.

Slit was slumped at the base of the door, his arm pulled at an awkward angle to allow for the position of his restraints. Dex reached him first and knelt down, gently raising Slit's sharp chin. There was a wide gash in his neck.

Warren bent over the body. "Who did this?"

Dex began first aid, wrapping ready-aid around Slit's neck. Warren reached down as Dex was pressing his hands over the wound. "You sure this is what you want, Dex?" asked Warren, "You sure you want to save this bastard?"

Dex didn't hear him. His life was testament to the struggle, the continual struggle, to maintain some kind of faith in the world around him; faith that good things are possible. Dex always aspired to that abstract concept of goodness, to overcome the evil, the inhuman, perhaps even the instinctive.

The medikit was quickly healing the wound, enough for Dex to press the first breaths into Slit's lungs. He heaved down on the man's chest, frantically trying to keep the blood flowing around his body. Dex worked Slit's body until he became dizzy from a lack of oxygen. He sat back on his haunches and panted for breath.

"Come on Dex," counseled Warren. "Be reasonable. He's gone, he brought this upon himself..."

Dex watched Slit's body. He knew Warren was right, Slit had made the decisions that took his life to the precipice. But if he could help it, Dex wasn't going to give him the final push, or let him fall away.

He threw himself back on the body, heaving on the man's sternum. The harder he worked, the more stricken Slit's body became. There was a parasite in the blood, a foreign body introduced by the laser-edge that was killing Slit from within, dissolving the walls of his veins, attacking the vital organs.

Dex never gave up, not even when it was obvious that Slit's body had. The paramedics arrived and watched from a distance as Dex pounded Slit's chest.

There was no moral or medical reason to keep going. Dex struggled merely because he could. Because that was his purpose.

The statement

A while later a young lieutenant was taking statements. "So you were over there with Captain Warren and Mr. Declan?" He pointed at the edge of the helipad.

Dan1 nodded. He was watching Slit's corpse being carried

away on a stretcher.

"Did you see this girl," he flicked the notepad, "Elenine, did you see—"

"El9," interrupted Dan1.

"Did you see her with a weapon of any kind?"

Dan1 shook his head. He had spent enough time with El9 to know why she did it—maybe he should have guessed that she was only ever interested in getting at Slit. But he was not going to tell this lieutenant anything new. He had nothing to offer.

"I didn' see 'er do it," said Dan1. "And I dunno where she got the laser-edge from."

"We already know it was her, we've taken samples from the weapon."

Dan1 could sense the lieutenant trying to gauge his reaction to this news. But it wasn't news. The deed was done and El9 was gone—back to the underground—back to wherever the hell she had come from; her project now complete.

Dan1 picked himself up. "Finished?"

"For now," said the lieutenant. "You can go."

Go where? Dan1 had no idea.

He'd seen a beastly side to himself, to Locky, to El9. He had betrayed Locky, who had been betraying him along. Locky tried to prove himself the apex predator on the battlefield— perhaps all he had ever tried to prove—and died in the process. Where was there to go from here?

He walked from the stadium and over the walkways towards the travelduct. Of the vast crowds only a few still lingered, confused by what had occurred. The hydra offered nothing but theories—no coherent narrative had formed. Dan1 felt the same.

He looked down at his hand and flicked out his pointer finger, briefly turning it into a rose. *The magician.* He grinned and wondered whether his condition could be permanently suppressed—whether he wanted that, whether he could ever satisfy the authorities, the Paris head office, the people of Melbourne, that he wasn't a danger.

Slit had called him a bag of chemicals, a machine. But when he faced down Wotan on the battlefield he was more than that. He was more than genetic coding - he had met his immaterial self. His genes, his material being, his clone, were mortal, destructible. His will was indestructible. Wotan would be defeated.

He stood above the travelduct and watched the train sliding from the westering sun, glistening like quicksilver. He didn't know where it was going and he didn't bother checking the hydra to find out.

E19 had taken what she wanted: Slit dead, Wotan out of hiding. He didn't begrudge her. She had given him a lot—the catalyst for a transformation. She had planted something in him that he would hold forever. It had given him a chance to immediately confront the fears Wilson's stories stirred in him: that he was nothing more than a genetically programmed animal, or worse, a machine; that he could never be more than a clone of his creator.

The train was coming and he prepared himself for the jump.

Back on the mare

E19 was galloping Northwest on the broad back of a fit Arabian mare, her father's arms wrapped around her waist, his head, collapsed on her shoulder, rolled listlessly from side to side.

She reached into her pocket and pulled out the small chunk of coral Dan1 had given her at the arena. The wind sheeted across her eyes, pushing tears from the corners of her lids.

Slit was dead and Wotan had been flushed out—the project was a clear success, but there was something unfinished.

Up to that point, she had never seen a moral dimension to anything outside of consumption—food and goods had moral dimensions, political consequences, and everything was to be sacrificed for their purity. But aside from living correctly, which meant consuming correctly, there was nothing more to life. For the first time, she felt she owed something to Dan1, felt that their relationship required it.

She craved Dan1. And it wasn't just the sex. She felt an obligation based on some connection, some intangible that had been established. She couldn't just wrap him up and throw him away, even if that's what her dad wanted. She folded the coral back into its pouch and shoved the package deep into her pocket—deep enough so no one would find it.

Epilogue

Bellum omnium contra omnes
[the war of all against all]

In the end

Slit's death was considered a tragedy. Biota had a statement out even before the police arrived. The Grand Final was canceled—ostensibly because of "an aggressive operation carried out by PETSO operatives that has resulted in the tragic loss of our most accomplished employee". Slit was given an elaborate funeral, attended by thousands in person, and millions through the hydra.

"This's me resignation." Dan1 passed the data intravenously to Ms.. Sundew, who slipped it into a file. Central security was immediately alerted.

"You will need to be escorted out."

"I could always fly out," chuckled Dan1.

Ms. Sundew looked at him suspiciously, her eyebrow arching like an arthritic cat's back. "Are there any personal belongings that you need to collect from the lab?"

Dan1 shook his head and walked towards the exit. He pressed his palm against the monitor and the door retracted. Ms. Sundew looked alarmed, taking a short sip of air.

"Security log must be behind," said Dan1, casually waving goodbye with a dainty hand—a hand that resembled Ms. Sundew's in every way.

Just the beginning

He approached the door and knocked loudly. Inside he heard frantic scratching, like claws across a polished wood floor.

"Yes guest, is the master expecting you, guest?"

A powerful black boot connected with the little helper's rump. The dog-wombat scampered off.

"Sorry about that," sighed Dex. "He's new."

"I thought the Biota Butlorg was recalled?"

"Yeah. It took me a while to find a store that stocked them."
Dex squinted and then looked away from Dan1. "What are
you doing here?"

"I want to track Wotan—thought you could help."

"Did Professor Wilson invite you?"

"No."

Dex swung open the door to his office. "Helluva coincidence."

Inside, Professor Wilson was examining a small, dead bird.
"What happened to the messenger?"

"Dogbat is defective," replied Dex. "Kills everything he
can—including himself occasionally. This is Dan1."

"I know." The professor nodded curtly. "It's nice we could all
get together. This message will interest you, Dan1. It's an offer
to join a mercenary army, authorized by Freyja von Bremen."

"Why would Freyja need a mercenary army?"

"Dex asked himself the same question. That's why I'm
here. And I can assure you that Freyja is not acting alone."
The professor drew a finger down his long aquiline nose.
"PETSO may consider Slit's death a victory, but it will have
consequences. Your friend may not know it, but she has just
joined a very long war."

"I'm here t'end it." Dan1 pulled the hood from his head and
threw out his mane of hair. "I'm gonna hunt Wotan."

"It's too late for that—you missed your chance on the
battlefield." The professor sighed. "We're going to need to beat
Wotan to the punch. An army isn't the only thing he's going to
want." The professor's tone was earnest. "I'm afraid this is just
the beginning."

www.ingramcontent.com/pod-product-compliance
Lightning Source LLC
Chambersburg PA
CBHW031101260626
47172CB00001B/165